The Upper Worlds

The Upper Worlds

The first novel in The Soul Survivor Series

VAN FORSON

Kingmakers Publishing
www.kingmakers.london
kingmakerslondon@gmail.com

ISBN: 1999859219
ISBN 13: 9781999859213

For Solomon, Louis and Ellie.
Your love and enthusiasm gave this story life.
Thank you for being the brightest souls in my
universe.

ACKNOWLEDGMENTS

With the fullness of my heart, thank you to Mellezia, Paul Angunawela, Atelisika. J. Dibi and Michael Van-Yeboah for proofreading my story.

To Sally, Sabina and all of my family and friends. Your kind words and positivity kept me going.

Thank you to Elisha Fagan for the interior book designs and Carlos. M. Burgos, whose original artwork was a constant inspiration.

Logo by Denise Simon at liber8design.
Website by Karl Stefan Hall at AGT.
PR and Marketing c/o Frances Mordue.

To the Giani Marg and the original storytellers Constance, Peter, Francis and Benedictus.
I learned from the best.
May the tradition live long and be passed on.

CONTENTS

PROLOGUE

ONE
The Upper Worlds

TWO
The Time is Now

THREE
The Living Dream

FOUR
The Crew

FIVE
The Portal

SIX
Underground City

SEVEN
The Prophecy

EIGHT
Madeleine Stone

NINE
The First Eye

TEN
Dot Pac

ELEVEN
Commania

TWELVE
Kimetic

THIRTEEN
No Retreat, No Surrender

FOURTEEN
Lock Down

FIFTEEN
Sub Zero

SIXTEEN
Urban Intervention

SEVENTEEN
The Long Goodbye

EIGHTEEN
Listen To Your Heart

NINETEEN
Me, Myself &...

TWENTY
I

PROLOGUE

Most people hope to live a long life, until a ripe old age, like Grandma and Grandpa status. I just about made it to my sixteenth birthday, and the prospect of celebrating another year isn't looking likely. But here I am, starting at the end of the story. Giving away the punchline before you've even heard the joke. The truth is though; my current situation is nowhere near funny. And when this all began I could never have imagined we'd end up here. So let me take you back, to a time when everything was normal. When I was regular. Before my life – or should I say all of our lives – changed forever.

My world is your world,

And your world is mine.

The only thing separating us,

Is distance, space and time.

ONE

The Upper Worlds

It was just another day at FB, or what is officially known as Falconbrook High. A sea of students flooded the forecourt ready to ride the wisdom wave.

The pristine outdoor sector was set out in an orderly fashion; a small row of tables on a raised plinth at the top end of the schoolyard. Columns of medium sized tables in the middle. And a large U-bend workstation at the lower end by the school gates.

Bright purple carnations, identical in petal formation and size, beautifully adorned the courtyard. Huge oak trees also neatly lined the area. A trace of the upcoming winter season, in the form of a gusty breeze, rushed through their auburn and yellow leaves as the branches swayed gently reaching for the sky.

"Have you seen Kid?" Philippe asked Brad as they sat together at the top end of the school on raised tables that looked like a stage.

"Not yet Big P, I'm waiting for her too." Brad, the all-star athlete, replied.

Having a rightful place here on this exclusive small table, which both Philippe and Brad did, automatically indicated their highly rated social status. Here you could be seen, and envied, by the entire school populace. The unspoken rule was that the Top Tables were reserved for only the most popular socialites and tastemakers.

"Kid's Coming of Age Day is around the corner," Brad paused, he paused many of his sentences for effect. "So maybe she's late because she *finally* blossomed and her Type kicked in overnight."

An array of adoring airheads giggled, fawning over Brad.

"You're so funny, Braddy." Madeleine Stone snickered, playfully punching his arm and allowing her hand to linger a little too long on his bicep.

"I know," Brad said, flashing a bright smile so dazzlingly that you would need to wear sunglasses if you intended on gazing at it for a while.

Whenever Brad spoke, it was always greeted with raucous laughter or a round of high fives, as if every word he uttered was either comedy gold or based on a profound wisdom. In truth, Brad wasn't particularly funny, smart or philosophical. But he didn't need to be because he was born to win the game of life. You see Brad was FB's lead Baller, captain of the foot, base and basketball teams. He was the classic, Super Jock Type and confidently owned his awesome athletic ability. Praise had been heaped upon Brad his entire life for doing what came naturally to him. Therefore his personality was not something he had ever worked on.

"So not cool Bro, you've got to stop teasing Kid about that." Philippe shot back, the protruding muscles that crept up the right side of his face rippled involuntarily like they always did when he was nervous.

"What did I say?" Brad grinned, totally unaware of his insensitivity. "I'm not teasing. Kid hasn't got a Code Type, which is kind of weird. Hopefully, she'll get one soon and be normal."

"Hmm." Philippe turned away from Brad.

He didn't want to continue this conversation or draw any more attention to himself. That was hard to do since Philippe stood at seven feet and two inches tall. His arms were as thick as tree trunks. His back so broad it blocked out the daylight. His pale purple skin stretched and strained to encase his huge designer muscles, which rippled bulbously throughout his entire body. Each of his visible veins revealed the blood coursing through him powered relentlessly by his two wildly beating hearts. Philippe's physique was jaw-droppingly incredible, and his strength was unrivalled by anyone in the playground. Yet he was the most sensitive soul at FB, the epitome of a gentle giant.

Philippe and Brad were easily the most popular boys at school, but they couldn't have been more different. Brad was devastatingly good-looking. Philippe was not. Philippe was kind-hearted and considerate. Brad was not. Brad was a bona fide, Gold Star Code Type – a premium superior being. Philippe was not.

Here on the Upper Worlds, a Code Type is a prearranged genetic disposition for greatness and superiority in one particular field. How it works is very simple. Parents choose what Type of child they want to have. Then, before birth, the baby's DNA is genetically modified to create the requested perfect offspring. This is the Code Type process. Whatever your Type cements your place in the world. It decides the life you will live. So, in essence, your Code Type is the most important thing about you.

When a genetic modification goes wrong, a person is born with mutations. They are deemed as inferior Code Types and known as Tachions.

Philippe is Tachion. His high-achieving parents had requested a superiorly athletic child, just like Brad, and had even paid top dollar for it. But in their quest for perfection, Philippe's DNA had been rigorously over-modified, resulting in his genetics mutating. So, unfortunately for Philippe, what compounded he and Brad's differences was the fact that they were supposed to be the same.

Philippe stood up to look across to the front gates for Kid. His gigantic frame on the raised platform gave him a vantage point to see all the way from where he stood, at the Top Table down to the other end of the schoolyard, and social spectrum. It was here by the U-bend workstations where the least popular kids at FB, like Max, congregated.

"One, two, three – stretch!" Bespectacled Max lunged on the spot in an awkward display of physicality. He was testing out his new metallic jumpsuit, self-designed for practicality, durability and comfort. No fashion or fad ever determined the way Max dressed; to him that wasn't logical.

16

"Good wrinkle free movement and storage action with your latest design Max." Boris, another Brainiac and fellow socially challenged occupant of the workstations, observed with an enthusiastic thumbs up.

"Yes, yes, thank you for your input, but I don't need verification on what I have already deduced," Max said, hastily checking his souped-up wristwatch, another homemade gadget. "Where is she?" He muttered to himself.

Max always kept a keen eye on Kids comings and goings. For him, she was the most fantastic case study. In all of his years observing her behaviour, Kid always arrived early to school. However in seven minutes and thirty-eight, thirty-seven, thirty-six seconds, according to his clock counter, she would be late. Tardiness displayed a critical error in one's judgement, which was not a mistake Max would ever make. But it didn't take someone of his superior, scientific, genius intellect, Code Type IE, to deduce that time is a terrible thing to waste.

Max made a quick note on his watch under the heading, *Subject K study, Day 1813* and resumed lunging and squatting on the spot.

A gaggle of sullen-looking Eee Cees trudged past Max on their way to the farthest end of middle tables. This was their designated section of the schoolyard, away from everyone else. The Eee Cees were nicknamed so because they were considered *Emotionally Charged*. They liked to think of themselves as mysterious Types who held a healthy disdain for what was considered the

17

norm. They dressed in all black, misshapen clothes in an attempt to disguise their true Code Type identity.

The Eee Cees avoided eye contact with the Brainiacs, not daring to interact with another from a different social group to their own. That was all Eee Cees apart from Sal.

Sal wore a black velvet hooded robe, which covered her from head to toe. Thick black eye makeup adorned her Geisha style whitened skin. The contrast made her emerald green eyes and flame red hair even more striking. She paused, folded her arms and watched Max's uncoordinated body movements.

"What in the world are you doing Max?" Sal asked with an uncharacteristic grin.

Max abruptly stopped his rigorous movements.

"Oh, Sal. Yes hi. This suit is a prototype, and I have to put it through its paces. Have you seen Kid this morning?"

"Nope." Sal replied flatly, her smirk turning instantly into a snarl.

Since Kids recent rise in popularity, Sal had hardly seen her at all, and she didn't want to let on that this bothered her. Sal never wanted to admit to anyone that anything ever upset her.

"Oh, well, you and Kid are usually inseparable, I thought you - "

"I said no Max," Sal said sternly turning on her heels sharply to catch up with the rest of the Eee Cees.

FB was indicative of society as a whole. Mostly everyone grouped with those of a similar Type. There were The Beautiful Ones, The Powerful Ones, The Smart Ones, The Creative Ones, The Workers and The Weirdoes.

Speaking of weirdoes, this is where my story begins. I'm the one they're all talking about, Keziah Monrova, but everyone calls me Kid. While my friends were waiting for me, I was soaking up what it felt like to finally be one of the cool kids. And there is nothing more icy than arriving at FB in a hot pink, drop top cruiser.

By making such an entrance, I was officially part of the elite Top Set. This kind of popularity had eluded me for my entire fifteen years. And it had taken a mixture of good fortune and a lot of hard work to attain this coveted social position. Nevermind the fact that I was sitting in the back seat of the car, and everyone was actually admiring my new best friends, the beautiful bombshell Twins, Mindy driving and Cindy riding shotgun. For me, there was still no feeling like this in the world.

As the cruiser entered the school grounds, the breeze rushed through my hair, flapping my long black ponytail messily in front of my face. What was once an intricately sculpted hairstyle, now resembled a windblown birds nest. I quickly brushed it away from my eyes and attempted to regain my cool.

"See, we made it on time Kiddie-girl." The Twins chimed in perfect unison; their dulcet tones carried like a melody duelled with a harmony to pleasantly play on one's eardrums.

"Yep, you were right." I said. "It was worth spending the extra three hours putting together a strong signature look this morning."

The Twins had dressed me in a rah-rah skirt and top combo which had several layered flounces. I had never worn anything like this in my life. I thought I looked like a pile of unwashed clothes. The Twins assured me I looked great.

"I told you, just like my mother always says, 'If you look good, you feel good.'" Mindy smiled cutesy at me through the rear-view mirror.

Although her eyes were hidden behind the latest huge designer shades, I knew her baby blues were shining brightly.

"So from here on in we'll give you a make-over every morning before school," Cindy added, squinting at the brightness of the sun.

She must have forgotten her shades at home.

"Consider us your glam squad. Yay!" The Twins cheered together.

"Great!" I smiled with an over-enthusiasm that sounded fake even to me.

We jumped out of the cruiser, and the Twins linked each of my arms. As we entered the school gates a troop of small, metallic surveillance Orbs flew overhead scanning our routers; checking our ID. Two bulky white Guardians - the robotic police – also approached us. They were the old kind, standard issue, who didn't usually see much action as the students at FB were exceptionally well behaved. Most times they were powered down, but now they buzzed and whirled into life, our near late arrival giving them something to do.

"Citizens Mindy and Cindy Lush offspring of Jane Lush and citizen Keziah Monrova offspring of Milan and Bibi Monrova, you have arrived at school under the ten-minute buffer before first period. Lateness is a violation of Truth seven nine four. It is forbidden to violate a Truth. Any laws broken will be marked on your permanent record and carry severe consequences." The first Guardian said.

"I'm very sorry Officer." I apologised for the three if us, "We won't cut our time so fine again."

"Indeed you won't." The second Guardian snapped.

"Sozzles." The Twins smiled sweetly.

They took the warning as seriously as I did but couldn't help but beam brightly. They weren't being disrespectful; they were just acting to Type. You see the Twins are Code Type Aesthetics, commonly known as the AEs. The AEs are genetically modified to be beauty personified. Smiling is the only expression that their face can genetically pull.

"Very well, be on your way." The Guardians dismissed us.

Although a unit of artificial intelligence, the Guardians seemed to soften after the Twins spoke. Their manner is so alluring that every person who meets them is captivated by their beauty. Evidently, their charm even works on robots.

"Phew - " Mindy said,

"- That was close." Cindy added.

"We'll never be nearly late again." I agreed.

"Composure girlies." Mindy said, puffing out her cheeks and preening her already immaculate, glossy hair.

Cindy followed suit whipping out a handheld mirror and applying balm to her lips. I awkwardly smoothed out my froufrou skirt.

"Let's roll." The Twins said together as they relinked my arms and strode graciously across the courtyard.

To reach the Top Tables, we had to navigate the rest of the students, who congregated in groups according to their Code Type status. You see here on the Upper Worlds, to keep everything functioning efficiently, there is a place for everything, and everything has its place. That's if you have a Code Type of course.

In junior school everyone would play together, putting genetic differences aside. But then somewhere during FB my friendship group had disbanded, each person gravitating to their own Type. I guess because my Code Type hadn't kicked in yet it was easier for me to remain friends with everyone because I didn't really fit in with anyone.

Yep, I said it. I'm almost sixteen years old, and I don't have a Code Type. Yes, it's embarrassing. Yes everyone asks me about it all of the time. My ma calls me a 'late bloomer' and says I shouldn't worry about it. But that's kind of hard to do when you're one of a kind, and there is no one else on earth like you. Oh, except my brother Jet. He hasn't got a Code Type yet either, but he's two years younger than me, and an utter odd bod, so he doesn't count.

By the workstations, where the genetically engineered geniuses sat building tech and arguing over theories – or whatever it is that Brainiacs do, I immediately spotted Max moving his body erratically. I stifled a giggle; he always made me laugh. Max was such a *neek* – the extremity of nerd and geek. He was a year younger than me but infinitely more intelligent than I could ever dream of being. I've been friends with Max for as long as I can remember, but lately, we had drifted apart. I missed him, but with my current social status, I thought it best to avoid Max, which was tricky since he's my next-door neighbour and also in my tutor group.

I attempted to strut past Max as effortlessly as the Twins who smiled radiantly as they sashayed through the courtyard like world-class runway supermodels. Being with the Twins gave me an automatic VIP status. That was something I could never achieve on my own. But it also highlighted just how out of place I was with them and the rest of the AEs. They are the beautiful ones. Their good looks being the only discernible talent and skill needed to navigate life. AEs are destined for fame and fortune because being really good looking was a trump card and lead currency on the Upper World.

Sandwiched between the Twins, I walked easily through the crowds. People stepped out of our way in awe and parted to let us pass as if we had a golden force field around us that gave us special privileges. In fact, we did have a super power, and it was called popularity.

"Where were you?" Sal said stepping across our path blindsiding me. "I came out of my way to give you a ride to school, but when I got to your house, your ma said you had left already."

"Oh yes, sorry Sal. I had something to do this morning, and I totally forgot our plans." I answered truthfully.

"Kiddie-Girl was with us," Mindy said.

"We gave her a surprise make-over," Cindy added.

"Kiddie-Girl!" Sal spat out the Twins latest nickname for me as if she had just swallowed a fly.

"Yeah, Kiddie-Girl," Mindy said, blinking cutely. "Don't you just love her new outfit?"

Sal looked me up and down with crossed arms that matched her cross face. I shifted uneasily.

"I mean come on Kid!" Sal said throwing up her arms in disbelief. "Really? I mean really what are you wearing?"

"It's vintage McQueen." Cindy chimed in factually. "But don't worry we can sort out your look another day. I can see you could do with some help. Ciao for now."

Cindy dismissed Sal and the Twins wheeled me away from her towards the Top Tables. I turned back to look at Sal who shook her head at me in disapproval. I quickly looked away. Yes, I had been spending less time with her lately, but I was tired of justifying my friendship with the popular kids. Unlike me, Sal felt no need to fit what society deemed as normal. In fact, she thrived on no one knowing her Type. I was different enough as it was, I didn't need to wear my oddness on my sleeve. I was just trying my best to fit in. At least I was able to physically do that, unlike the Tachions.

Tachions usually lived and went to school in Sub Zero. Sub Zero was a district on the outskirts of town. Most Upper Worldians preferred it that way. I've heard adults speak about how unsightly and unruly Tachions were. Although branded inferior, there is this unspoken fear of Tachions, a palpable sheer panic by most Code Types that one day the Tachions would somehow hurt them by using their undiscovered genetic ability. My ma, who works in Sub Zero, told me that Tachions never dared to find out about their latent power. Doing so was a direct violation of Truth number one, the first Law of the Upper Worlds which states, *'Tachions must never harness their power, in any way or at any time against a Code Type.'* If a Tachion ever broke that law, they would be fuzzed, meaning annihilated by the Guardians on the spot. The small group of Tachions that attended FB stuck together and didn't mix with us Code Types. That was all except for my friend Philippe.

Philippe didn't hide away in Sub Zero. His parents were both high achieving, well-decorated athletes and had raised him to succeed despite his genetics. He had lived his whole life amongst the elite and Philippe wore his difference like a badge of honour. I had a longstanding admiration of him for that.

"... And that wasn't the half of it." Philippe chuckled, in full comic rendition as we reached the Top Tables.

"You're so funny Big P." Madeleine Stone tittered loudly.

Madeleine was the leader of a band of AEs so shallow they made a puddle seem deep. They called themselves the 'Pretties' due to how good-looking they were. I called them the 'Prees', not to their face of course, because they liked nothing better than to pree, which was to stare and judge. Kate, Lottie and Porsha were the staple of Madeleine's airheaded army and were quick to shoot down anyone with a catty comment or a sarcastic snicker. They were merciless and cruel to everyone they deemed unworthy, and because I didn't yet have a Code Type, I was a prime target for their flawless foulness.

As the Twins and I approached, Madeleine's eyes darted to Brad. She was desperate to monopolise his attention before he noticed that we, by that I mean Mindy, had arrived. Madeleine quickly turned on her heels and walked away, rudely interrupting Philippe's story. The Prees dutifully followed suit. Although they had been giggling with Philippe, a second ago, he was now dead to them. Philippe looked momentarily dejected as the Prees ditched him for Brad like so many other people had done on so many occasions. He took it all in his gargantuan stride, literally, and was standing by another group of elite Code Types, who also liked the danger of being associated with such a fierce looking Tachion. In a matter of seconds, he was relaying his funny exploits to them, and they were rolling around in stitches.

I strutted, as best I could, to keep in step with Mindy and Cindy as we walked towards the table where Brad and the other jock and cheerleader Types were sitting. Madeleine and the Prees had beaten us to it and looked the Twins up and down assessing every aspect of their attire. They were beautifully turned out in matching outfits. Obviously.

I wasn't a threat to Madeleine's top rated status, so she glanced at me with a look of annoyance rather than envy. I twitched nervously under her scrutiny.

Tick.

I had been practising my plastic smile every day after school. It had taken a long time for my fake smile to read as cute, but I had finally achieved it. Whenever Jet, my little brother, caught me grinning to myself he would say I looked like I belonged in UC, which was an underground prison for deranged criminals.

"Ewww! What's that weird thing you're doing with your face?" Madeleine shrieked, wrinkling up her perfect button nose in sheer disgust.

I attempted to ignore her, trying with all my might to fit in by holding the prettiest smile my face muscles could muster. Holding the perfect smile was no easy feat, I can tell you. There was no way I would ever be able to maintain the cutesy cute, look that the Twins did so effortlessly. I just wasn't born that way.

Tick.

There it went again! The face spasm that made it clear that I didn't belong here at the Top Tables amongst the elite Top Set, those who lived an amazing life due to their genetics. The tiniest facial movement betrayed me, letting everyone know my life was a lie.

Tick.

Sugar! The nervous tick was not letting up. I had been holding my fake smile for far too long. For the briefest moment, the corners of my mouth turned down into a frown.

"Why are you, like, doing such crazy things with your face?" Madeleine squealed in high-pitched disapproval. "You look so – like – *UGLY*!"

Madeline had drawn unwanted attention to my far from perfect face. Others around the table stopped their conversations to stare at me. She had once again made it blatantly obvious just how out of place I was among the stunningly beautiful girls.

I tried to regain my smile, but another cheek spasm gave the game away completely. I sucked my cheeks in hard and pouted my lips. That would have to do while I tried to fix my facial muscles back into a pleasant smile.

"Like – seriously, what is that?"

"That's right, work it!" Mindy and Cindy clicked their fingers and jovially chirped in a sing-song unison swooping in to once again save me from utter humiliation.

"I saw a model recreate that look yesterday on Fashion Focus on TEN - " Mindy said.

"- Duck face, old school selfie pose. It's retro. You're bang on trend, Kid." Cindy completed her sister's sentence as she so often did.

The Twins imitated my pained expression but somehow managed to look like Goddesses. Not at all uncomfortable and awkward like I was.

Madeleine narrowed her eyes but then seemed to buy the cover as Kate, Lottie and Porsha copied the Twins' model pose.

"Well - 'kay!" Madeleine gave in - but not before shooting me, what she could only wish would be, a cutting look.

I was grateful for the Twins helping me out. But I didn't like pretending to be someone I wasn't. The old me, the one not concerned with fitting in, would have put Madeleine in her place. I didn't like being this meek.

Brad greeted the Twins and me with a hug and smiled his brilliant white-toothed grin. I called Brad's trademark smiles 'dazzlers' because that's exactly how you felt when he shot one at you. Dazzled.

"Good morning, Bonitas." Brad beamed arching an eyebrow.

"Good morning Braddy." The Twins sang in girlie unison.

"Hey, Brad." I blushed.

"Hey, Kid." Brad said grabbing me by my shoulders and spinning me away from the Twins.

He pulled me into the centre of his teammates.

"Look, your muscles are getting bigger. I told the guys earlier your Type is kicking in. Hey, maybe you'll turn into a Jock!"

Crimson flashed through my cinnamon skin.

"Lol, Brad." I said dryly, denoting that he wasn't funny in the slightest.

Madeleine joined in with a high-pitched cackle,

"You're so funny, Braddy." She said batting her eyelashes and twiddling her hair.

"Kid is gonna get hench and try to challenge me for FB captaincy."

Brad had quickly gotten into his favourite new pastime, which was baiting me in an attempt to get Mindy's attention. He would make a joke at my expense, something he knew I could handle as we had been friends for so long. Mindy would protect me by telling him to stop and after much of the Twins insisting he would say, "*I'll stop, only because it's you*" and shoot Mindy a dazzler. Mindy would cutely curl a lock of her golden hair around a perfectly manicured finger, and Brad would be mesmerised by her effortless beauty and grace.

But this time Brads little game had not worked because Philippe had joined us and made a beeline straight for Mindy. He whispered a joke that only she could hear. Mindy giggled uncontrollably, leaving Brad entertaining Madeleine and the Prees.

"What's so funny?" I asked, making my escape from Brad.

"I was just telling the Twins that I was going to nominate myself as a contestant in the next Miss Teen Upper Worlds." Philippe joked.

"You're like, so silly, Philly." Mindy giggled.

"I think I've got a chance to win that golden tiara, don't you?" He winked a muscle-laden eyelid at Mindy.

She batted her eyelashes back. Cindy followed suit.

"You're definitely in with a chance, I'd vote for you." I laughed.

I instantly felt relaxed in Philippe's company. He knew how to make us all feel good about ourselves and put a genuine smile back on my face. Now I was calm and ready to join the schoolyard banter.

And that's when it happened.

School is for learning.

1 + 1 makes 2.

*But when you question all
you know,*

What are you going to do?

TWO

The Time is Now

A harlequin-clad figure agilely scaled the school fence, and front flipped effortlessly into the forecourt. It moved with the grace of a ballerina and the silence of a shadow.

The Harlequin hurtled through the air like a red and white chequered whirlwind. The movement across the schoolyard was so rapid that the Harlequin reached the Top Tables before anyone, even the floating surveillance Orbs, could detect any unusual activity.

The catapulting figure came to a stop and kneeled directly in front of Kid.

"You must be in action," The Harlequin spoke in soft tones and a strange accent.

"Oh, my!" The Twins gasped in unison as they and the Prees backed away from the mysterious intruder.

"Only you can save us now. Only you can save us all." The Harlequin announced urgently, although the speech was barely a whisper. "Kid. The time is now!" The Harlequin said, before springing to its feet.

"Did you just say my name?" Kid gasped.

Taken by complete surprise, the cumbersome Guardians were slow on the uptake. They fumbled with their armour before launching a white lightening population control ray. In that instant Kid was knocked from her spot and hurtled eight feet away from the tables. The pop con laser instantly turned the spot where Kid had sat, into a clump of smouldering ash.

Kid had not been blasted by the Guardians, but rather it was the hulk of Philippe that had swept her off her feet, knocking her to the ground and out of harm's way. Philippe covered Kid and the Twins, sheltering them from the chaos.

The Harlequin somersaulted majestically into the air and landed agilely on the Eee Ces table.

"Wow!" Sal mouthed awestruck.

The Eee Cees usually expressed a nonchalant disdain for life, but even they couldn't hide their shock. Nothing like this had ever happened at FB.

The second wave of old school Guardians whirled into action. They usually sat inactive near the U-bend workstations. They had never had cause to be fired up before. The surge of activity led to a drain on the mainframe, which resulted in the image of the carnations and oak trees to flicker in and out, momentarily revealing the reality of the schoolyard. The recreation area was no more than a mess of grey concrete littered with plastic motion sensors. FB's picturesque courtyard, with flowers in bloom, was in actuality a virtual reality holographic simulation.

The Harlequin flipped across the forecourt in leaps and bounds. The entire forecourt erupted in panic as students ran screaming and hiding under tables in an attempt to avoid the reckless blasts from the Guardians. The Harlequin took a tremendous leap of faith from the Brainiacs workstation towards the school gates and freedom. But before the Harlequin's feet made it to the ground and safety, a gamma ray racked through the intruder resulting in instant annihilation.

Ash intertwined with clumps of red and white material fell to the ground. A deafening silence descended across the forecourt, and every pair of eyes turned to look at the person the intruder had held onto. Kid.

Pause.

Bibi, my father, grabbed the controller and stopped the onscreen playback of the incident at school.

"I don't know why you insist on continuously watching this back Milan." He scolded my ma. "We have the facts; this security footage from the Orbs, the report from the Guardians and the account from the Principal. This incident was nothing more than a case of mistaken identity. A mad man at the school gates."

"It was a woman dad," I replied flatly. "A young girl at that."

"It's a figure of speech Keziah." Bibi sighed as he paced the metallic floor of our pristine living room, which we only used when we had important company.

After the incident, it was a blur, but I was marched to the Principal's office by the Guardians, questioned, cleared, debriefed and sent home. Principal Farley had explained to my parents that this was the actions of a lone assailant, and I should return to school on Monday as normal.

My dad took the facts as they stood and was willing to move on. My mother, on the other hand, had burst into tears, called a family meeting and not let me out of her sight. So far she had replayed the incident seventeen times.

"I just want to make sense of it. My angel could have been hurt." Ma cried, throwing her arms around my neck and cradling me like a newborn baby.

"I can't breathe," I huffed.

"Let's not get hysterical," Bibi said with a furrowed brow frown.

My dad is a scientific Code Type – deriving conclusions based purely on data, which he called fact. My dad said the word 'fact' a lot.

"The *fact* is Milan, you mollycoddle these children and what you're doing right now is just making matters worse. Keziah was unharmed. The school is fine. The perpetrator was caught. The end!"

"Yes, it could have been the end, the end of our daughter!" Milan wailed. "If it wasn't for Philippe who knows what would have happened to her."

My mother was a Compassionate Code Type. Modified to be charitable, caring and kind. There wasn't much of a demand for her Type anymore. She was a rarity and many of her views outdated.

"That boy is just so amazing, so wonderful, so special!"

It was due to my ma that I had close Tachion friends in the first place. Not just Philippe, but people like Wain who lived in Sub Zero. She had always campaigned for Tachion rights and equality. She said the way Tachions are treated on the Upper Worlds by Code Types was inhumane.

"How is Philippe? He wasn't hurt at all, was he? And the Twins? Are they ok?"

My friends always said I was lucky to have a warm-hearted mother, but on days like this, it was just truly annoying.

"He's ok ma, like I've already told you, no students were hurt."

"And you precious one, how are you *really* feeling?"

"I'm fine ma." I lied, freeing myself from her suffocating sympathetic grip.

"Icy. Check out those garms on the girl that got fuzzed," Jet, my little brother, excitedly grabbed the controller, "no one around here dresses like that."

He sat so close to the screen that it lit up his face as he rewound the footage in slow mo.

"Everyone's talking about it," Jet said as he played the incident for the eighteenth time. "People are saying the intruder could have been from UC!"

This was the most animated I had seen Jet in years. He spent most of his time sullen and joint at the hip to his one and only friend, Skye.

"Stop playing that footage Jet!" Bibi demanded grabbing the controller.

Delete.

Bibi erased the clip from the screen. "There! It's done. No more mention of this will be made in this house."

"Dad!" Jet threw his hands up in protest. "That was excellent training research you just destroyed."

"Training for what?" Bibi asked.

"Never mind, you wouldn't understand anyway…" Jet muttered underneath his breath, skulking away from the screen.

"Just because you deleted the clip it doesn't mean it didn't happen. I can't believe I'm once again the talk of the town." I cringed

"Keziah, I can assure you that it's only this household who are blowing everything out of proportion," Bibi said. "The fact is this incident hasn't even been reported on TEN local. I can assure you if it were of any importance it would have been on the news."

My dad's words were not comforting. He wasn't the one who had to face my friends and somehow explain this mess. I had just clawed my way to popularity at school, instead of just being the weirdo without a Code Type, and now here I was once again the centre of negative attention.

"Dad, you don't know how it feels to have the entire school talking about you behind your back like you're some sort of freak!" I exploded. "I swear I'm never going back to school."

"Of course you are," Bibi snapped.

"You can't make me!"

"Of course we can Keziah, stop being so dramatic. The Authorities are happy this incident

39

has nothing to do with you. I suggest we drop this. Now!" Bibi yelled.

"Will everyone please stop shouting," Milan said. "A life was lost today in that schoolyard, right in front of Kid's eyes. It's a deeply upsetting time for us all."

"A criminal was annihilated by the Guardians before any real harm was done. Those are the facts so will everyone please stop being so emotional before this gets silly."

Milan shot Bibi as stern a look as she could muster. "It's ok Kid, you've got the weekend now to relax, and perhaps you can take a few days off school next week, to let this all die down."

Bibi turned to his wife disapprovingly, "We can't do that Milan. We cannot constantly shield her from the real world. That's the problem with your Type, you're just too soft."

"I'm not soft," Milan protested unconvincingly, "I just don't want Kid to go through any avoidable harassment. The world is so cruel these days. Perhaps it's not such a bad idea for her to stay away from school for a while?"

"If Kid gets time off then I'm not going to school either." Jet jumped in.

For Bibi that was the final straw.

"Jet, your whining isn't helping matters. This is about Keziah, not you."

"It's always about Kid! You never listen to what I have to say." Jet hollered.

I rolled my eyes, "Stop being such a drama queen and grow up." On this one occasion, I agreed with my dad.

"I'm not a drama queen. I'm thirteen, and I am grown up. I'll show you; I'll show all of you!" Jet stormed out of the room, slamming the door shut behind him.

Milan started after Jet. Bibi stopped her in her tracks.

"Let him go. This is exactly what I mean when I tell you our children are far too sensitive. That's why I keep insisting we should have them Code Type tested. I'm sure they've got far too many of your compassionate genes and far too few of my logical ones."

"No Bibi, I will not allow it," Milan finally put her foot down, "the process is too painful to inflict on them. Their Code Type status will become apparent, with time."

"But Kid is almost sixteen years old, and she's showing no signs of a Type."

"I know her Type should have become apparent by now, but she is a slow developer."

"Argh! Would you guys stop talking about me like I wasn't here," I snapped. How embarrassing that my parents were discussing my private issues in front of me.

"I'm sorry sweetie. This is all too much for all of us. I really don't feel comfortable leaving you tomorrow, so I'll stay home." Milan decided regretfully.

"You can't miss your annual general conference this weekend Milan, you're the guest speaker. If anyone stays at home with the children it'll be me." Bibi huffed, "I'll catch up on some research data or something."

I really didn't want to be a burden. My parents had been excitedly planning this trip for ages. Plus it would be awful for my ma to go and dad to stay behind at a time like this, he would be annoyed and therefore annoying the entire weekend.

"Look, I'm fine. Ma you shouldn't miss your conference. *Both* of you should go."

"I suppose we could put Auto Nan in charge of the children for the weekend." Bibi offered as a logical solution.

"That's totally not cool. We're not babies; we don't need a nanny to look after us." I protested.

"Ok, maybe there's another option - " Milan began.

"It's not up for discussion," Bibi wouldn't allow his wife's people-pleasing ways and his daughter's strong will to deter him from his decision, "Auto Nan will watch over you for the weekend and report back to us. If there are any problems, we'll be on the first light speed transit back."

"Okay, whatever," I mumbled. I had no fight left in me.

"Darling are you sure you're alright? Help us to help you." Milan pleaded.

I stopped myself from snorting ironically at ma's constant concern yet lack of a backbone. In the end, she always gave in to whatever my dad decided. It wasn't her fault. She was designed that way.

"I'm tired. I'm going to bed."

I left the room under my ma's worried gaze and my dad clapping his hands together to conclude the matter. "Well, that's that then."

Upstairs, in my room, I flopped wearily onto my bed.

"Track fourteen," I instructed and the latest song from my favourite band, the Allstars, played.

I exhaled loudly. I couldn't get the Harlequin's face out of my mind. Everyone kept saying it was a dangerous intruder, but I had looked right into her eyes, and I refused to believe that the child staring back at me was a threat. In any case, she had spoken to me, told me the 'Time is now!'

Time for what?

I curled up into a ball and hugged my pillow tightly for comfort. The day's events weighed heavily on my mind until I drifted into an uneasy sleep.

Dreaming is a must,

Where truths are softly spoken.

So in the land of nod,

Keep your third eye open.

THREE

The Living Dream

Bright artificial light bounced from one transparent or reflective surface to another. The glare stung the witchy-looking woman's eyes. She blinked rapidly surveying the premises. The maternity hospital was a completely see-through building. She shifted uneasily in her polyester nurses uniform. She didn't like being so exposed or the pristine manner of the Upper Worlds.

The nurse smiled politely at her co-worker, a Guardian model Neil 2000, who made small talk in its predictable pre-programmed way.

"A lovely set of newborns aren't they?"

"Yes." The nurse agreed, keeping a watchful eye on the parallel rows of several glass incubators, each crib containing a new life.

"Beautiful bundles of joy," the robotic security said enthusiastically.

"Mmm Hmm." She nodded in agreement, scratching her long, wart-ridden nose.

"So perfect in every way." He blabbed on.

"Quite true." The lady yawned loudly, exposing the golden teeth in the back of her mouth.

She glanced at the clock projected into the middle of the room, it read; 02:00 hours. Right on time two men, a tall one and a small one walked down the long shiny silver corridor towards the nursery. The tall man had luxurious mahogany toned skin. He was dressed in an expertly tailored bright purple suit. He glided smoothly across the walkway, taking powerfully elongated strides, which kept his majestic six foot five frame moving at a steady pace. The small man's crooked body rested heavily upon a twisted cane as his little feet pattered in quick succession to keep up with his companion. His receding hairline sprouted an impressive waist length silver ponytail, which waved behind him gracefully as his cane scraped along the metal floor, not so gracefully. The tooth grinding sound echoed around the clear clinical walls and alerted the lady and the Guardian of their arrival.

"Excuse me Nurse Zono," Neil 2000 said politely as he exited the secure plastic partition and approached the two men.

"You're excused," Zono said, watching the Guardian like a hawk.

"Good day Sirs," Neil said cordially reading their eye scans.

Neither pair of irises matched the hospital system, or any database on the Upper Worlds.

"Access denied," Neil reported sternly. "You are trespassing. State your business or leave the premises immediately. Otherwise, you will be annihilated."

Such talk was an idle threat to the likes of the tall and the small man. The powers vested within them could wipe out a thousand of this type of old fashioned robotic machinery. But they didn't have to move a muscle. The lady, Zono had this one covered.

The nurse appeared behind the Guardian, "Sorry, Neil. Your chat bored me to tears, but I still don't like to have to do this to you."

With one flick of her bony wrist, she created an ionised field that powered down Neil 2000, and he fell to the floor with a thud. The action was as effortless as swatting a fly. Zono swept a mass of frizzy black curls back underneath her white cap, overriding the system and releasing the emergency button to let in her guests. Unperturbed by the commotion, the tall man and the small man sidestepped the broken robot and walked into the glass inner sanctum.

Without speaking a word, Zono extended a long, knobbly index finger and the men followed her direction. The three cohorts walked through the nursery in silence until Zono stopped abruptly in front of a cubicle. There they stood in a triangle formation around the crib as they held counsel.

"A female offspring has been born to the Monrova family. XX donor mother Milan, a Compassionate Code Type and XY donor father Bibi, a Superior, Scientific Code Type. They have named their baby girl, Keziah." The automated birthing report informed them.

All three gazed at the newborn in awe. And fear.

"So the miracle stated in the lost scripture is true." Zono finally spoke to her companions.

The small man slapped his forehead in disbelief, "I never thought, not for a moment, not for a million years that the teachings from the Vortex of Souls would manifest in my lifetime."

"She was the only female born on the Upper Worlds today." Zono whispered as if someone could be listening to their conversation. "No mutations and not a trace of a Code Type."

"If she is truly without Type, that would make the impossible possible. Can she really be made of the same magical stuff as the ancestors?" The tall man asked, his deep bass tones reverberating around the room.

"Let's not be too hasty, let's, not be, to-oo, hasty." The small man dithered. "Indeed there is no such thing as coincidences, but we have waited a long time, a very long time, too long, for her. We have to be certain, very, very certain that she is the one."

"If she is the one she will have to work quickly." The tall man said urgently.

"The Elders established many guiding parties, and the task has fallen to our Trinity to protect her." Zono reminded her guests. "I always knew we would be bestowed with the honour of watching over her."

The three peered intently at the infant.

"Such little hands and such tiny feet. What a great weight to bear on shoulders so small?" Zono mused.

"Only time will tell how much she will be able to take," The tall man added.

"But time, time ticks on, continuously. And ticking time is not something we have the luxury of." The small man said.

Just then, the baby opened her almond-shaped, big brown eyes and looked into the faces staring down at her. She drew a sharp breath, and her lips quivered.

"Now, now little one," Zono said as she rocked the crib.

Before she could soothe the infant, her tiny face scrunched up. Tears streamed down her rosy cheeks as she let out an almighty wail. The three mystics looked at each other.

"The battle cry of a leader." The tall man said defiantly. "And so it is, and so it shall be; mark this advent in history. From this day *The Prophecy* has begun!"

"Aaaahhh!" The baby cried.

"Aaaahhh!" I jerked bolt upright in bed. It took me a moment to realise where I was. The Allstars music was playing on repeat. A froufrou outfit, I would never wear again, strewn on the floor. Several screens broadcasting all the latest Upper Worldian happenings were switched on. Yep, I was definitely in my bedroom, and it was just another bizarre dream.

I squinted adjusting to the early morning brightness. Heaving myself out of bed, I stumbled out of the room and padded barefoot down the levitating steps.

"Good morning, Miss Keziah." Auto Nan sprang into action as soon as I entered the kitchen.

"Morning," I mumbled rubbing my eyes and searching the fridge. Vitamin granules, O2 vacuums, powdered greens and pulses filled my health conscious mother's cooler.

"You're up early." Auto Nan said checking the digital display projected in the middle of the room. "It's 5:01 in the AM."

"Bad dream," I grunted, my head still buried amongst the provisions.

I was not in the mood for conversation.

"Not another one, Miss Keziah." Auto Nan said sympathetically, making a note to add to the report for my parents. "Well, this should help you feel better."

Auto Nan zoomed into action and in no time at all produced a warm, soothing beverage.

"This is for you with two sweeteners. Just how you like it."

I smiled, receiving the drink gratefully. It was exactly what I needed, "Thanks, Nan." I said sipping the sweet liquid and warming to the idea of being babysat.

It wasn't so bad having a domestic Guardian to look after us while my parents were away. Ma had obviously programmed Auto Nan that morning, for that I was thankful. If it were down to my dad, Auto Nan would have instructed me to clean the house sensors or complete some other menial task as soon as I woke up.

I carefully cradled my drink and took a seat at the kitchen table. On the desktop wedged between my father's science textbooks, my IM - Interactive Messenger - flashed. I pressed play. The message was from Jet and his being beamed out in front of me in a holographic simulation.

"Look lame-o. I didn't appreciate the way you spoke to me last night. Ma and Dad have gone and so have I. Skye's taking me to UC to find out what the Harlequin wanted from you. Don't tell anyone. I'll be back soon. Sayonara."

The image faded to blackness.

"What?!" I glanced conspiratorially at Auto Nan who was busy tidying the kitchen.

I ran to the house security monitor and quickly scanned Jets bedroom. In his bed I saw a lumpy bump as if he was asleep under the covers. But I knew my brother far too well to be fooled by that.

"Zoom into the bed and x-ray scan," I whispered.

The camera zoomed in, and sure enough, the lump in the bed was nothing more than a row of pillows. My heart jumped into my mouth. I sat down at the terminal to track Jets router. It didn't blip anywhere in the house. Now alert, I typed in Jet's coordinates which would show me wherever he was located. The scanner bought up a map of our entire neighbourhood.

'Blip. Person Not Found.'

I widened the search, and the map expanded to include the surrounding areas.

'Blip. Person Not Found.'

Desperately I checked the entire city,

'Blip. Person Not Found.'

Panicked now, I checked the net and quickly found the coordinates for the Outer Limits and typed them in furiously.

'Blip. Jet Saint Monrova Identified.'

52

On the map, I saw a blue spot representing Jet. He was nearly off the radar on the Outer Limits crossing into UC.

"No!" I screamed in horror, dropping the mug on the floor sending the beverage splatting everywhere.

Auto Nan zoomed into the room. "Whatever is the matter, Miss Keziah?"

"Nothing. I'm fine. Well, not fine."

"What can I help you with?" Auto Nan went to work cleaning up the mess.

"Nothing! Er, sorry about that Nan, I'm still a bit shaky from the dream."

My goodness! Jet was in grave danger. Nobody *ever* went to UC. I couldn't believe he was foolhardy enough to venture down there. I needed to get him back home to safety and fast! I couldn't figure out how on earth to solve this mess. But I knew someone who would.

"I think I need some fresh air. I'm going to pop outside."

I bounded past my Automated Nanny and shoved Jet's rocket sneakers on my feet. I wouldn't be caught dead in them on an average day; there was nothing chic about these gnarly flying boots.

"But it's 5:06 AM." Auto Nan said.

"I know, just need to clear my head. I'll be in the garden," I said hoping her lie detector was not switched on.

"Well put your coat on. The weathers turned, and it's chilly outside."

"Yeah, sure," I said flying top speed, out the back door.

53

I crossed the yard and raced up the side of Max's house to his bedroom and knocked loudly on the window. Within seconds a light flicked on, and his blind sprang up.

Max looked at me, more bug-eyed than usual, before cautiously letting me in. He was fully alert. No yawning or early morning disorientation, Max was ready to go as soon as he opened his eyes. I appreciated his Code Type's efficiency at times like this.

Max checked his self-designed wristwatch, which measured all manner of things, the least impressive of them was time.

"I'm assuming you are aware that it is 5.07 in the AM." He stated as I hovered mid-air in his room.

"Those things are a waste of essential energy." Max looked at the boots disgustedly.

I powered them down. I didn't have time for a lecture on the energy crises. I launched straight in, "Max I need your help, Jets gone to UC! My parents are away at a conference, Nan is sitting for us and has no clue that anything is wrong. I need to get him back home safely and in one piece before she realises and calls my parents."

Max's pupils darted to mine reflecting massively in his spectacles.

"You're a bit old for a Nanny aren't you?" He chuckled.

"Don't change the subject; we're wasting time," I said.

He had missed the vital point that Jet had run away. And, I was embarrassed that this little

54

neek, dressed in his self-designed grey sleep suit, with a pile of tech in one corner of his room and a mini lab in the other, was laughing at me.

"Jet has done crazy things before, but this takes the biscuit. What are we going to do?"

"We?" Exclaimed Max, "There isn't a *we*. *You* are going to inform your parents of Jet's escapade, and I am going back to sleep." Max took off his spectacles and returned to a horizontal sleeping position.

I didn't bother to control the whine in my voice like I might have done if it were another of my friends, "Max, you know how overprotective my parents are. If they find out about this, my dad will ground us for life!"

Max sat up and put his spectacles back on, pushing them up the bridge of his nose, like he always did when he was thinking.

"Kid, I can not get involved in the pursuit of your younger sibling, it's just not a logical course of action. Why has Jet gone to UC anyway?"

Max took his spectacles off again and laid down as if getting ready for a bedtime story. I looked at the counter clock impatiently before answering.

"He's trying to get to the bottom of why the Harlequin came to me in the schoolyard. Last night we had a major family discussion about it. Ma was crying, Jet was being annoying, Dad got upset. There was even talk of getting us CTT'd!"

Max quickly sat up and put his spectacles back on acknowledging the seriousness of the situation.

"Not the dreaded Code Type Test! From my research, I believe it's an unbearably painful process. Your father is a legend in the scientific community; he could probably carry out the procedure at home."

"Exactly! How would you like me to come into school on Monday and be regened like some lifeless zombie?" I crossed my eyes and pulled a silly expression, before flopping onto his bed.

Max smirked at Kid's dramatics. But he knew she was right. Her father could easily request a Code Type Test, and if something in her genetic makeup was askew, her father could authorise for Kid to be Re-engineered, regened for short. It was a process where the person was never quite as they used to be. They looked and sounded the same, but were someone entirely different on the inside. Max was so fond of Kid he wouldn't like it at all if that happened to her. But he couldn't afford to let his emotion rule his mind, and he never did, he wasn't genetically constructed that way.

"Aside from the punishment your parents could administer if they found out about Jet's escapade, going to Underground City is not logical. It is a forbidden, frightful territory. You've seen the news and heard all of the stories. That tyrant, The Res, runs the city with the rule that lawlessness is the law. How could we possibly go there?"

I nodded. There were daily news reports on the screens about how terrible UC was. The Res was a sworn enemy of the Upper Worlds, his intrigue even more sinister due to his identity never being revealed. And even though no one on the Upper Worlds knew what he looked like, everyone was in firm agreement that he was truly terrifying.

"We're not even permitted to the Outer Limits. How on earth are we going to find Jet? We wouldn't know where to start. If you ask your Nan to call your parents and take care of this situation, instead of trying to sort it out yourself, I think that would be a very pertinent course of action." Max finished his logical argument and took his spectacles off.

"Yeah I know Max, you're the genius. I wouldn't even know how to get past the PGs. I don't know what I was thinking." I conceded.

The PGs were the Portal Guardians, mainly Code Type enforcers who guarded the portals to UC making sure no one entered or exited. Some of the elite Top Set at FB would boast about having gone to UC to try and stack up cool points. But we all knew such braggadocious claims were a lie. The truth was, the PGs would never let teenagers pass to UC. I had no idea how Jet and Skye could have wangled their way in.

"On the other hand, a counter argument, hypothetically speaking of course, is that you may not be able to get past the PGs, but your friends might." Max said slowly putting his specs back on and pushing them up the bridge of his nose. "Did you call Mindy and Cindy?"

"Why would I call them?"

I was surprised that he even mentioned the Twins. I couldn't imagine their daintiness anywhere near UC.

"Everyone at school seems to do exactly what they ask of them. Everyone emulates the way they look, dress and talk," Max chose his words carefully. "Perhaps they could be useful in influencing the PGs decision to let you into UC."

My face twisted into a knot as I thought that through.

"No, I could never - "

"- Do you want to get Jet or not?" Max cut me off.

I looked up at him; his bespectacled face had taken on an odd look. I couldn't quite put my finger on it, but something about his usual unassuming demeanour had changed.

"Of course I want to get Jet. I wouldn't have come to you otherwise. It's just that - "

"Your friend Philippe would be good too," Max interrupted again, "his super strength would certainly be an advantage in a hostile environment. Captain Brad as well. I'm sure his athleticism could come in handy if you were serious about venturing into the unknown."

"Oh yeah, why don't I invite Sal to join the party and everyone else on my speed dial." I joked.

Max pushed the bridge of his spectacles, "I have no idea what her Type or talent is, but she seems pretty unconventional, she might be good for something."

I glared at Max. "Is this your inappropriate attempt to make new friends, my friends, at the expense of my brother's safety?"

"The only one of your friends that I have any interest in conversing with in a social setting would be the one who lives in Sub Zero. What's his name? Wain. You should definitely call him if you're committed to this expedition. The working of his incredible two brains has always fascinated me."

I narrowed my eyes at Max, why was he making this about him?

"And, Wain's first-hand knowledge of the Outer Limits would be useful in plotting the way to UC and back," Max added, clawing back his argument.

I got the sweats just thinking about having all of my friends together in one place. They were all so different. How would I buffer the conversations, how could I be normal around everyone who knew a different side to me? I couldn't be as cynical as I was around Sal, the Twins would just not get it. If I started acting girly, Sal would roll her eyes. I couldn't be as dismissive of the Code Types superiority complex as I was around Wain, Brad would surely take offence. I couldn't be as profound about life, the universe and everything as I was with Philippe, as no one else would understand the deep stuff. And I couldn't be as goofy as I was with Max. That would freak everyone out.

Max cleared his throat to get my attention, "So what do you think about the alternate theories I've presented?"

"Ma would never let us out of her sight again, and dad would have us CTT'd for sure if they ever found out that Jet had gone to UC."

"Then you know what to do," Max said with a twinkle in his eye.

That's when it dawned on me. Max was looking at me as if I was a walking talking science project. He pushed his specs up his nose slowly.

"Why so helpful all of a sudden? What's in it for you?" I asked.

"You probably won't even get passed the PGs, but if you miraculously make it into UC it would be the most interesting species study I've ever conducted. My analysis of alternative environmental conditions with the first-hand contact from differing variables lacks a field trip."

"So you're doing this for science?" I asked dryly.

"What other reason is there?" Max asked.

"I don't know Max, our friendship, how much you care for me." I joked.

Max's cheeks flushed red, "Well that is a variable I have also taken into consideration."

Now it was my turn to blush. I knew Max had a soft spot for me.

"I'm surprised you came to me for help," Max admitted.

"You're the first person I thought of."

"Oh." Max looked bashful. "I don't often see you; now you have your new friends."

"I haven't replaced you, Max," I said gently sitting beside him. "I've just grown up a bit and hang out with people my own age now."

"Yes of course. The Top Set." Max adjusted his specs. "Logically you'd want to be in the company of those exciting people. In any case, I've been keeping myself busy. There's always lots to do, to evaluate, to hypothesise," he said gesturing to the half-finished, long equation written across his wall, "I'm still trying to figure that one out."

"You're right; my friends are ace. But after the Harlequin who knows if they'll even want to know me anymore, let alone go with me to UC!"

Max shrugged, "Why would anyone blame you for the rogue intruder? I don't know what precisely occurred as I was observing all variables from approximately twenty feet away but I believe the perpetrator was on a mission of confusion and destruction. The Harlequin didn't single you out. You were an innocent bystander in the commotion."

I was about to tell Max that the Harlequin had spoken directly to me, but then quickly decided against it.

"I don't understand the complexities of social groupings, especially the social hierarchy you're climbing. So, I have no idea how your friends will react. But if your brother is in danger and your friends could help, I'm sure they would. Hypothetically speaking of course."

"And what if this wasn't hypothetical, what if we now were speaking practically?" I asked.

61

"Well to turn this theorising into action, you have one immediate problem." Max took off his specs one last time before making his final point. "As soon as your bionic babysitter gets wind of what's happening she'll report it to your parents. How are you going to get around that one?" Max rested his spectacles, and his case, triumphantly.

"Well, that's where you come in." I smiled cheekily.

"I really must insist - " Max protested.

"No, you mustn't." I placed his specs back on his face. We had wasted enough time talking.

"Get dressed and meet me at mine."

I powered up the rocket sneaks, darted out of Max's bedroom window and flew across the yard, to my house. I had an urgent call to make to my seven closest friends that would test the mettle of our friendship.

*Be careful of the company
you keep.*

*For what they sow is what
you reap.*

FOUR

The Crew

Back in my bedroom, I made my distress call. I synched in each one of my friends, and they holographically appeared before me.

"No-oo Kid!" The Twins squealed. "You can't see us without our make-up on!"

They were sitting in identical pink bedrooms, in different wings of their mansion house. Even first thing in the morning they looked flawless.

"Like, I mean no one sees us – " Mindy began,

"- Au naturel" Cindy ended.

To my relief, the Twins were their usual mega friendly selves, totally unfazed by the Harlequin at school. My dad had been right, only in our household had we blown the entire thing out of proportion. Once the Orbs and the Officials gave you the all clear, your slate was wiped completely clean. Upper Worldians readily fell in line with whatever the state told them.

"What time do you call this?" Sal grumped from underneath her bedcovers. "It's too early in the AM for a social call."

Her red mane was a fuzzy ball. Gone was her Eee Cee clothing that exuded toughness. Before she shrouded up, Sal looked soft, even - dare I say – fragile.

A shirtless Brad, who was already up and working out, smiled a dazzler, "Are you calling because you wanna join me for a quick sweat session?" He asked mid one-handed press up.

"Oh, Braddy." The Twins cooed shielding their eyes from his well-toned physique.

Philippe, who was also genetically engineered for extreme workouts, curled a two-ton dumbbell, the weight of a car, in each hand. He was far less self-absorbed than Brad and realised my call was not a social one.

"What's the matter, Kid?" Philippe asked sensing something was wrong.

"It's Jet. He's run away to UC."

"What?" Wain, who had a massive heart-shaped cranium indicating the formation of his two brains, piped in panicked, "That place is dangerous yo! Even us Tachions don't go down there."

Wain always looked and sounded startled even when he was calm, but on this occasion, he had a good reason to be alarmed.

"I know," I moaned. "I need all of your help to get him back home safely, and there's no time to waste."

"Ok!" Wain jumped on his hoverboard, "I'm on my way," he synched out.

I was happy Wain was willing to help without question. He lived way out in Sub Zero, and I needed him here fast.

"Jeez! Who was that guy? He looks like my dogs armpit." Brad chortled tactlessly.

"You're such a bonehead." Sal snapped, surfacing from her bed and cracking her knuckles.

"What did I say?" Brad asked flashing a dazzler, unaware of his insensitivity.

Sal gave Brad a cutting side-eyed look. Although also annoyed at him, the Twins fluttered their eyelashes and smiled at Brad. They had a range of smiles from little pouty ones to wide bright ones, but to frown was out of the question.

"One day the freaks will inherit the earth," Philippe dryly quoted the Tachion mantra. He didn't take offence to Brad's Code Type superiority complex. He was used to it.

"Oh yeah? Well, Tachions can bring it any day, because we all know that Code Types rule!" Brad goaded Philippe.

They were sporting teammates at FB, and their competitive friendship was both on and off the field.

"Whatever, Captain." Philippe dismissed Brad with a smirk, but the muscles rippling in his face betrayed his emotion. "You know whatever you need us to do Kid, we've got you."

"Affirmative. I deduced that you would want to assist Kid with her perilous pursuit." Max said scuttling around his room, shoving various tech into an oversized backpack. "I suggest you all bring provisions for this expedition."

"The King of the Neeks speaks." Brad chuckled.

He was annoying everyone. Sal rolled her eyes. Philippe's muscles flexed. The Twins smiled sweetly.

"At your service." Max nodded, acknowledging the derogatory title that I suspected he was secretly fond of. Max liked to be in charge, so being the king of anything was probably a good thing in his book.

I'd had enough of Brad's showboating. This was a serious matter and nothing to joke about.

"How quickly can you get to mine?" I asked urgently.

Philippe answered for the whole group, "We'll fly to yours at the speed of light."

***

"I'm glad you made it here first Wain." I high fived him as he walked in through the back door.

"No worries. I dodged the Orbs and flew down as quickly as I could." Wain said slapping his three palms in quick succession into my hand.

Wain is like a brother to me. We had known each other since we were babies. Wain was raised in the orphanage that my ma facilitates in the Tachion community, Sub Zero. Ma is well respected there and campaigns tirelessly for Tachions to have the essential species rights, like an education, nourishing food, adequate clothing and shelter. Wain's mother was an activist for the Tachion Liberation movement, the TL. They hold rallies calling for an end to what they believe is the tyranny of the Authorities on their community. Wain's mother was fuzzed by the Guardians when he was four years old, so Ma took him under her wing. I once caught my parents arguing over Wain. Ma wanted to adopt him, but dad wouldn't allow it. She cried for months over that one.

"I'm so worried. Can you believe Jet would do such a stupid thing?" I said ushering Wain into the house.

I checked the house monitor. Nan was upstairs in my room diligently folding all of my clothes that I had deliberately emptied out of my wardrobe and onto the floor to keep her occupied.

"I can actually," Wain chuckled. "Jet's a live one. Is Skye with him?"

"Yep, but just because they have each other, it doesn't mean they're safe. I could really do with your help."

"Whatever you need, I'm here for you," Wain said wide-eyed.

"I hate to ask, but can you please pull *The Face*. We need to get out of here fast, and I need to shutdown Auto Nan first."

"Your parents still make your Nanny look after you?" Wain asked in disbelief.

"I know!" I cringed "My parents still treat us like babies."

Wain shook his head, "Code Types are weird, yo."

A soft knock on the back door interrupted us. It was Max dressed in a self-designed camouflage jumpsuit and a huge backpack bursting at the seams with homemade gadgets.

Wain noted his garments," I didn't know we had to come in fancy dress."

"Neither did I," I said dryly.

"Affirmative." Max nodded.

I grimaced slightly. I hoped he would dial down that kind of talk around the rest of the crew.

"If I must, against my better judgement I might add, venture into dangerous pastures unknown the best thing I can do is be fully prepared for this once in a lifetime fact-finding opportunity," Max stated matter-of-factly.

"Naturally." Wain marvelled. To the mainstream, he was considered odd, but by his account, Code Types were the strange ones.

"And Wain, it is an honour to be undertaking this study of you. I...I mean *with* you." Max said as he grabbed each one of Wain's three hands and shook them vigorously.

"So back to business," I whispered.

"Wain, you pull *The Face* to disorientate Auto Nan. Max, you shut her down, then I'll erase my home security data, and we head to UC. Get Jet and Skye and head home without my parents ever knowing a thing."

"Disabling Auto Nan is no problem," Max said confidently. "The rest of your scheme is somewhat simplistic and will require a more thought out plan."

"He's right yo, but don't worry. I'll pull *The Face*; we'll find Jet and Skye. UC is pretty scary but - "

"Who's down there?" Auto Nan called out from the top of the stairs. "I hear more voices than the two audio tones programmed into my system."

Nan scanned Max and Wain's Codes,

"Why are your friends Maxwell Schneider and Wain Walens here so very early in the AM?" Nan inquired.

"Erm, for a school project," I lied unconvincingly.

"Wain doesn't attend your school."

Of course, Nan was right. Although Wain was academically brilliant, he wasn't accepted at FB because his face well and truly did not fit. I thought he was extraordinary looking in the best way. But by the Upper World standards, he was grotesque.

"There's no mention of that activity in the program from Milan. I'll just contact your parents to -"

"Wain, you're up!" I said pushing him to the front of the levitating staircase that Auto Nan was descending."

The Face Wain! Pull *The Face!"* I yelled.

"Ok yo!" Wain called out. "Shield your eyes!"

I covered my eyes, Max did the same but set his camera to record. No doubt he was collecting data to analyse later. Wain, did as I had requested and unleashed *The Face.*

The Face is a hideously frightening take on Wain's already out of this world appearance. It's the closest Wain ever got to experimenting with his latent Tachion talents. We discovered *The Face* by accident when we were little kids. I would blow raspberries, and in his attempt to match me, he would pull *The Face*. It was kind of funny back then but as we grew up it got more terrifying. His

71

ears grew, flapping over to hide his entire head before springing back to reveal his eyeballs bulging out of their sockets and spinning on their stalks. His head split in two, and his tongue corkscrewed out of his mouth a metre long. *The Face* was not for the faint-hearted.

Nan attempted to read Wain's expression but had never encountered such a sight, "I cannot compute."

The Face sent Auto Nan into maximum overdrive. She lost her footing and toppled to the bottom of the stairs.

"Fascinating!" Max gasped peeking at Wain through his fingers. "But illegal. That is a direct violation of the First Law of the Upper Worlds. Truth number one states that Tachions are not permitted to use their powers."

"It's not a power – it's just a face!" I defended Wain.

But Max was right. There were dire consequences for Tachions if they used any of their powers without a permit. I shuddered to think of how helping me could have gotten Wain into serious trouble if there had been any Orbs or Guardians around.

"You've been warned," Max said, before going to work cross wiring Auto Nan's circuitry. He took advantage of Auto Nan's system rebooting as it tried to process the inexplicable data of Wain's face. The doorbell rang just as Wain moulded back to his regular look.

It was Sal and Philippe.

"Good timing guys, you just missed Wain pull The Face, I relayed to my friends.

"Thank goodness we missed it," Sal cracked her knuckles, "I hate it when he does that thing."

"Don't hate, appreciate. He's just making use of his Tachion talents." Philippe said. "Contrary to popular belief it's not only you Code Types that are special."

"I know," Sal muttered, "it just feels exploitative to make someone do that just because they're different."

"What's up yo." Wain greeted Sal and Philippe with an elaborate three handed high five. Although he didn't go to FB, he was still very much part of my crew.

Philippe slapped Wain's tiny palm with the minimal amount of effort, but the force still sent Wain flying backwards.

"You're crazy strong, yo!" Wain marvelled.

"Sorry." Philippe looked down sheepishly.

He tried his hardest to play down his strength and agility. So much so that he opted out of running for captaincy of the teams at FB, allowing lesser athletes, like Brad, the ability to bask in what could have been his limelight. Not many people apart from me knew things like that about Philippe. He was never one to boast.

Max clipped out a wire from Auto Nan's brain circuitry and typed furiously in the air on his aero pad.

"Your automated nanny's internal processing unit is tough to crack. Its hardware cannot be easily disconnected," Max exclaimed as he grappled with the electronic device. "So what I'm doing is bypassing the mainframe and inserting my personalised program to defrag the factory settings and upload timed data on my command."

"In simple terms Max." I said.

"I've put Auto Nan into sleep mode for twelve hours. We'll have to be back with Jet by then; otherwise, irregularities will show and Nan will check the back-up data and see something is amiss."

"I understand," I said wheeling Auto Nan to the side of the room. "Basically there's no time to waste," I said, throwing on my backpack.

The doorbell rang again, Sal opened it.

"Hiya," Mindy and Cindy piped together, bright eyed and bushy tailed. "Like what'd we miss?"

"Nothing much." Sal murmured amazed at how much makeup the Twins were wearing at this early in the AM; she had barely brushed her hair.

"You missed a display of my exceptional brain power." Max boasted, pushing up his spectacles.

"Like, ok, but who are you?"

"I'm Max, I'm in your class, and I have been since pre-school."

"Oh." Mindy and Cindy shrugged.

Max shirked smaller, physically affected by the unintentional put-down.

"Morning Twinnies." Philippe smiled charmingly.

Mindy's eyes sparkled back.

74

"Hiya Philly." They chirped in unison pushing past Sal and running to hug him.

Sal rolled her eyes, "Did you both set your voice to irritate mode this morning?"

"Ha!" Wain laughed.

The Twins may have been offended, but no one would ever know as they blinked and smiled brightly.

I looked around; someone was missing.

"Where' s Brad?"

"He's out front." Cindy pointed to his silver space cruiser in my driveway.

Brad waved, flashing an early morning dazzler.

All of my friends had assembled just for me. Their friendship warmed my heart. This motley crew were a carnival of souls. There was Sal, the tough, mysterious one. Max, the neek. Wain, the highly strung super brain. The Bombshell Twins. Philippe, the gentle giant and Brad, the insensitive jock. A group of Types as diverse as this wouldn't usually work together, but I couldn't have wished for a better team.

Brad beeped his horn, "Let's roll Kid, Twinnies, Big P and the rest of you freakazoids, the engines running."

Leaving this reality and stepping into another dimension,

Takes a paradigm shift to prepare you for the ascension.

FIVE

The Portal

"So here we are, the Outer Limits." Wain announced as we arrived at the central portal that led to the Underground City. It was set next to the sewage system downtown in the desolate wasteland next to Sub Zero.

"The point of no return," Max said.

Wain jerked his three thumbs at him, "Ha! What's wrong with this guy?"

"Just stating the facts," Max said unperturbed by the ridicule. "Underground City, or Chesterton Workhouse as it was formerly known, was constructed to be a prison of no return to the Upper Worlds for the jailed convicts sentenced there. The criminals escaped from their cellblocks and took over the prison and its surrounding areas. Labelling themselves 'Urbanities', they remained underground and carved out a city filled with the worst people in the world!"

"But that was then - " Mindy began.

" - And this is now!" Cindy finished her sister's sentence like she so often did.

"Nowadays it's a place of trickery and illusion. A cesspit, a hell hole, a haven for the seedy underbelly of society," Max said.

"So they're really all murderers down there?" Brad asked with uncharacteristic trepidation.

"Nah, I heard these days only cool people hang out in UC." Philippe waded in supporting the Twins.

"And how many of those so called *cool people* who've been to UC and returned to the Upper Worlds alive have you spoken to?" Max asked.

"None." Philippe admitted.

I wrenched my hands; I needed to diffuse the situation quickly before everyone became fearful. "It's all hearsay. None of us knows what goes on in UC since none of us has been before."

"Well, actually I have." Sal mumbled.

Everyone turned to her in disbelief.

"Like when?"

"Like how?" The Twins asked. "Gooooo team Sal!" They squealed in unison; clapping as if rehearsing with the cheerleading squad.

"That's just totally rad, dude!" Brad said trying to fall in line with the Twins enthusiasm for the place.

"How come you never told me?" I said.

"I didn't think it was worth mentioning," Sal shifted awkwardly.

"It's only like the edgiest place in the whole world, and you've been there and didn't tell anybody?" Mindy gasped. She always wanted to be on the cusp of whatever was considered cool. And dangerous was really in at the moment.

"What's the point of doing something totally rad and not letting everyone know about it?" Cindy squeaked.

"I don't believe you, on how many occasions?" Max stared suspiciously.

"A few times…" Sal petered off uneasily.

"What logical reason would you have to go to UC?"

"For this and that…" Sal trailed off again, cracking her knuckles.

The scrutiny was making Sal uncomfortable, and the crew's attention was swaying from what we came to do.

"We can discuss this later. Time is of the essence and we need to find Jet and Skye." I said.

"You're right Kid. We're going to need a tightly run plan," Philippe said.

"Affirmative." Max responded like an army sergeant.

Wain bobbed his head at the notion. Although they were both brains, they had different belief systems of logic. Max was more syllogistic meaning he would weigh up the merits of different approaches of an argument and go with what he deemed the best one. While Wain was a lateral thinker meaning he solved problems more creatively.

"In UC we need to keep our wits about us and look out for each other, but first we have to get past the PGs," Wain said.

"The who?" Brad asked.

"The Portal Guardians. They're the ones who guard the entrances in and out of UC." Wain explained.

"Oh," Brad said. He spent all of his time on the playing field and paid no attention to this kind of stuff.

Max sized Wain up and made a note on his aero pad.

"What are you doing there, Bro?" Wain asked.

"Keeping a record of everything you say and do," Max answered bluntly.

"Why?"

"Because you're fascinating." Max said pushing his specs up his nose.

"Oh, thanks, I guess," Wain said feeling uncomfortable under Max's bug-eyed stare.

"So if we don't get past the PGs then we can't get into UC?" Brad asked still trying to get to grips with the situation at hand.

"Yes dunderhead." Sal mocked.

"Got it." Brad sighed, confident that the rescue mission would be thwarted by the PGs before it even got started.

"What do you have to barter with the PGs?" Sal rummaged around in Max's backpack without his permission.

"Hey get out of there. I've got nothing for them. Everything in my survival kit is vital. I - "

Before Max could finish his sentence Sal pulled out a miniature radio.

"This'll do," she said trotting off.

"Hey! I just made that." Max protested.

Sal stopped dead in her tracks and cracked her knuckles impatiently.

"Do you want to help Kid or not?" Sal asked narrowing her piercing emerald eyes.

Max's steely blue eyes gazed into Kid's big brown ones. How could he let her down?

"Go forth," he breathed out helplessly.

"Thanks, Max, you're the best." I smiled at him and saw his cheeks flush.

"I'll handle them. Wait here." Sal jogged across the dusty gravel floor towards an unassuming circular gate etched into the side of a hill.

Two thick set Code Types were stationed at a makeshift checkpoint by the portal. They were dressed casually in black slacks and duffel coats and didn't look like Officials. But their bald heads, thick necks and big structures looked menacing all the same.

"This is so-oo exciting." Mindy yelped watching Sal like a hawk.

"Yeah, I mean like what is Sal going to say to them?" Cindy squealed enthusiastically as if first picked for the cheerleading squad. She was never picked first for anything, Mindy always was.

"We should go with her," Philippe said. "Safety in numbers."

"She said to wait here, so let's wait. The Eee Cee knows what she's doing," Brad said. "I only came along for kicks and giggles. And here we are begging to be let into a city underground full of crims. I mean, does anyone else think this is crazy?"

"Like, whatever!" Mindy attempted to wrinkle her nose in disapproval of Brad, like she had seen Sal do about ten times today, but failed miserably and ended up looking even cuter with a nose twitch like a bunny rabbit.

"Kid needs us. It's just like on the football field, we've got to roll as a unit and have each other's back. One team, one dream." Philippe levelled.

"Ok, you're right," Brad shot out a dazzler. "It's just that I've got ball practice later and as Captain, I can't miss it." Brad tried to mask his fear.

"It's ok if you want to go home," I said. I didn't want to force anyone to do anything they didn't want to.

"Yes, I understand why you're afraid," Max said. "The danger of UC is real."

"But fear is a choice," Wain replied, "just like courage. Choose which emotion you want to feed."

Max made another note on his aero pad.

"Me? Afraid? I'm not scared of anything!" Brad called out, the shrillness of his voice betraying he was. "I'm staying," he said, not wanting to look like a wimp.

Out on the sporting arena with his adoring fans, Brad was the definition of bravery. But out here in the real world without a ball to kick, throw or bounce, it was a different game altogether.

Sal jogged back to the crew.

"Here's the deal," she delivered the news to us out of breath. "Earlier today a PG was knocked out and the surveillance destroyed, but the guys on duty can't remember a thing."

"Ha, pathetic yo!" Wain laughed.

"How could scrawny Jet and tiny Skye knock a big man out cold?" I asked.

"I dunno, but that's how they got in I reckon," Sal said. "Also moves are afoot in UC. Something big is going on down there. The PGs don't know what it is, but they've been warned to keep the city shutdown."

Brad dazzled, relieved. "Mission over, homeward bound."

"Yeah but, no - " Sal caught her breath. "- I managed to persuade the PGs to let us in."

"How did you do that?" Max said.

"Forget about it," Sal said fixing a gaze on Max.

Max adjusted his specs, looked confused and forgot what he was saying.

Sal continued, "We've got until five in the PM when these PGs change shift. If we're not back in the Upper Worlds by then..."

"Then what?" Brad asked anxiously.

"Then we better get used to living like Urbanites," Sal said flatly, cracking her knuckles.

"I know I'm asking a lot of you and if you want to turn back now I understand," I said.

Everyone knew that UC was a dangerous place. *Fact*, as my dad would say, and here I was leading my friends on a hazardous journey. I had no way of knowing how to find Jet, and what we were going to encounter. All I had was a gut feeling to do this.

"Yo! We're in this together. We're here for you." Wain said reassuringly.

"Even in opposition to my better, logical judgment," Max added. "With what Sal says, I'm even more intrigued by what we might encounter on this trip."

"And with all the powers vested in us," Philippe said flexing his ginormous muscles.

"And to be the most daring AEs in the whole Upper Worlds and give the Top Set something to talk about." The Twins giggled.

"We're right behind you." Brad feigned enthusiasm. "Way behind you," he added underneath his breath.

All eyes turned to me. This was my mission, my call. I looked around at my friends' expectant faces.

"Let's do this."

And with that, the eight of us walked across the gritted wasteland towards the hole in the side of the mountain. Sal fixed the PGs with a mean stare, and the burly men sprang to their feet opening the heavy circular rusting portal to let us in. The door rolled behind us with a clanging thud, and in total darkness, we descended into the murky dirty depths beyond the portal.

"It's so dark in here I can't see a thing!" Brad yelped, sounding as high pitched as the Twins.

"Here, take these." Max said.

Luckily for us in his bag of gizmos, he had thoughtfully packed enough light beams for all of us.

"That's better." I said shining the light in front of me.

I led the way, and Brad bought up the rear as we stepped down the rusting steel escalator. The clanky machinery juddered spiralling downwards in a zigzag formation. The steps seemed endless, and in the near darkness, we could not see the bottom.

"Have you guys noticed something?" Max said.

"What!" Brad screamed dramatically, his voice echoing loudly around the cold, grimy steel walls.

Philippe looked back and shook his head. "Not cool buddy, so not cool."

"This escalator only goes down," Max continued.

"So?" Brad asked in a deeper voice trying to regain his composure.

"So how do we go back up and out of UC?" Max asked.

Sal smirked knowingly. "You don't find your way out of UC, the way out of UC finds you."

"What does that mean?" Brad whined.

"You'll see," Sal said without further explanation.

"For a Code Type, you're really starting to sound like a Sap, they all speak in riddles," Wain said.

"What do you know about Saps?" I asked. "I've read about them but never actually seen one before."

"I've met a few in my time," Wain said. "Sometimes the Saps come to Zero and bring us food. They're really friendly people and wise too.

Well, that's if you can decipher the puzzles they speak in."

"Remember the project we did on the Saps in Social Studies Twinnies?" Philippe said, "Apparently Saps can't survive in the Upper World, so they live beyond the trees in that nature stuff."

"You're like so knowledgeable." Mindy gushed.

Philippe suddenly felt embarrassed. He wasn't used to having all of Mindy's attention. The muscles on the side of his face lightly rippled.

Max did not like being outdone in the intelligence stakes and chimed in eagerly, "That's quite correct Philippe. I haven't encountered any of the Sap population in person, although I have researched them extensively. The Saps have less genetic modifications than Code Types, therefore they are physically weak, unable to survive in our environment. Even breathing is a difficult task for them. So they must live in the trees, which provide them oxygen.

"Their leader is Dr Stoneway, rumoured to be the oldest man on Earth. The mysterious land they inhabit is called Commania. As indigenous peoples, they have many customs and traditions including a belief that their dream state is as important as when they are awake and - "

"Do you like totally know everything in the whole entire world?" Cindy cut Max off, as she stepped carefully down the stairs in her stiletto heels, which kept getting caught in the ridges of the slow moving escalator.

"Yes well, I like to stay abreast of a range of social, cultural and philosophical theorems. It makes fine light reading when I'm not studying my scientific texts." Max said pushing his spectacles up his nose. "In fact, I know a lot about this place," he said enthusiastically shining his light around him. "Would you like to hear some fun facts?"

A glaring silence greeted Max.

"I'll take that as a yes then." He cleared his throat before he began his history lesson to a captive audience.

"Underground City is a debauched district, which runs underneath the Upper Worlds."

"Ha! You don't say, Plato!" Wain ribbed.

"Even I know that." Brad laughed, momentarily forgetting his dire situation.

"If you're going to do anything at all, you should do it properly, so I'm starting from the beginning," Max said slightly disgruntled but continued his lecture anyway.

"Two hundred and fifty years ago UC was a metropolis of prisons called Chesterton Workhouse. It was constructed underground as the prisons over ground were already bursting at the seams with petty criminals. That was before our current government and our brave leader; His Excellencey William Admiral restored law and order to the Upper Worlds.

"All of the criminals kept at Chesterton were violent convicts, thought to be too dangerous to be rehabilitated, so they were sent underground for life."

"This is like worse than Mr Egan's history lesson." Mindy yawned.

"Like totally B to the O to the R –I –N –G." Cindy cheered.

"Yeah, quit it, King Neek," Brad called out. "If I wanted to know this I'd watch it in on a screen."

I smiled to myself. Whether Max was doing it on purpose or not, his lecture was helping to calm nerves as we journeyed deep into the heart of darkness. I was thankful for this distraction.

"Go on; I'm listening." I encouraged him.

"Me too. It's *fascinating*," Sal mocked.

"Me three," Philippe called out. "I never pay attention in class, I'm too distracted by the perfection that is Mindy's face," he said charmingly. "And yours, of course, Cindy, since you've got the same one."

"Oh yeah?" Mindy giggled and batted her eyelashes. "Well, this face needs plenty of rest to look this good. And since we woke up so early I didn't get enough beauty sleep. Plus these shoes are so not made for walking."

"Well, why would you wear high heels to UC anyway?" Sal asked irritated.

"Because fashion is life!" The Twins answered in unison.

Sal rolled her eyes and cracked her knuckles.

"Ha! You Types are crazy yo!" Wain laughed, thoroughly entertained. He'd never spent this amount of time with friendly Code Types, and although they were self-centred and weird, he was enjoying their company.

"Such a precious beauty should never be tired." Philippe said playing along with Mindy. "In fact, she shouldn't have to walk at all." And with one hand he playfully scooped Mindy up in his arms and carried her with ease down the steps.

"Oh, my!" Mindy held onto Philippe beaming like a beacon.

She enjoyed being held by him much more than she let on to anyone.

Brad looked on annoyed by the blossoming friendship.

Cindy clicked her fingers to get his attention. "Like, Hel-lo Brad, what about me?"

"Oh, yeah." Brad lacklustrely mirrored Philippe's moves sweeping Cindy, the less sought after twin, off her feet.

"This is so totally the way to travel." Mindy and Cindy piped in unison.

Sal rolled her eyes at the Twins' helpless girly display, "Please continue Max," she said through gritted teeth.

Max cleared his throat again, happy to finally have everyone's attention.

"Many moons ago, after several revolts, the Authorities pulled out of the city, leaving it a law unto itself. The portals were shut off fearing the Urbanites would rise and run amok in our world.

"Over the decades UC became synonymous with the dregs of society. It's well documented that teenage misfits unable to achieve the high standard of Code Type living run here to hide and partake in activities outlawed on the Upper Worlds, such as Capsing."

"What's Capsing?" Cindy asked. She only ever spoke to cool kids and had never paid so much attention to a Brainiac.

"Capsing is the process by which Tachions who are unhappy with their mutations, go into capsules and through a painful process, temporarily alter their DNA. They give themselves a regular appearance and pretend to have a Code Type identity so that they'll be more accepted by society."

"Whoa! People do that here?" Brad said.

"Yes, it is a commonly known fact."

"Jeez." Brad loosened his collar, once again feeling the fear of the underground.

Max continued, "Ganglords operate different factions, but the resident in charge of UC is a terrifying, unidentified man known only as The Res."

"*The Res*," Philippe said in awe. "The name alone strikes fear into my hearts," both beat wildly as he held Mindy close.

"Yo! The Res is the ultimate villain. I heard he's able to kill a man, just by thinking it." Wain shuddered.

"No way!" Brad gagged, "I'm not feeling so good."

"You know what's going to make you feel even worse?" Sal said.

"What!" Brad screamed, dropping Cindy to the floor.

"Ouch!" She wailed.

"We're here," Sal said as the rickety escalator stopped abruptly.

A red neon light crudely signposted the unassuming entrance. The circuitry cut in and out and the sign flashed and buzzed cheaply, reading simply, UNDERGROUND CITY.

In an unknown city, where
no one knows the rules,

It's best to mind your P's
and Q's.

SIX

Underground City

Standing before us was a darkened sprawling metropolis illuminated by artificial lights.

"Wow. Is this it?" I asked.

"Yup," Sal confirmed.

"Eewwwww!" The Twins cried out. "We thought it would be way cuter than this."

"What did you expect? It was once a sprawling prison!" Max was exasperated. His expert tuition was wasted on their fickle minds.

The darkened city with its strange sounds, toxic smells and weird brick and iron buildings was extremely intimidating.

"This is creepy yo," Wain said.

"Where are all the people?" I asked.

"I don't know," Sal said anxiously. "It's never usually this quiet."

"How will we even know which way to go?" Philippe said, the sight of UC stripping him of his earlier bravado.

"We have to stick together," Brad said nervously.

"Logically we can't," Max answered flatly setting his backpack down and tapping furiously on his aero pad. "If we're going to cover all dimensions of the city in our time limit, we need to split up."

"You're right Max," I agreed. "Sal, you've been here before, you take Philippe, Mindy and - "

"Me!" Brad volunteered, not wanting to leave Mindy and Philippe alone with each other.

"Okay," I said shooting a look. Brad was acting weird, but I was far too worried about Jet to be concerned by it.

"Sal, you guys head to the parts of town you know. Max, Cindy, Wain and I will head in the opposite direction."

"Fine, I'm going to head towards the Main Square. It's the hub of activity."

"Party over here!" Mindy beamed forgetting the predicament we were all in.

Sal gave her a scornful look.

Max typed into his space keys before announcing, "According to my coordinates that's due East, so we'll head West."

"Keep in radio contact," I said waving my IM.

"They don't work down here." Sal said, "No transmitters."

"Great! How are we going to call for help?" Brad whinged.

Sal gave him a dirty look. Mindy smiled at him, as that's the only face she could pull, but Brad's lack of bravery was getting on her nerves.

"I have come prepared, as always," Max said sticking homemade tracking patches on everyone. "This way I'll be able to trace you on my aero pad."

"And we'll keep in touch with each other in our mind," Wain said to Philippe.

96

"Erm. Ok." Philippe nodded unsure of his ability to use the Tachion power of telepathy. "I haven't ever tried ESP before, with it being outlawed on the Upper Worlds and all. It might not work."

"It doesn't matter where you grew up my Tachion brother; our skills never leave us," Wain assured him.

"Time restrictions guys," Sal said impatiently.

"Let's get busy," Philippe said scoping the area.

"Whatever happens we meet back at this spot at four in the PM." I urged.

"Not a millisecond later," Max added setting his watch.

"Hopefully someone will be around by then to show us out," Sal said cracking her knuckles.

"Right, let's do this," I said.

The Twins hugged each other tightly, "I'll miss you Twinny!" They cried in unison.

I couldn't believe they had agreed to split up; they were never apart.

We all formed a circle and high-fived before separating into our respective groups. Sal, Mindy, Philippe and Brad headed east. Max, Cindy, Wain and I go west.

***

Main Square was grimy. The dirty concrete floors were stained with sticky splatters and trash was strewn all over the ground. Here the most incredible looking people roamed the streets. Pole thin, barrel fat, one-eyed, four-legged. Some of the more spectacular looking Tachions made Wain look as aesthetically pleasing as the Twins. These types of people were usually banned from the Upper Worlds and hidden away in Sub Zero.

"Are you sure you know where you're going?" Brad whined, shaken up by the unfamiliar sights and loud sounds.

If she could, Mindy would have rolled her eyes the way Sal did. But the best she could muster was to bat her eyelashes in disapproval of Brad.

"If I have to tell you one more time to shut it, Brad, you're going to taste my fist in the shape of this knuckle sandwich." Sal huffed.

Although she had a tough exterior, she was also afraid in UC.

"Relax everyone, enjoy the scenery." Philippe joked to lighten the mood.

The displays of the glass-fronted shop windows were obstructed by crudely erected wooden beams or corrugated iron bars indicating that the stores were regularly looted. When the crew did get to glance at the goods inside, they couldn't identify what most items were. Bizarre food substances and knick-knacks that held no discernible value were on sale. Nothing like this was available on the Upper Worlds.

People hung around street corners talking in peculiar accents. Music blared from every orifice, and there were so many darkened nooks and crannies that led off into even more dank and secret places. There wasn't a surveillance Orb,

Guardian or trace of a pop con missile in sight. There was no way to keep control of this city.

Mindy concentrated extremely hard trying to digest the atmosphere in order to relay every detail back to the Top Set at school. But UC was something you couldn't explain. It had to be seen to be believed.

"Like, what are those eggy shaped things?" Mindy said pointing to the well-worn, boulder-sized silver pods that lined the pavement.

"Capsules." Sal answered shortly.

"Why are they everywhere? What do they do?" Philippe asked.

"Just watch this," Sal said. "It's easier than me explaining."

The crew stopped walking and observed as a blubberlicious, red, Tachion squeezed its jelly-like form into one of the metal capsules in front of them.

"Don't stare so much," Sal whispered harshly noting the disgruntled look on the red Tachion's face because of the small audience it had drawn.

The capsule door closed and it begun to shake rapidly turning 360 degrees and vibrating violently. The blob inside was screaming for dear life.

"Is it some new form of extreme sport? Can I have a go?" Brad asked upbeat that he may have found one thing he liked about UC.

Sal rolled her eyes, "No Brad, It's not a game. Just watch."

The capsule reopened with a steaming fizz. Through the haze, an attractive woman stepped out of the pod. She smoothed down her hair and straightened out her clothes before vehemently sneering at the teen quartet, "You didn't see a thing."

"Like, oh, my, gosh! What in the world was that?" Mindy squealed.

"Yeah, where did that massive blob go and where did that hottie come from?" Brad asked just not getting it.

"That *blob* and that *hottie* are the same person. That's what you call Capsing." Sal said. "She's a Lappion, a Tachion that passes as a Code Type. That effect won't last forever, it'll wear off, and she'll need another fix."

"Whoa! A Lappion?" Brad said.

"Like, oh, my, like, gosh!" Mindy spluttered again, her vocabulary going into under drive. "I mean I've never seen a real life Lappion before. I thought they were like folklore, made up or something."

"No Lappions are real alright," Philippe said trying to sound knowledgeable, but he too had never witnessed anything like that with his own eyes.

"Well, I wouldn't know a Lappion if I saw one," Brad said.

"Well duh," Sal snapped. "The whole reason that they're Lappions is because they Caps and transform in secret. They're ashamed of themselves and don't want the whole world to know what they truly are."

"How come you know so much about Capsing?" Brad asked Sal.

"Forget about it," Sal said eyeballing Brad, and he did.

"Like it must be so-oo hard to be a Tachion and wanting to change yourself so badly that you'd put yourself through that," Mindy said trying to be sympathetic but sounding like she was giving a pep talk to one of her poodles.

"It's cool. I'm fine being a Tachion." Philippe said all too aware of his bulky, oversized muscles that he had unsuccessfully tried to hide under a baggy baseball shirt.

"Good for you," Sal said earnestly. The corners of her mouth slightly turned up in her attempt at a genuine smile.

Mindy fluttered her super-curly eyelashes, "Yeah, you're like so-oo perfect as you are Philly, I wouldn't want you to change a hair on your head."

Mindy and Philippe shared a secret smile, the muscles in his face twitched.

"Yeah good for you Big P," Brad said playfully punching Philippe's arm in a macho show of affection. "But I'm sure happy to be a bonafide Code Type, aren't you girls?"

Sal narrowed her eyes, and Mindy fluttered her eyelashes, both trying to warn Brad from making a tactless comment. But he didn't get the hint.

"I mean, I'd hate to be as gross as that creature that entered the capsule."

"Shut up, Brad." Sal pushed past him signalling the end of the conversation.

"Yeah, just like zip it," Mindy added tottering after Sal.

"What did I say?" Brad smiled chasing after Mindy, totally unaware of his insensitivity.

Philippe was left standing alone. He looked wistfully back at the dented silver pod and caught a glimpse of his cumbersome frame in its dull reflective surface. He stared at himself wondering as he often did what he would have looked like if he had been born a Code Type.

"I am what I am, and I'm proud of me," Philippe whispered his personal mantra before turning to catch up with the rest of the group.

***

Max, Cindy, Wain and I had walked away from the bright lights of the downtown district, and found ourselves in a dilapidated shantytown. Dirt roads sprouted crudely constructed plastic houses, which had broken glass windows and sticky tape holding doorframes together. The houses were empty, and there was no one to be seen.

"This is so eerie, yo. It's so quiet here," Wain gulped shining his torchlight in front of him.

"Too quiet." I said.

"Let's just count our lucky stars that we haven't come across any bother and hope that we find your troublesome little brother soon and get out of here." Max said taking another snap with the night vision button on his spectacles.

He was gathering lots of data to analyse later.

"Like, I hope we find Jet soon, these pumps are pinching my toes!" Cindy wailed as she hot stepped it down the potholed street.

The clicking of her heels coupled with the scent of young blood alerted the hidden locals that there were new people in town, who weren't from around these parts.

***

"So how do you know so much about Capsing?" Brad asked Sal again as he jogged to keep up with her along the busy street.

Sal turned and stared deeply into Brad's eyes. "What did you say?"

Brad gave a quizzical look as if trying to recite the alphabet backwards. "Umm, urgh? I don't know what I was saying, I just forgot."

"Braddy, you're so forgetful today." Mindy squealed, "But I'm so-oo glad you're in a better mood." She added sweetly.

"Yeah, I feel better, especially when I'm with you." Brad flashed the most magnificent dazzler.

"That's too cute." Mindy giggled.

Philippe felt a ball of jealousy plummet in his stomach. Now Brad was back on form; he was sure Mindy wouldn't pay him any more attention. He knew his looks would never win Mindy's heart, but his personality just might. He looked up and read the hand-painted sign above a rickety wooden door. It read *BARRACOON. Live music here!*

"Hey, let's go in here," Philippe said upbeat.

"Why?" Sal said testily. "We're not here to have a good time; we're here to find Jet and Skye."

"Well, this area is full of Capsules and Jet's a Code Type so wouldn't need to do that, but he sure loves playing his string music box thing so I reckon he'd head somewhere like this," Philippe said.

"Oh, my, gosh! Like a real-life music joint, where they play real live music!" Mindy piped joyously, "Madeleine Stone and the Pretties are going to die on the spot with envy when I tell them this!"

"Yeah, like totally awesome idea dude," Brad added.

He didn't care about the music; he just wanted to get off the streets and into less hazardous territory.

Sal stared hard at the music spot with all her young wisdom.

"Ok, you're right. Let's give it a shot," she nodded, bravely leading the way into the Barracoon.

***

"Who goes there?" Came a low whiney snarl from amongst the shadows. Mindy, Max, Wain and I froze mid step. No one dared breathe.

"I said who are ya?" A scraggy looking man morphed from the shadows, accompanied by several of his gaunt looking Goons.

They encircled us, looking like they lacked a decent meal and smelling like they needed a good bath.

"I'm Maxwell Schneider from 23 Glycena Avenue, nice to make your acquaintance sir. And you are?" Max said formerly extending his hand.

"I'm Grimm, Mr Grimm to you, the mayor of this town, and y'all are trespassing in my neighbourhood."

"Yup." The Goons nodded in agreement with their leader.

They were dressed in murky raggedy clothing and had greying sallow skin, which enabled them to camouflage into the bleak surroundings perfectly.

"Alright, we'll be going then," Wain said turning to leave.

"Not so fast," Mr Grimm and the Goons blocked our path. "What have ya got for us?"

"Nothing. Sorry to bother you, sir." I said.

Mr Grimm swiftly moved his whippet like body and saddled up next to me. I held my breath not wanting to inhale the pungent fumes emitting from his scarcely toothed mouth.

Max sprang into action typing furiously onto his aero pad.

"It seems we have entered a residential area unable to be seen by the untrained eye."

"And?" I whispered.

"They have allowed us, rather lured us, into the centre of their community, much like how the Achaearanea tepidariorum, commonly known as the house spider captures her prey in the centre of the web."

"Why don't you just make your point yo." Wain hissed his two brains racing.

Max gulped, "We are in danger guys, grave danger."

***

Inside the Barracoon was an old rundown amusement arcade littered with broken bumper cars, a carousel that no longer spun and a dismantled roller coaster.

The venue was jam-packed with colourful people of all Types. At the centre was a stage. On it, a compare dressed in a bright red tailcoat jacket and black top hat yelled into a handheld microphone.

"...The day is still young, the night yet to come, but whatever the weather we party!" The Ringleader roared as the crowd erupted into a raucous round of cheers.

"Next up for your listening pleasure is the best to ever do it. The greatest of all time. The one, the only – *Paisley Parade!*"

On stage, a troupe of performers - whose hair on one side was swept back - blew, plucked, struck, strummed, banged and rattled a variety of musical instruments as the lead singer danced and sung his heart out.

"Wow!" Sal said.

The crew were captivated. They had never experienced such musical genius.

Everyone in the place was dancing with unabashed glee. Necks were bobbing, waists rolling, arms waving, feet shuffling, hands clapping, fingers snapping; the revellers knew how to have fun. Unrestrained laughter rung out all the way from the dancefloor to the rafters.

"Now this is my kind of place!" Philippe shouted enthusiastically over the music as he tried to join in with the dancing.

"Like, oh my." Mindy covered her eyes with her hands, yet peered through open fingers in sheer bashful delight.

"This place is the bomb zee," Brad added enjoying the music but not quite knowing what to do with himself.

"It's the ultimate cool." Even Sal lost herself to the mind-blowing infectious groove. The vibe was electric. "Let's head to the balcony for a better look."

"Look over there!" Brad pointed tactlessly.

Sal saw a striking blue Tachion kissing a stunning Code Type Ae girl.

"So they're smooching, big deal?"

"I think they make a cute couple," Mindy said smiling coyly at Philippe.

Philippe looked down at his feet, the muscles on his face rippled.

"Not them. There!" Brad pointed further towards a person who had a lion face, a man's torso and robotic legs.

"Wow wee." Philippe was flabbergasted, "It can't be?"

"I think it is," Sal said.

107

"What is it?" Mindy asked.

Today they had seen the most extraordinary beings, but nothing came close to this.

"It's an AniMaTron. A hybrid of animal, man and machine. They are one of the rarest species on the planet." Sal said.

"I know!" Brad said happy that he was finally knowledgeable about something. "Last year at the world games in Freeca we played ball against an entire team of AniMaTrons. They are born warriors, the stiffest competition we've ever experienced. They completely thrashed us."

"Those guys are tougher than tough, practically undefeatable." Philippe agreed.

The AniMaTron was in deep discussion with a Lappion who was on the come down halfway through a Capsing transition. Half his body was a young strapping Code Type, while the other half was an old silver wrinkled Tachion.

"Amazing." Mindy marvelled.

The Barracoon was violating all kinds of Truths laid out by the Authorities. No such gathering would be permitted on the Upper Worlds.

"So this is what we've feared about UC the whole time," Philippe shouted over the music.

"Fun!" Brad said snapping his fingers.

Mindy threw her arms around Sal and hugged her tightly.

"Thank you for bringing us here. It's the best place ever!"

Sal was taken aback by the warm gesture, "That's cool, I didn't do anything."

"Yes, you did. I'll never forget this day as long as I live." Mindy beamed.

Just like any other mere mortal, Sal couldn't help but feel happy that she had pleased Mindy. Her sweet personality was contagious, and she had just made herself a new fan.

Paisley Parade ended their performance, and the crowd cheered in appreciation. Turntables levitated in the middle of the dance floor, and the Ringleader started spinning some tunes.

"It's so like, free, here. You don't have to fit a Type; you can be whoever you want to be. Just look around you. It's beautiful." Mindy said poignantly.

Sal looked at her, surprised by her thoughtful comment. Philippe smiled affectionately; he knew there was so much more to Mindy than just good looks.

"You're right." Philippe agreed, "This gathering certainly would never happen at home. Any difference is rejected because it scares people."

"You're both so right. It's crazy that we try to fit in with someone else's ideals of perfection. Who made the rules anyway?" Sal flashed a rare smile.

Perhaps the oxygen levels were low in this place, but she felt good, lightheaded, without a care in the world.

"You know, I've never experienced anything like this before in UC. Things are exceptionally smooth today."

"I hope the others are having as good a time as us," Mindy said.

"Yeah, they might have even found Jet and Skye by now." Brad was hopeful.

"Maybe but Wain said he would let me know telepathically," Philippe said, unsure of exactly how that would work.

"I almost forgot what we came for," Sal said. "We should get going. We've got work to do."

"Aww," Brad moaned losing his new found rhythm.

"Let's get a drink before we go. My head's pounding, maybe because this cool music is so loud." Philippe said.

"Ok, just the one." Sal retook charge of the mission.

They walked away from the balcony and approached a long, glass-topped bar.

"What can I get you?" The bartender, an eight-armed Aqua Tachion with the name badge, *Seymour* slurred without looking at them.

His four pairs of hands were busy pouring drinks and wiping down glasses.

"Four H_2O to go," Sal ordered extending her thumbprint for payment ID.

"You only want water? Hard times huh?" Seymour chuckled chewing absentmindedly on a cocktail stick.

He looked up at each of the crew individually, and his eyes widened. The cocktail stick dropped from his mouth.

"I don't believe it!" He exclaimed, "You've come! You're here!"

Sal, Mindy, Philippe and Brad looked at each other puzzled.

"Look, we don't want any trouble," Sal said, on high alert.

Seymour boomed a hearty laugh before jumping on the bar and waving his arms madly in the air.

"OSEYI! OSEYI!! OSEYI!!!" He bellowed to all in the Arcade. "They have come, THEY ARE HERE!"

The Ringmaster scratched the music to a stop, leaving an ear piercing silence. Everyone in the Arcade stopped partying and what felt like a million pairs of eyes looked from Sal to Mindy to Philippe to Brad.

Brad's body became rigid. He prepared for what was surely his pending doom. "Maaan! I knew this was too good to be true."

Sal looked around for an escape route. Philippe pulled Mindy behind him protectively and put up his dukes, ready for a fight. He had never fought anyone in his life, but he was big and strong, maybe he could protect them all.

"Like, what is going on?" Mindy squealed.

People always admired her beauty, but this attention was different, intense. The Arcadian Urbanites stared at her in a way she had never seen before.

"Let's, go, now!" Sal said tightly, making a beeline for the exit.

Seymour's arms blocked their path.

"What the -" Sal huffed.

Before the crew could move another muscle, the entire crowd of Arcadian Urbanities dropped to the ground on their hands and knees and bowed before them singing in awed unison, "You are welcome!"

***

"I'm sending distress signals telepathically to Philippe, but I don't know if he's receiving them," Wain said wriggling to free himself from the ties that bound him.

We were strung up together in the middle of the dusty shantytown. A raging fire flickered eye-wateringly close. Mr Grimm and his Goons had left us to go and squabble over the gadgets from Max's backpack.

"Like I hope Philippe gets the message soon, I'm too beautiful to die an ugly death." Cindy yelped.

I shifted trying to undo the tight knot binding my hands and feet. I was truly sorry to have gotten my friends into this mess. What was I thinking anyway? It was so stupid of me to come all the way to UC, to look for Jet. It was a forbidden territory for a reason. I had foolishly followed what my ma would call my instincts. Perhaps what my dad always said was right, maybe when I finally got my Type, I would act more rationally. I couldn't wait for my Code to kick in. Then I wouldn't be so impulsive.

Mr Grimm morphed from the shadows.

"So ya bought us nothing except this junk." He said tossing Max's aero pad in a heap with all of his other belongings.

"I'll have you know that is not junk? It's state of the art gadgetry, I made it myself."

Mr Grimm sneered. The Goons salivated, globs of spittle hung from their mouths like rabid dogs.

"Eh hem," Max coughed nervously at his outburst. "Perhaps, good sirs, this would interest you?" He said offering up his state of the art IM. "You can have it, use it, sell it and we'll be on our way - as soon as I've copied over my hard drive. Give me ten seconds." Max bartered.

A Goon with yellowing eyes indicating iron deficiency and rotting teeth indicating a deficiency of toothpaste snatched the IM and bit into it. Shards of his enamel flew to the floor as his teeth broke off.

"If we can't eat it, it's no good to us," the now toothless Goon guffed.

"Do you know how much that costs?" Max said astounded that his high tech was now a pile of rubbish.

"Shaddup!" Mr Grimm screamed. "We don't need those machinery thingamajigs. They can't help us survive."

I shifted uneasily as Mr Grimm's scrawny figure ambled around the group.

"Look what living in the Upper Worlds has done for ya. Y'all so alive. All that oxygenated air, drinking all that H_2O, the abundance of sunlight! We have none of that. We're dying here."

Mr Grimm sniffed around us like a tracker dog.

"Look at your skin." Mr Grimm said poking my chin with a bony finger. "All that melanin. Do you know how I crave that richness?"

I pulled away disgustedly. He lifted up Max's chin and examined his chattering teeth.

"And look at your healthy canines and molars. There's enough calcium for the whole town in your gob."

"And your," He paused looking at Wain, "your bountiful grey matter." He said tapping Wain's enlarged cranium like a drum.

"Ow, yo!" Wain complained.

"I could live for another fifty years from those cells."

"And you." Mr Grimm licked his paper thin, dry lips and held onto Cindy's delicate face, "Ya look good enough to eat." He salivated baring his discoloured dagger-shaped teeth."

"Ewww!" Cindy squealed.

"We need the regeneration from your stem cells. And we'll have ya roasted, fried or even stewed," a Goon cackled.

"Oh, my! Like whatever you do don't stew me, my skin goes all wrinkly in hot water." Cindy stated seriously.

Max and Wain looked at her in disbelief,

"I don't think you've grasped the seriousness of the situation," Max said perplexed.

"Yeah. Seriously yo? We're about to be eaten, and you're worried about how you're gonna look?" Wain asked incredulously.

"Of course. On-trend until the end!" Cindy said with an air-headed smile.

"Aw Cinds!" I buried my head in my hands.

Mr Grimm and his Goons wheezed and spluttered, roaring with unhealthy laughter.

***

Sal, Mindy, Philippe and Brad were seated on golden jewel encrusted thrones in the centre of a Great Hall. The palatial room ran underneath the Barracoon and was decorated ornately. Diamonds and pearls hung from the chandeliers. Priceless artwork from the early 20th century rose period adorned the high windowless walls. Ancient handcrafted Persian rugs, aristocratic Ghanaian Kente cloth and the finest Chinese silk, were strewn over the floor and ruffled between the Grecian pillars. Treasures from the Seven Wonders of the World were displayed on hieroglyphic columns. No one would have guessed that such a decadent setting would be hidden beneath such a run down amusement arcade.

"This place is the ultimate in awesome." Brad's dazzling smile had returned with a vengeance, lighting up his face.

"This is one million times better than being crowned prom queen!" Mindy squealed, waving at

115

the Arcadians below as if she was an actual princess.

A regally dressed Urbanite appeared on the stage before them. He looked like a textbook Sap - old and withered. The robed man bowed before them.

"Dear ones. I am Ecclesiastes. We your faithful followers have waited a long time for your coming. You are welcome."

"Yeah right back at you, buddy." Brad joked.

"Shush!" Sal warned Brad scornfully, trying desperately to comprehend what was going on.

Ecclesiastes continued, "We will do everything in our power to serve you."

"Like really? My feet are so-oo hurting and – "

Before Mindy could finish her sentence two Arcadian Urbanites were on hand to remove her shoes, a bowl of warm water was rushed in, and her feet massaged.

"Like, oh my goodness!" Mindy yelped in delight.

"Dude, are you like The Res or something?" Philippe asked cautiously.

The very mention of his name made the entire room of Urbanites bow once again in submission.

"The honour of The Res being does not dwell within my shell," Ecclesiastes said respectfully. "But we are your loyal subjects, not his."

"Maybe we're not who you think we are, and this could be a severe case of mistaken identity," Sal said.

"Your identities could never be mistaken," Ecclesiastes said. "Please regard this." He instructed gently before unveiling the wall in front of them.

"What the - " Sal muttered.

The muscles in Philippe's face trembled.

Brad's dazzler drooped.

"Oh, my. Like, what?" Mindy spluttered.

"Is that me?" Brad moaned.

"This doesn't make any sense," Sal murmured, "You need to tell us what in the world is happening here."

"Yes, of course - " Ecclesiastes began, but before he could continue. Philippe cried out in pain.

"Aaargh!" He grabbed his head, lost his footing and came crashing to the ground.

"Big P!"

"Philly!" screamed Brad and Mindy simultaneously, rushing to his side.

"What's wrong?" Sal cried out, totally losing her cool.

"It's the others," Philippe wailed through gritted teeth. "I'm receiving multiple distress signals in my head. They're in big trouble."

***

"...Look at it logically." Max pleaded, "You can't eat us. We would take ages to cook, and we

117

wouldn't even be tasty. Our bones are too hard and - "

"Shaddup!"Mr Grimm commanded fiercely. "I've had enough of pussyfooting with y'all. Stoke up the fire boys, and get that barbeque blazing. This one first." Mr Grimm yanked Cindy up by her hair.

"Like Aww!" Cindy was fearful but unable to cry; instead, she pouted prettily.

"Listen," I said attempting to stand up. "This is all my fault, take me and let my friends go. My father is powerful. He's a high-ranking experimental biologist on the Upper Worlds. He will get you all the DNA you want, the lab where he works has tons of that kind of stuff."

"I'm not leaving you," Max said. "Against my better judgement I came here with you and I'm sticking with you."

I shot Max a sideways glance. He appeared to be thinking outside of his logical framework, acting out of Type, which was something unheard of.

"We roll as a unit or not at all," Wain agreed with Max.

Mr Grimm grinned, amused by the show of solidarity.

"Well if that's how y'all wanna play it, you can perish together."

He threw Cindy back down.

"So it'll be you first." Mr Grimm cut my ties and dragged me towards the fire. "Let's see how brave you are now!" He hacked and wheezed.

"Enough!" A voice boomed as a tall man stepped from the shadows. A bright maroon light illuminated the noble looking figure.

The shantytown Goons cowered.

I knew this man. I had never seen him before on the Upper Worlds but I had met him plenty of times in my dreams. He held out his hand expectantly, and Mr Grimm removed me from his vice like grip.

"Nice to make your acquaintance Keziah." The tall man said.

He was dressed in a well-tailored purple suit and had shades on in the dark.

"Who are you?" I asked astounded.

"I'm known as The Res, and this is *my* city."

"The Res." I gasped in shock.

Max wiggled himself free and walked up to The Res gawking,

"Fascinating." He mouthed, adjusting his spectacles. "This field trip is even better than one could have wished for."

"Boy, are we glad to see you. I thought we were done for." Wain breathed a sigh of relief. Then covered his mouth with his three palms for speaking out of turn. This man was rumoured to be so bad that he could destroy an entire neighbourhood just by clicking his fingers.

"Certainly there are others you'd like to see more," The Res beckoned behind him.

Jet and Skye sheepishly stepped out from his humongous shadow.

"Jet!" I cried, grabbing and hugging my brother. I pulled Skye in too.

"What do you two think you're playing at?" I laughed and cried. I had never been so happy to see these little dorks.

"It's good to see you too, Sis." Jet smirked mischievously.

"Hey, Kid." Skye rasped shyly in her husky voice.

She hardly ever spoke, and when she did, it was usually only to Jet.

The Res folded his arms, "I've been tracking your movements since you and your compadres entered Underground City. You would never have come to any harm. You just had to go through this experience so I could see what you were made of. Now please excuse me."

The Res turned from the group and strode up to Mr Grimm and his Goons.

"Jeez! If that's The Res, shouldn't we be afraid of him or something?" Wain asked wide-eyed.

"I don't know, but I don't think so," I answered.

I couldn't explain that The Res always helped me in my dreams. That would sound way too weird.

"I can't wait for school on Monday when I tell the entire Top Tables what went down," Cindy said poofing out her hair and reapplying lip-gloss, unfazed by the mayhem all around.

Max and Wain looked at each other unbelievably.

I pulled Jet to the side.

"Seriously Jet, what do you think you're playing at? You can't go running off like that."

"I'm not a drama queen." Jet said flatly still hurt by what I'd said yesterday.

"Ok, ok. I'm sorry," I knew that Jet was as sensitive as I was. "But you didn't need to run off to teach me a lesson."

"I wasn't trying to teach you a lesson. I wanted to find out about the Harlequin, but I got sidetracked. There's so much to see and do down here. I went to a music arcade and played my guitar with real musicians. They taught me ancient music chords and everything," Jet said excitedly. "This place is incredible!"

"That's all well and good that you had fun, but it's so dangerous down here. It's no place for us." I argued feeling like I sounded like our ma, or worse still our dad.

"It hasn't been scary for us at all. Skye and I have been with The Res the whole time."

I looked over at The Res who was sternly talking to Mr Grimm and his Goons.

"How did you find him?"

"I didn't, he found us as soon as Skye and I entered UC, he had the Torpedo waiting for us at the bottom of the escalator."

"What's the Torpedo?" I asked.

"It's a-a-a. It's too hard to explain, you'll see." Jet said.

I frowned. None of this made any sense.

"Why was The Res waiting for you? Why does he care who you are? Why has he rescued us? How did he know to - "

"I don't know." Jet interrupted with a shrug.

Jet's dismissiveness annoyed me. Why was he acting so blasé amidst so much trouble?

"You put us all in danger. The whole crew came out to get you and Skye home safely, and all you can do is smile like an idiot!" I yelled.

Jet shrugged again and walked off to join Skye.

"Don't be upset with your brother; anger is such a wasteful emotion."

I heard The Res speak to me, but when I turned to look his way, his lips weren't moving.

"All of this was meant to be." The Res continued coolly, his voice inside my head. *"You have many questions; all will be answered in time. Now please, give me a moment."*

The Res refocused his attention on the Shantytown dwellers. He glared at Mr Grimm and his Goons whose spindly legs trembled in fear.

"I've warned you before about this kind of behaviour Sidney. Now, what do you think I should do with you?"

"Errm maybe let us go with a stern talking to? Let's call it a final warning. We'll never break the law again, Your Honour, Mister Res sir." Mr Grimm wheezed nervously.

"No, I think you should be punished." The Res said coolly.

With one flick of his index finger, he made several of the Goons' hair and teeth fall out. The Res swiped his finger the other way and sewed their lips together, pulling a zipper across their faces.

Some Goons at the back of the mob tried to escape. By wriggling his little finger, The Res turned them into paper-thin shadows of their former selves and one by one they fell to the ground like a row of dominoes. The Res blew out a soft puff of air, and the Goons closest to him inflated like helium balloons and floated high into the sky.

"Woah!" I gasped.

The Res had hardly moved a muscle.

"I don't like wasting my time or my talent." The Res bellowed. "Let that be a lesson to all of you."

He turned to Mr Grimm and addressed him quietly, "Don't let me have to embarrass you in front of your clan like that again Sidney."

"No Mister Res, I mean yes Mister Res." Mr Grimm trembled feebly.

The Res left Mr Grimm and his now oddly shaped mob quaking in their boots and strode, long powerful steps, towards me.

"That was spectacular." I gushed.

The Res smiled a perfectly symmetrical grin that seemed out of place on his stern face.

"Thank you. Please excuse the minor distraction."

"All of my tech is ruined," Max said picking up his broken aero pad from the heap of gadgetry destroyed by the Goons. "I have no idea if the rest of the crew are okay."

"Oh my goodness! Where's my Twinny?" Cindy wailed, finally showing concern for the scary situation.

"Your Twin and your friends are all fine." The Res assured us as he flipped out his phone.

"Now!" he commanded, and in a split second a shiny, oblong-shaped vehicle appeared.

It was completely sealed with no indication of wheels, windows or doors and levitated in the air silently. With its state of the art design, it was the most impressive cruiser I had ever seen.

"That's the Torpedo." Jet smiled.

An entrance in the Torpedo, the closest thing to what you could call a door, opened up to reveal a spacious interior that could not be detected from the outside.

"Hey, Langston." Jet greeted the driver who was fully kitted out in racing gear.

"Yes, young squire." Langston high-fived Jet, then saluted The Res as he entered the vehicle.

"This is phenomenal!" Wain exclaimed, throwing his arms in the air.

"Take a seat." The Res ordered.

Jet and Skye scrambled straight in. Wain, Max and Cindy ventured into the Torpedo in awe. I remained on the dusty sidewalk with the disfigured Goons wailing in agony behind me.

On the Upper Worlds, The Res was regarded as the number one enemy of the state. How could we trust him? The Res stared at me poker-faced.

"I think it would be wise if you joined us, Keziah. You must have many questions, and your explanations are long overdue."

"What does that mean?" I asked.

Wain and Max stared wide-eyed looking back and forth from me to The Res. Jet and Skye lounged comfortably. Cindy buffed her chipped fingernails.

"Playtime is over, so please sit!" The Res commanded.

I realised he meant business and quickly hopped in. The doors closed instantly, and the Torpedo pulled off at top speed.

***

"This is a place of divinity," The Res said as he opened the door to the Great Hall revealing Sal, Mindy, Philippe and Brad.

"Cindy, you're safe!" Mindy squealed in joy at the sight of her sister.

She ran and threw her arms around her Twin.

"Oh, Minds it's been just awful without you." Cindy sniffed sadly, smiling all the while.

"Ditto Twinny," Mindy said, but if truth be told she was having the best day ever.

The Res stepped aside as the rest of the gang were reunited. Everyone hugged and high fived each other, excitedly all talking at once.

"...Then the blob came out of the Capsule and was a seriously hot chick." Brad slapped Max on the back.

"So the Goons had us tied up, and I wasn't scared at all, yo." Wain boasted to Philippe.

"...Look at the thrones; they're pure gold! It's better than being voted Ms Teen Upper Worlds." Mindy gushed.

"...And the rumours are true, they dance down here, like this." Philippe demonstrated to Wain.

"Has anyone got any blotting powder? I'm like all shiny" Cindy queried.

"Fascinating," Max said making a mental note of what was being said since he had no more working tech to record anything on.

"Kid's friends are so lame," Jet snorted.

"Be nice; I think they're ok." Skye rasped softly.

"Do you?"

"Yeah, they're always cool with me."

"Well, if you like them I'll try and make an effort." Jet relented. He would do anything for Skye.

"We are your loyal servants. You are most welcome." The Arcadian Urbanites threw themselves at my feet.

"What's all this about?" I asked.

"Pretty cool isn't it?" Jet was amused as more people dropped to their knees as we walked by. "People have been doing that to me all day."

"You can stand up guys." Unlike Jet, I was uncomfortable with this intense attention.

The Arcadians rose on my command.

"You will lead us to victory." A part elephant, part man, part machine said shaking my hand with his trunk.

I had never seen such a being and gawped in speechless awe.

Sal urgently pulled me to the side, "You have to see this."

"Brace yourself Kid, this is going to mess with your mind," Brad warned.

"You guys come and look too," Philippe signalled the others.

"That's so old, Skye and I have seen it already." Jet tutted.

"It is icy though." Skye fidgeted, linking his arm.

"What is it?" I smiled in anticipation; everyone seemed to know what was going on apart from me.

"This." Sal slowly turned me around.

The main wall of the Great Hall was a shrine. Several portraits were displayed majestically in jewel-encrusted frames. The works of art were beautifully crafted, hand-drawn paintings on old-style paper. It took me a moment to compute and then I realised that the pictures were of us!

My image was the centrepiece. I was seated on a beautiful throne, looking over my shoulder at Jet. Jet's portrait was of him as an adult. He looked rugged and serious. His eyes were not their usual brown but instead reflected silver. A line of people I had never seen before stood behind him. Skye was next to Jet linking his arm like she always did. She too looked older and wiser and sat cross-legged levitating above the ground.

On the right-hand side of my image stood Sal, she had two heads. Philippe's painting blew me away. It portrayed how he would look if he had been born as a bonafide Code Type without any mutations. He was dashingly handsome with dark brown hair and piercing blue eyes.

Next in line were the Twins. Mindy was smiling, but tears streamed down her face. Cindy had a frown, which was so odd as it was an expression she could never genetically pull.

In his portrait, Brad was laden with many sporting medals, but instead of his buff physique, he had the body of a Sap - small and scrawny.

Max stood at the head of an army of scientists. He was dressed in the official Authoritarian issue white coat and safety goggles.

Wain stood at the end of the line. His arms outstretched with three fists in the air, in the Tachion Liberation victory salute.

I gazed at the paintings in amazement.

"My Mind is officially blown."

"Why are all our pictures here, yo?" Wain asked, wide-eyed.

"Like they could have drawn a better picture of me," Cindy squealed in horror. "My face is like totally distorted."

"Forget you, look at me," Brad shuddered. "How come I'm Mr puny?"

Max walked around eyeing the paintings. Then he began a slow handclap.

"Bravo, you've got us this time Kid, you trickster, you. I get it. Where are the TV cameras?

Is this being filmed for one of those prank shows on TEN?"

"This is nothing to do with me; I didn't set it up," I said as utterly bewildered as the rest of them.

Everyone started talking at once, pointing to the pictures of themselves and discussing why they looked the way they did.

The Res strode up to the shrine. As he did so the Arcadian Urbanites once again dropped to their knees and cowered, this time in fear and not reverence.

"I...I...I don't understand. I don't get it." I said, searching The Res' face for answers.

"Ha! It's got to be a big joke, right?" Wain laughed nervously.

"This is not an elaborate hoax." The Res addressed the group seriously.

"Then what is going on here?" Max said. "These portraits of us look ancient. That is just not logical."

"Do not question me, boy!" The Res said ferociously.

"Sorry Mr Res, sir." Max gulped fearfully.

The Res' sharp tone hung in the air as a hush descended across the room. He turned his scowl into the most uncomfortable rigid smile. It wasn't a smile with genuine warmth; rather it looked like one that a great white shark would give you before it gobbled you up in the ocean.

"All has meaning." The Res said more cordially. "Ecclesiastes, please make sure our young guests are well looked after and told *precisely* what they need to know."

"Yes Your Honour, Chief Resident in Charge." Ecclesiastes bowed knowingly.

My stomach flipped, I wanted to be sick. I was scared and intrigued at the same time. I needed answers to questions that I didn't even know to ask.

The Res must have read my mind and said, "Let me explain."

What's the use in trying?

*When there's nothing more
you can do?*

Just Be.

*Embrace the Humankind in
you.*

SEVEN

The Prophecy

I sank into a soft cushioned chair in The Res' dwellings. It was a strange den decked in purple and black velvet materials and old paper books. The very few forms of modern gadgetry, like the transporter, looked out of place in this museum piece.

The Res took a seat in a wooden chair by a hole in the wall that simulated a roaring fire. He rocked gently back and forth as he chugged on a pipe.

I dragged Jet to my side, and he flopped down on the sofa beside me.

"I'm never going to let you out of my sight again," I vowed.

Jet smirked and fidgeted with his hands IMing Skye exactly what was happening.

"Messaging won't work down here," I told him.

"I know," he said without looking at me. "She can read them later, I don't want Skye to miss out on any of the action."

"How did you and Skye get past the PGs?" I asked.

"We overpowered them." Jet said nonchalantly, not even bothering to look up from his IM.

"What? That simply isn't possible. I saw how big they were. You guys are too small to take them on."

Jet finally looked at me and chewed the corner of his lip nervously. "Skye used her powers and took them out with a single note."

"Jet! Have you lost your mind? You know Tachions aren't allowed to harness their powers! Why would you let Skye do something so reckless?"

"It's not reckless. Skye and I have been in training for a while. She can do the most awesome things with just her voice."

"Jet!" I shouted. "You've gone too far now."

"You get Wain to pull *The Face* all the time. What's the difference?"

I shifted uncomfortably, "Pulling *The Face* is not against the law it's just something special Wain can do."

"Really? Well, try explaining that to The Orbs and The Guardians, see if they'd agree with you." Jet fired back.

The Res cleared his throat loudly. We stopped bickering and stared at him.

"I'm sure it's a challenge to take this all in." He said calmly.

"I don't understand what is going on," I said, leaving my agitation with Jet, for now.

"Indeed." He puffed out a blue vapour. "I'll begin shall I?"

The Res had a way of asking questions that made me feel like he didn't require an answer.

"Yes, please. I'm baffled by all of this too." Jet chimed in goofily.

"Young Jet," The Res boomed, "your time will come. But for now it's Keziah's time to lead the way, and you will take your cue from her."

"Cue for what?" I said. "I don't understand? How did you know we were coming to UC?"

"Because I sent Tia to your school to awaken you."

"The Harlequin?" Jet and I both gasped.

The Res nodded, "Yes Tia is her name, she is an Arcadian Urbanite."

"But she was fuzzed!" Jet blurted out.

"I am aware of that," The Res said without emotion. "It was for the greater good."

Poor Tia I thought. She had risked her life, wasted it for no reason, all because a bunch of entertainers who gathered at a run down amusement arcade were mislead into believing that I was somehow, something special.

"She knew what part she had to play," The Res continued. "Lady Zono told us. She predicted this meeting in UC. But it was taking too long, so I sent Tia to speed up the proceedings. I knew someone would put the pieces of the puzzle together and come to UC for answers. I'm glad Jets adventurous spirit got the ball rolling."

"Who's Lady Bono?" Jet said.

"ZO-NO." The Res said loud and clearly, taking the pipe away from his mouth.

"What does this lady have to do with me?" I asked.

"Lady Zono is the mystic who can read the signs from The Prophecy."

"What Prophecy?" Jet and I asked together. We were starting to speak in unison like the Twins, which was so not cool.

"The Prophecy of the Soul Survivor," The Res said as he stopped rocking and looked directly into my eyes.

"And what has that got to do with me?" I asked.

"*Everything.*" The Res bellowed.

"Icy! That sounds way cool!" Jet stood up throwing his arms in the air.

His IM slipped from his hand, flew across the room and knocked a crystal ball from the desk. It fell to the ground and smashed into pieces.

"Jet! Stop being so careless and just sit over there in silence!!" I yelled.

All of this talk of a Prophecy had put me on edge. Instead of clearing things up, The Res was making everything more confusing.

Jet sheepishly retreated to a corner of the room and sat on a mat on the floor.

"With all this erratic activity, it's as if the scatty witch is here with us." The Res murmured to himself.

He waggled a finger, and the broken pieces of crystal floated back onto his desk.

"That crystal ball belongs to Lady Zono. She'll get it back in due course, although I doubt she'll be too pleased with what you've done to it. She loves those things."

136

"I'm sorry about that Mr Res, sir," I said awkwardly. "We Upper Worldian Code Types have never done anything like this before. We're kind of nervous in UC."

"You Code Types? What Code Type is that then?" The Res asked stroking his goatee.

"I'm not sure," I began feeling under pressure. I always felt embarrassed when I was forced to have this conversation about my Type.

"My ma says I'm a late bloomer as my Code Type isn't apparent yet - "

"That's because you haven't got a Code Type." The Res interjected. "Neither has Jet."

"What?" Jet and I said together astonished.

The Res shook his head disgustedly.

"Pah! You think you're *Code Types*?" He spat like it was the most absurd thing in the world.

"It's obvious the time is well overdue for you to understand The Prophecy." The Res said, pressing his index fingers and thumbs together and resting his chin atop the triangle his hands formed.

I hugged a cushion tightly to my chest. Jet sat mouth agape on the mat. He had our full attention.

The Res relit his pipe and started rocking before he spoke.

"The evolution of humanity will lead to its eventual elimination.

For man is too busy in the construction of destruction.

Too concerned with dying to live.

But the purest soul, born of Human flesh,
Will lead the way that saves the rest."

He paused for effect looking at Jet and I. We looked at each other puzzled.

"I suppose you've never heard that verse before?" The Res asked.

"No." Jet and I shrugged.

We had no idea what he was on about.

The Res exhaled deeply creating a large blue smoky ring above his head.

"That's about as far as I get memorising quotations," he muttered to himself before levitating a weathered leather bound, paper book from the book shelf to his hand.

"This is The Vortex of Souls. It's our book of divinity written aeons ago," The Res said leafing through the exquisite hand scribed book, which had ornate inscriptions in a language I couldn't read on the cover.

"It's essentially a manual from our more forward thinking ancestors who kept important information to hand down to subsequent generations. Ah! Here it is."

The Res found the passage he was looking for and read the text aloud.

"Slaying the three-eyed beast will pave the course of change.
One Soul shall survive, come what may.
Tenacity, strength but mostly grace.
A leader will emerge to change the face,
Of the universe, for the next million years.

Have faith, have passion, but have no fears.
For everything is everything, what will be will be.
Trust that the Soul Survivor dwells within you and me."

The Res closed the book shut with a thud and dust plumed from it, joining the smoke rings in the air.

"What in the world does that mean?" Jet asked.

"You know nothing? Nothing at all about this?" The Res seemed somewhat perturbed for the first time.

We both shook our head.

"You have no conscious comprehension of who you are, do you?"

"No." I answered feeling more confused with every word The Res said.

"I guess the Authorities have done a total number on your parents." He muttered before becoming deadly serious.

"This is *The Prophecy of the Soul Survivor*. It states that a time is coming, in fact it's upon us now, where the world will be totally uninhabitable to us all. Code Types, Tachions, Saps, Lappions, AniMaTrons, Morphers, every being, every animal, every insect, every plant, every life form, every soul on earth will perish."

He stood up and begun to pace the well-worn room, "You see our predecessors sold us out a long time ago. They cared nothing for us in the future. Back then they took everything this world

139

had to offer, leaving us, their children's, children's, children the scraps of civilisation.

"Their selfish actions played us, destroying everything we would need to survive in this world. However in life, as in any good game, if the cards are not stacked in your favour, you might just have to find a cheat, to win." The Res paused looking from me to Jet.

"What does that mean?" Jet said, looking as worried as I.

"It means you're our trump card. You are the exception to the rule. You're the one that no one accounted for. Our ancestors didn't factor you into the game as they couldn't conceive you'd even be a player.

"You're the one the mystics predicted, the philosophers theorised about, the Alpha the Arcadian Urbanites and free thinkers the world over revere.

"You're not a Code Type Keziah, or Tachion or Sap or a combination of any other life form on earth who are only able to successfully harness one major talent, or are flawed and defected. Your soul survived progress, technological advancement and the destruction of our ancestors. You are the Soul Survivor, a bonafide genetic throwback.

"You, my dear, are Purely. Wonderfully. Incredibly. Human."

"What?!" I bugged out.

Humans no longer existed on earth. Yes, they were our forefathers but were extinct many moons ago. My dad had bored Jet and me about his job on so many occasions that we were well versed on the extinction of Humankind.

Humans once populated the earth. They came in many shapes, sizes and hues, spoke many languages and had many differing customs. They were chaotic and destructive, but on the upside, each Human did have the ability to be brilliant at many things. This is what my dad called, 'The Human Potential' and lamented that it was scientific progress greatest loss.

Back then Human scientists were always looking for ways to improve the species. In essence, they wanted to create perfect Human beings. They began manufacturing humanoids with enhancements. The early humanoids were defected and carried mutations. They became what we now know as Tachions, like Wain and Skye.

The Human scientists continued until they successfully engineered the humanoid into what they thought was a state of perfection. Ultimate beings extraordinary in one particular field in which they would excel. They were what we now call Code Types like Brad, The Twins, Max and Sal.

The Human scientists also created Tech like the robotic Guardians and the Orbs and even Animal, Tech and Code Type hybrids like the AniMaTrons.

The trouble was that in perfecting only one particular Human attribute they had unwittingly bred out the extraordinary multi-faceted potential of Human beings, people with the ability to create endless possibilities. Put simply, the capacity to be

141

awesome at many things. It was only Humans who had that potential. The Human scientists discovered that being perfect in every single area did not exist.

In their constant pursuit of perfection, Humans had created many things, but ultimately their search for progress had eradicated themselves.

"Eww, I don't want to be Human!" I cried out.

"But that's what you are." The Res said sternly, "It's something to be very proud of.

"With your Human kindness, you have the power to save us all. You must capture the three-eyed beast, spoken of in the Vortex of Souls and set us all free. That is your entire reason for being born Human. It is your mission on earth."

I gulped before I could find my voice to speak,

"The Res, sir. Me, the Soul Survivor, Human? This is a big mistake. Someone's got it very wrong."

"There's nothing wrong." He answered swiftly, "Everyone, even me, has their part to play in The Prophecy. All those close to you, even those who vex you," The Res glanced at Jet, "have a vital role in the mission. That is why I didn't immediately stop the shantytown dwellers nonsense. I needed to see what you were made of. And you proved yourself to be selfless. No Code Type, unless re-engineered for senseless bravery, would ever do what you did for your friends."

I looked at The Res open-mouthed. This was crazy! Here I was with the most notorious man in the underworld, the sworn enemy of the Upper Worlds and he was telling me I was the Soul Survivor, the chosen one who was born Human to save the planet!

Maybe he was a mentalist. The Res was charming, but in no way was he friendly. He was incredibly powerful and fearsome. Not someone I should be getting cosy with in UC.

Jumping up I threw the cushion to the side, "It's time to go Jet."

"But The Res hasn't finished, he was telling us about - "

"Get up Jet!" I ordered through gritted teeth.

"So finally you're truly afraid." The Res said returning to his chair. "It's taken you a long time to get to that emotion. That's good, very good. A great leader should be fearless."

"I'm not afraid," I lied, "this is all a bit much to take in, especially from you. You're The Res! No disrespect but where we come from you're known as a wicked man."

The Res looked at me thoughtfully before answering.

"Do you think I'm wicked?" He asked with a piercing stare.

His earlier uncomfortable cheeriness had well and truly departed.

I answered cautiously, "Well no – you protected us and have been very hospitable."

"But perhaps Mr Grimm would think so because of the way I chastised him?" He continued, stroking his goatee.

"Yes, but they were going to harm us, so I'm glad you stepped in."

"Exactly," The Res snapped his fingers. "All has meaning. What is *good* and what is *bad* are all relative, different interpretations for each person. That is not to say that bad things do not happen, and goodness is not a virtue, but be watchful of the judgements you make."

What did that even mean? I stood rooted to my spot. Jet looked from The Res to me. The Res continued rocking in his chair.

"In your world, I have to be viewed as bad - a villain, as I'm opposed to your leader The Admiral who is regarded as good - a hero. But those two things are just different sides of the same coin. The definition lies in your perspective."

What The Res was saying astounded me. His Excellency, our president William Admiral, was the all-knowing commander of the Upper Worlds. He had written the New Truths, the laws that everyone lived by. He had revolutionised our world taking us from the dank days of the past into a brighter future with structure, perfection and uniformity. He had been in power for many moons and was continually re-engineered as his being was too virtuous to cease.

"What are you saying? His Excellency, William Admiral, is evil?" Jet asked.

I was glad Jet was on the ball asking questions. I felt like I had lost the power of speech.

The Res stroked his chin again thoughtfully. "This is neither the time nor the place to speak of The Admiral. Just consider that in your world nothing is as it seems."

"How can you say that?" I asked accusingly. "You live here underground, what do you know about the Upper Worlds?"

"I know much about your world," The Res boomed. "It's full of trickery. It is as synthetic as the holographic simulations that adorn every home, store, and institution. Our reality is limited to our perception. And you must decipher your own reality, even if it is oppositional to what the Authorities tell you, what you learn at school, what you watch on the screens. Each soul is the driver of their destiny. I have power in the Underworld, The Admiral controls the Upper Worlds, Madam Water has dominion over the seas and Thurgood the skies; but The Prophecy states that *you*, the Soul Survivor, will master us all."

I wrinkled up my face. Who were all these people The Res had mentioned, what was he talking about?

"But if Kid is the Soul Survivor how will she know what to do?" Jet asked.

He seemed to be getting this much more than I was.

The Res stopped rocking, "The missions will present themselves, and you will deal with them in your own, uniquely Human way."

"How do I know if I can trust you?" I asked meekly.

The Res puffed on his pipe and blew blue smoke out before answering.

"You do not have to trust me. But you must trust yourself."

"But what if I get it wrong?"

"This is not the time for error Keziah, nor is it the time for doubt." The Res stood up and strode across the den. "It's late, time to get you home."

"But, but there's still so much to learn," I said.

"And you will. But I do not have all of the answers. You do."

The Res showed us to the door.

"Now." He commanded into his flip phone.

"Will I ever see you again?" I asked annoyed at myself for spending my valuable time with him either disbelieving everything he said or in a state of total confusion.

"When you most need me, I'll be there." The Res said, making it sound like more of a threat than a promise.

The Res opened the door to reveal the crew waiting outside the Torpedo. They stared at me as if I were a total stranger.

Brad broke the awkward silence, "So do we have to start calling you *Oh Great One* or something?"

"Yeah, you're some big shot, yo!" Wain looked in wide-eyed awe.

"No, I'm just the same regular me," I blushed.

"Yeah, Ecclesiastes said that we're all super spesh," Mindy smiled.

"Can you believe we're like superstars in UC." Cindy chirped.

"Madeleine Stone is so going to have a cow when she hears this!" They clapped in unison.

"So what did The Res say? Did he tell you what Type you're going to be?" Max asked intrigued.

"No, he said - "

"Silence is a virtue." The Res spoke directly into my head. *"Your friends do not know that you are Human. Be wise with whom you share your secrets."*

I blinked. The crew were all looking at me, frozen mid sentence in silence.

"Yes, please continue?" Max prompted.

"Erm, he said that he's sure it'll kick in any day now." I smiled feebly.

"Alrighty then," Max said, pushing his specs up his nose.

"Aren't you freaked out by this whole thing?" Sal asked, "Cos I sure am."

"I've never been more confused in my entire life." I levelled.

"All aboard, it's time to go," Langston said.

Philippe scooped up the giggling Twins and carried them into the cruiser.

Jet took a pew next to Skye, and she linked his arm.

"What went down in there?" She rasped.

"I'll tell you later." He whispered back.

I turned to The Res, "You have put a lot of faith in me, but I don't think I can capture any three-eyed beast. I don't even know what it means."

"You are Human," The Res said as softly as he could, "embodied within you are endless possibilities. You can do anything you want to. But you must truly believe it to achieve it. So, Keziah, the real challenge is not what you can do, but will you do it? And that my dear is an entirely different question."

I tried to understand what he was saying but feared I was just not getting it.

"Here, take this." The Res said dropping the broken pieces of the crystal ball into my hand. "Perhaps when you meet Zono, she'll be able to guide you better than I, and you can explain to her what happened to her property."

The Res gave me one last sharky grin and closed the door to the den.

"Hey Kid, let's go," Philippe called out.

Feeling utterly dazed and confused, I climbed into the Torpedo, and the vehicle deftly glided away.

A rare beauty.

A true beauty.

Does not settle on ones skin.

A fine beauty.

A deep beauty.

Comes from within.

EIGHT

Madeleine Stone

"...So to conclude," Miss Peach droned on, "think about the Youth Corps and where you would like to be stationed for National Service next year."

We were in class at FB, and I could hardly focus on anything my teacher was saying. My mind constantly raced since UC. I still couldn't make sense of what The Res had told me.

The IM on my desk flashed. It was yet another message from Max, even though he was sitting right next to me.

'I have deduced another logical explanation for the fascinating series of events at you-know-where.'

Max was in denial about the whole Underground City experience and did not believe it to be real.

'What now?' Wain, who was the only one of my friends not in the class with me, messaged the group chat.

Max texted hastily, *'When we entered the portal, we stepped into the most realistic virtual reality simulation, which joined all of our brain waves together and created a group fantasy.'*

'In short Max.' I texted back.

'The whole you-know-where experience was an elaborate fictional illusion.'

I could have proven it to be real by showing Max the one thing that had survived our time in UC, the shattered gemstone. I didn't dare though. I hadn't really shared anything that The Res had said with the rest of the crew. Especially not the bit about me being Human.

'So we still can't tell Madeleine and the Pretties?' Mindy texted.

They had been bursting to boast to the Top Set that we were all underground superstars.

'I would strongly advise against it. At least until I can get a conclusive argument formulated. You wouldn't want egg on your face.' Max warned.

'Ok. Maxi.' The Twins agreed.

A few days ago Mindy and Cindy didn't even know Max existed. But since UC we had all bonded on a whole other level and now everywhere we went we rolled as a tight-knit team. Much to the sheer disgust of Madeleine Stone.

"Five-minute stretch break." Miss Peach announced, and the class became a hive of activity with everyone talking amongst themselves.

"Explain to me again why *they* are sitting with *us*?" Madeleine asked the Twins.

"They're cool peeps." Philippe jumped in defence of Max and Sal.

A Brainiac and an Eee Cee sitting amongst the Top Set was unheard of.

"Yeah." the Twins chimed in unison, "Sal's bohemian look is the ultimate in chic," Mindy said.

Sal and Mindy smiled at each other. Their time in UC had cemented their friendship.

"Ewwww! No way. Run along little neek and take your spooky looking friend with you." Madeline demanded.

"Very well," Max stood up to dismiss himself.

"Sit down Max," Sal said cracking her knuckles and glaring at Madeleine.

Sal was usually ready with a witty comeback, but everyone knew it was lunacy to go against Madeleine Stone. Madeleine ran FB. If you challenged her, she would fix it so your social life at school and beyond would be over. Her father was some big shot, billionaire, music exec, so she threw the best parties, wore the latest designer clothes and had met every famous person under the sun. No one disrespected Madeleine Stone, ever. Well, at least not to her face.

"C'mon Madeleine they're my friends, and I asked them to join us," I said protectively, but not wanting to upset her.

Madeleine's eyes narrowed, "Since when did you, like, get a say about who sits with the Top Set? I don't even know what you're doing here. You and your friends should find a pew in the front with the other losers."

"Who? These guys?" Brad said throwing his arms across Max and Sal's shoulders. "These guys are *legends*!" He said flashing a dazzler.

"Oh, Ok Braddy." Madeleine backed down immediately.

It was no secret she had a massive crush on Brad, half the school did. With his endorsement,

Sal and Max had gained themselves an official place with the Top Set.

"But Braddy, you don't have a space." Madeleine said saccharine sweetly.

"I'm cool right here thanks," Brad said pulling up a chair and wedging himself between Mindy and Philippe.

"Bro!" Philippe exclaimed as he was barged out of the way.

"What did I do?" Brad dazzled back.

"So let's resume class," Miss Peach brought us all to order, "Without further ado, I have the results of your work placements."

It was compulsory that all year eleven students completed a week-long employment to experience what it was like to be an adult citizen of the Upper Worlds. In the real world, your job was determined by your genetics. You had to fit in with what society had predetermined your life would be. But on work placement, it was a potluck, and you could be stationed anywhere. The entire class waited for the announcement with bated breath.

"Cindy Lush will be placed with Philippe Christopher at the extinction zoo."

"Yay! I love those fluffy, furry and feathered things." Cindy squeaked.

Philippe's face muscles flexed, he loved seeing the cloned animals that once roamed the earth but no longer existed too, but would much rather it be Mindy then Cindy he'd be spending one on one time with.

"Maxwell Schneider and Boris Davies will work at the state run Techno Corp." Miss Peach continued.

That's where my dad worked. I couldn't imagine a more hideous work experience. My dad's job at the governmental scientific institute had to be the most boring on the planet. Max turned to me and did a mini fist pump. His workplace suited his Type to a tee.

"Brad Windsor and Jefferson Anderson will assist Captain Tate from the National Triple Ball team."

"Yeah! Woo hoo!! In your face!!!" Brad yelled out amidst a round of high-fives. "It'll be good to check out the competition. I'll be taking that old timers job as soon as I leave FB."

A few more placements were read out, and I was trying to quiet my racing mind to listen out for my name.

"Madeleine Stone and Sal Mackinte will be placed at the Centrale Music Emporium."

"Oh great. Me and my new BFF can get extra cosy." Sal whispered sarcastically.

Mindy giggled.

"And finally the most coveted work placement at T.E.N, The Eye Network..."

TEN was the state-run multimedia company that provided everyone on the Upper Worlds with information, gaming and entertainment. It broadcast everything from new music, the latest fashion trends, sports and the news. TEN transmitted on every screen in every home, every street and institution, non-stop twenty-four hours a day, seven days a week. It was the coolest. Anyone who got a work placement there would receive kudos ratings forever.

"Yay!" Mindy squealed excitedly, clapping her hands.

I clapped too. It was only right Mindy got such a coveted spot.

"We did it Kid!" Mindy beamed.

"Did what?" I asked.

"Didn't you just hear Miss Peach? We've been selected to work at TEN."

"Me?" I gasped. I couldn't believe my ears.

"Bravo," Madeline Stone slow clapped bitterly, "I see TEN went for the cosmetically and genetically challenged by employing you two."

"I thought I looked good today." Mindy blinked upset.

Cindy jumped up and started preening her sister's immaculate hair. None of the AEs could take on Madeleine. They didn't even know how to. They weren't engineered that way.

But I wasn't an AE or any other Type, and I'd had enough playing nice to her.

"Oh get off your high horse Madeleine. We got the best work experience, and you didn't. Deal with it."

"Settle down girls." Miss Peach said.

Madeleine shot her a sharp smiley glare. Miss Peach sat down at her desk. In the hierarchy of life, Gold Star status Code Type Madeleine by far outranked the basic educating Type Miss Peach, and our teacher knew not to upset her.

Madeleine drew her attention back to me.

156

"Ooo. Mmm. Gee! I would think very carefully before you speak to me again freak," she sneered. "One word from my daddy and he'll have your daddy regen you into a proper Code Type, you weirdo."

"Oooooh! You got burned!" Porsha, Madeleine's third best friend, laughed in my face.

Madeleine tossed her luscious, silky hair over her shoulder triumphantly.

"Chill out Pretties," Philippe tried to play peacemaker.

"Leave them. This is fun." Brad dazzled, his teammates high-fived him in agreement.

"It's not worth it. Just leave it, Kid." Sal said.

Usually, I would have sat down embarrassed and taken the loss. I wouldn't have wanted to draw any negative attention to myself. But now I knew my worth. I am Keziah Monrova, a legend underground. The Soul Survivor. Pure Human. I wasn't going to let this beautiful bully take me down.

"Mad," I shortened her name knowing full well Madeleine hated being called that. "Why do you have to be so mean all the time? Doesn't it get tiring being so bitter and in competition with every other girl for attention?"

Madeleine would have looked shocked; if her face could pull that expression. She certainly was not expecting my comeback.

I twiddled my hair around my fingers, batted my eyelashes and smiled inanely like an airhead, imitating her.

"So like duh, OMG, like, no way, like Ewww! Yes, I might be different but I embrace that. And yes, your father may well be some relic in the music industry, and you've met all of the cool bands by riding on his coat tails, but that isn't something to boast about. It just confirms how utterly talentless you are.

"Next week, Mindy and I will have the greatest work experience at the coolest television station, where we get to meet the hottest people on the planet. And guess what? We got there on our own merits, not because of who our *daddy* knows."

"OOOOOOOOOHHHHHHHHHH!" Rang out from the entire classroom.

Madeleine gasped, clutching her chest in sheer indignation. No one had ever spoken to her like that before.

"Mad, you've just been burned, boiled, toasted, baked and fried!" Sal chuckled.

ZEEP, ZEEP, ZEEP, ZEEP!

The beeps signalled the end of the class, but nobody moved. Everyone waited for what would surely be Madeleine's killer comeback.

"A–A-A," She squirmed, "Yeah… Well… Like. Aaahhhh. I'm going to tell my daddy about you!" Madeleine squealed, storming out of the class with the Prees following shamefaced after her.

"Yes, Kid." My friends and the rest of the class high fived me because someone had finally been brave enough to stand up to Madeleine.

"What you just did was like so-oo cool," Mindy giggled in my ear. "Madeleine went like one

158

hundred places down in the cool stakes, and we got work experience at TEN, all in one day. Yay!"

"Yeah, that is pretty cool," I giggled too as the excitement of my life set in.

***

The TEN studios were located slap bang in the middle of Centrale, the trendiest part of town.

"Wow." Mindy squeezed my hand as a beefy Code Type security guard took our eye scan and led us through the outer sanctum of the building.

"The entrance is through there." The security pointed to a waterfall.

"But my hair will get wet," Mindy said aghast.

"It won't." He replied gruffly.

Mindy noticed his bad temper and changed her voice into a more sugary tone, "Kind sir, I spent two hours styling my hair this morning, I can't risk it frizzing." She smiled sweetly.

I made a puking face at Mindy's girly act. But it seemed to work a treat as the security guard's stern face cracked into a grin.

"My daughter's the same. Don't worry about your hair; it will be fine. All is not as it seems at TEN. Now go ahead, they're expecting you."

"Thank you ever so much." Mindy smiled reassured.

The security guard smiled back, happy to have been of assistance.

I smiled too, Mindy could charm anyone.

As Mindy and I stepped in front of the wall of water, it parted to reveal a long white corridor decorated with chic oxyinomum, the most precious metal on earth. Underneath our feet was a glass floor with all manner of exotic brightly coloured fish. As quick as a flash a raven haired mermaid swam to the surface. With her iridescent aqua marine and fuchsia fins, she was the most beautiful being I had ever seen.

"Wow wee!" Mindy and I gasped.

The mermaid waved at us before disappearing into the dense coral.

"This is unreal," I said, trying to take in all of the sights.

"It's, like, the most incredible thing I've ever seen." Mindy marvelled.

Further along the brilliant white corridor, which led to the main TEN building, the tech was state of the art. Life-sized holograms of all our favourite celebrities lined the walkway.

"Good morning and welcome to TEN." Viv Reen, the teen heartthrob presenter of the Twins favourite show *Fashion Focus* greeted us.

Rouge burned my cheeks and Mindy fluttered her eyelashes wildly, smiling coyly at him.

"Good morning Viv." We chimed.

Viv gave us a mini salute and ushered us on down the corridor.

"Nice to see you lay-deez." DJ Dan of The Allstars said.

He was mine and Mindy's favourite celebrity; all our screens saved his image.

Mindy stopped in her tracks and dramatically clutched her heart.

"Kiddie-girl, I think I'm going to die right here of happiness." She whispered.

"Remember Minds; they're just Vir Sims, they're not real." I reminded giving her a reality check. But she was totally awestruck.

I had to admit the Vir Sims – Virtual Simulations – at TEN were incredibly life like. Their density and movements made them seem like real living beings.

"Hi Dan, how are you?" Mindy fluttered her eyelashes and gave her brightest dimpled smile.

The Dan simulation smiled and repeated his programmed words, "Nice to see you lay-deez."

Ross of The Allstars joined Dan, "Hey, do you want to take your picture with us?"

"Sure! We'd love to," Mindy squealed enthusiastically as if being asked on a date.

Her response fit the automatic speech decoder and Vir Sims of the entire Allstars band, Dan, Ross, Kyle and Gio gathered around Mindy.

"Does my hair look ok?" Mindy asked nervously running her hand through her perfect mane.

"Prestigious as always Minds."

"Yay me!" Mindy clapped for herself before thrusting her IM at me.

She stood in the middle of the group next to Dan and smiled more perfectly and broadly than I thought was possible.

I snapped the image and then projected it for Mindy to see.

"Wow, it's like uber realistic." Mindy was amazed.

I gave her back her IM, "Yes, everything is fake here, but it all seems so real."

"But like no one needs to know that." Mindy said. "I'm going to post the pic right now and pretend that I actually met the Allstars. Madeleine Stone is going to have a cow when she sees this. Yay!"

"Have a nice day now lay-deez." DJ Dan said.

Mindy blew him a kiss. I laughed and dragged her away.

"Let's go; our contact will be waiting for us. We'll be late if we stop to speak to all of the stars."

" 'Kay." Mindy reluctantly agreed.

We quick stepped up the long white corridor and passed more celebrities. Mindy squealed in delight whenever she saw someone she liked.

"Just one more pic," she said several times snapping photos constantly and posting them immediately.

I spotted Tainted Stone. They were musicians from many moons ago, and old folks still listened to their music now. It was the only band Jet liked because they played the same string instrument thing he did. Jet despised all of the music I liked. I snapped a quick image of them; Jet wasn't impressed with much, but perhaps a picture with Tainted Stone would please him.

Mindy and I finally reached the end of the corridor, which opened into a reception area. It was an awesome looking foyer decorated with marble and golden statues of all the famous people on TEN. In the centre was a glass tower. The tech all around was so advanced that I didn't even know what most of it was. Even the Guardians were sophisticated and made from platinum. They were way sleeker and more advanced than the bulky white plastic ones in my neighbourhood.

"This place is magical." I said taking it all in.

"Like, so incredible." Mindy agreed.

Out of nowhere a stunning man, in full makeup, wearing an asymmetrical dress appeared in front of us. He was holding a lazer projecting our images.

"You must be our W dot E from F to the B." He trilled in a voice almost as high pitched as Mindy's.

"Yes we are, I'm K - " I began, but before I could finish introducing myself the man bypassed me and launched himself at Mindy.

"You. Are. Gorgeous!" He stated the obvious as if Mindy didn't know what she looked like. "I just love your bangs!" He said fluffing up the front of her hair.

"Why thanks, it took me like all morning to get it right." Mindy squealed revelling in the compliment.

Mindy got told how beautiful she was several times a day, but I never saw her tire of it.

"Just simply divine dah-ling!" The man said pushing me out of the way.

"I'm Ivan, I'm your contact and I'll show you where you will be working for the week."

"I'm Mindy, Mindy Lush." Mindy pouted.

"Yes. You. Are!" Ivan clicked his fingers, punctuating his words.

"I'm Kid," I shouted from over his shoulder.

Ivan whipped around with dramatic effect as if I had startled him.

"Ye-ees!" He said slowly looking me up and down.

I nervously smoothed down my side ponytail suddenly feeling inadequate. Maybe I should have made more of an effort on my appearance like my dad had told me too. *'The fact is Keziah, there's only one opportunity to make a good first impression,'* he had warned me before I left the house. But I was comfortable wearing a hoody. It kept me warm.

Ivan turned back to Mindy and gushed, "We have the perfect work experience for you, right here in the heart of TEN in the studio. And girlfriend that is where it's at! You'll meet all of the stars and like gorgeous people and you're so beautiful I'm sure I'll even get you a feature in one of our shows. Your face fits honey. You are perfect!"

"Really? Oh, my!" Mindy yelped in sheer delight.

Ivan was definitely a Code Type AE. Mindy had found her male equivalent. Ivan half dragged Mindy to the glass tower elevator. I was left standing by reception.

"What about me?" I called out.

Ivan whipped around as if he had forgotten I was there. He sashayed hastily back to me and looked me up and down again.

"You're not quite right for the tower," he decided. "I wouldn't want to bring facially challenged people there; you'd only feel out of place. What Code Type are you?"

Now I was flummoxed. How could I possibly tell him that The Res had said I was Human?

"She's a brain." Mindy interjected saving me from further embarrassment.

"Oh, my!" Ivan announced throwing his hands up in the air, exasperated that he'd wasted precious time talking to an Intellectual Type.

"Well the beauty can come with me and the brain can take that corridor down to your left, someone will be there to meet you. Have a nice life!"

Ivan sashayed away dragging Mindy with him to the elevator. Mindy turned back to me.

"See you at lunchtime," she waved with a happy twinkle in her eye.

"Bye Minds." I managed to say just as the elevator door closed in my face.

In typical fashion, Mindy had gotten the best job due to her looks. She was my good friend and I cared for her deeply, but the way our genetics predetermined our lives annoyed me greatly.

Everyone at TEN was rushing around looking beautiful, important or both and I was a nobody. I couldn't possibly be this Soul Survivor that the Arcadian Urbanites revered.

"To the left or was it right?" I muttered to myself feeling like a total and utter loser.

A group of Techies walked through a door on the right marked 'TX'. Not knowing where else to go I ran in behind them. The door swung shut behind me and I was alone in a long dark hallway full of grey steel doors. The glitz and glamour of the foyer were gone.

"Hello?" I called out.

My echo reverberated down the long metallic walkway but the Techies were nowhere to be seen. I turned to go back to the reception but the heavy steel door was locked.

"Just great." I sighed. I walked slowly up the hallway to find another way out.

All of a sudden a door flew open. A ginger haired Techy ran out and grabbed me.

"Are you my new assistant?" He asked manically.

"Erm? I guess so." I said unsure of exactly where I was meant to be.

An illuminated sign above the door flashed *Sector Seven.*

"I'm James, and you are?" He said with a hurried handshake.

"I'm Kid," I said happy to have at least one person at TEN interested in me.

Inside the room, behind James, I saw hundreds of TV programmes, films and music videos playing on a multitude of screens.

"The hired help are getting younger and younger," James said to himself, "But I'm not one to question."

The images on the screens had me transfixed.

"Don't just stand there, come in," James ushered me into the room. "There is so much to do. Here take these," he said handing me two blue circular plastic patches.

I looked at the inch long objects not sure what to do with them.

"Put them on," James instructed.

"Where do they go?" I asked feeling stupid.

This first day of work experience at TEN was no way near the fun I thought it would be. I looked towards the exit in two minds whether to stay or make my excuses and leave. That would make Madeline Stone's year if I decided to quit my work experience on day one. I decided to stay.

"In your ears of course," James said tetchily, "I'm frequing, and you don't want your head crammed with all of this nonsense."

"Right, right." I nodded not understanding the technical talk but going along with it anyway.

I placed the plastic patches in my ears, and instantly the room spun. My body lurched forward as if I had been catapulted into the air and was tumbling to earth at a great speed. I grabbed hold of the wall in an attempt to keep my balance.

"They're probably not what you're accustomed to in training college; these are the new kind. They take a little while to get used to." James said.

The pit of my stomach dropped and I wretched fighting to keep my breakfast down.

"It's always the same with new employees. You'll be okay in a mo," James was unconcerned. "Then you can help me Freq these new 'mercials. The Yuletide season is coming and we've got a massive backlog."

James' words were appearing to me in visual text rather than audible sound. Rather than hear, I could read his speech.

"W-Wh- What have you done to me?" I managed to say, my voice occurring as colours rather than words.

This was unbelievable. My senses were all scrambled. My legs wobbled, and my body shook. I was engulfed by a million distorted voices, but I couldn't identify where they were coming from.

I squinted my eyes and focussed my attention on the screen directly in front of me. The disorientation grew more intense. Then it clicked. The hundreds of voices were coming from each of the TV screens. But this wasn't the regular sound matching the film being shown. This was hundreds of other voices hidden within each scene.

My knees hit the floor. I grabbed the patches, and I tried to take them off. James was still talking to me, and I concentrated enough to read his words,

"If the patches are at a high frequency turn them anticlockwise, it blocks out the signals."

I turned the dial, and the voices stopped abruptly. The wild ride ended, and I instantly regained orientation.

"What was that?!" I spluttered flopping into a chair.

"You were experiencing the coding," James said seated at a giant mixing desk with lots of buttons, switches and levels. At the centre of it was a long digital number.

"The patches decode the subliminal messages. What you were hearing was the televisual output in its natural state before we do the frequing."

"So when you say *'frequing'* what is it exactly that you mean?"

James looked up exasperated,

"Your training appears to be rather limited. Techno Corp is getting very slack these days. But I'm not one to question."

James took a deep breath and sputtered,

"I don't have time for an encoding 101 session but the basics are, in this department we change the frequency of all the TEN output, music, games, films, programmes, adverts - everything so that the masses can't hear the subliminal messages that are being transmitted."

I sat bolt upright as Techy James continued,

"The patches allow us to listen to what is actually being said and our job is to raise the frequency – freq until all the messages are hidden. Then they are broadcast, and the citizens of the world buy, eat, think and even love in the way TEN tells them to. Subconsciously of course."

"So there are hidden messages in what we watch," I gasped.

169

"Of course," James said matter-of-factly. "That's the easiest way to control people, by making them think they have free will, when in fact they have none at all. Citizens of the Upper Worlds would freak out if they knew we formed all their habits and opinions for them. Well, probably not. They'd react exactly how we'd tell them to." James chuckled to himself hunched over his mixing desk like a mad scientist.

"Their brains are all re-engineered and they don't even know it."

"Why?" I asked helplessly.

James looked at me aghast,

"You just said W-H-Y." He spelt out the word suspiciously. "I'm a Code Type Dg, a doer, modified not to question. I thought you were a Dg too, a Regen from Techno Corp. But you can't be if you said the 'W' word. Because we never question our superiors."

The jig was up. James had given me all of this information voluntarily because he had mistaken me for someone else. I couldn't own up now or surely there would be dire consequences to face.

A screen in front of me displayed an advert for holidays in outer space. I quickly thought on my feet.

"No, I'm not questioning. I was about to say Why –tes, you know, the space tours. I would really love to go on a moon cruise." I nervously pointed to the screen.

James looked at the screen where The Whytes tours advert was running.

"Your patches aren't frequed correctly. The signals are still getting through making you want to consume. Turn the dial anticlockwise some more that should completely block out the messages."

I pretended to do the action.

"That's much better." I said.

"These patches are miracles; I wish we could take them home. But alas before we leave work we hand them in and then get decoded."

"Oh yes, decoded." I imitated his forlorn expression pretending to understand what the term meant.

"You know I wish we didn't get decoded." James said wistfully, "I don't like my memory wiped, forgetting everything from the working day. Sometimes I think it would be nice to remember, but I'm not one to question." James said accepting his place in the Code Type hierarchy.

"Yes, I'm not one to question either," I said mirroring his motto.

"We can't spend all day with our chins wagging, there is a lot of work to do, so let's get on with it," James said before training me on the mixing desk and showing me how to freq.

With all of life's to-ing and
fro-ing.

You still get to where you're
meant to be going.

NINE

The First Eye

I sat in front of the TV screen in my bedroom trying to comprehend the day's events. I pressed the zapper in a daze watching the programs flip from one to another. I could barely remember anything from my first day of work experience. I knew I worked with a Techy called James, but I couldn't for the life of me think of what we had done. My mind was completely blank.

"Wake up Zombie!" Jet clicked his fingers snapping me back to reality. "Ma said you had something cool to show me."

"What? Oh yeah. Look at this pic I took with Tainted Stone." I gave Jet my IM, and he projected the picture I had taken earlier.

"Well, it's not the actual band, it's just an image, so what's so cool about that?" Jet shrugged.

I should have known he wouldn't be impressed.

"The Vir Sims at TEN are so lifelike. The tech in that place is off the chain." I said.

"Meh." Jet said, sitting on the corner of my bed. "So how was your work experience?"

"Good. I think." I said rubbing my weary head.

We sat in silence for a moment, and I went back to my mindless changing of the channels.

"All you do is stare at the screen all day." Jet mumbled.

"I'm just doing what everyone else does."

"Well not me, I never watch screens," Jet said.

I sat upright, and I looked at him properly. That was true. Jet rarely watched any screen unless it related to his homework or those music boxes he liked to play. And Jet was so odd. Different from everyone I knew.

"Why are you looking at me so weirdly?" He asked.

"Why don't you like watching the screen?" I said.

He eyed me suspiciously, "Why do you care?"

"Can't I take an interest in my little brother?"

"Well if you must know it bores me. I mean what's so great about watching other people's lives and gossiping about them? That's what most TV shows are about. Plus Skye and I have so much going on." Jet brightened like he always did when talking about Skye.

"We've got her secret power training, and we do band practice. I haven't got time to be staring at screens all day."

I looked at Jet squarely, as if seeing him for the first time. He was so different from me. If he didn't look like me, I would have sworn that we didn't share the same DNA.

"But Jet, everyone watches screens. It's just the thing to do."

"For you and your friends maybe but Skye doesn't have any screens in her house, not one. Her mum says something weird happens to you when you watch too much telly."

That was it! I remembered!! Something *did* happen to you when you watched too much telly. And I knew that because I had spent a whole day making sure that it did.

"That's why you're so strange!" I exclaimed, "Because you don't watch screens like the rest of us, it doesn't affect you."

"What are you talking about? What doesn't affect me?" Jet asked puzzled.

"That." I said zapping off the TV set. "Come," I said dragging Jet behind me. "I need help to figure this one out."

***

"...So you mean to tell me subliminal messages are being encrypted into television output to brainwash everyone?" Max concluded pacing up and down his bedroom.

"Yeah, that about sums it up," I said sitting on his bed. "But if you are privy to that information they decode, I mean, erase your memory at the end of the day so you can't remember what you've done. I think my decoding was only temporary because I'm not a Dg Code Type, genetically modified to follow orders without question. I think Dgs are the only ones allowed into Sector Seven."

"Fascinating." Max raised his eyebrows and pushed his specs up the bridge of his nose.

"Like, that's not how I saw it, and I was there," Mindy said.

She was synched virtually into the room, while physically sat at home in her bedroom.

"Yeah, but you were busy in the studio while I was downstairs in transmission," I countered. "You wouldn't know what goes on down there."

"Are you like sure that you're not just jealous because I was with the cool people and you were stuck with the Brainiacs?" Mindy griped.

Today had been the best day of her entire life, and now it was being tarnished.

"Well, technically if what Kid says is true Techy James is far from a Brainiac. He's a do-er with minor technical ability, and that is a huge difference." Max corrected her.

"Like whatever," Mindy said dismissively. "Aren't you just a little bit bitter Kid?"

"Well yes, my work experience sucked big time, but that's not the reason why I'm telling you this. I'm saying it because it's true." I knew how farfetched it all sounded.

"Yo! I've got plenty of literature I could give you to read which says the same thing." Wain, who was also synched in, piped up.

Finally, his Code Type friends were speaking his language. He had always been aware of what he saw as the oppressive regime of the Upper Worlds, but this was the first time Kid had shown any interest in something like this.

"There are people here in Zero who have been claiming this to be the case for the longest. The Upper Worlds controls us all. Not just us Tachions, but you Code Types too."

"Well, I believe you, Sis. This could be the first mission The Res spoke about." Jet jumped up enthusiastically.

"Hush!" Max whispered loudly. "We agreed we wouldn't talk about that whole unconfirmed *you-know-where* experience until I can conclude my findings."

"Who made you the boss of me?" Jet said annoyed.

"Let's forget *you-know-where* because TEN is like way cooler. I met so many celebrities today." Mindy gushed.

"Real life or Vir Sim?" Max asked.

"Like that doesn't matter. All that counts is that from my pics people are so jealous of my life. Yay. Go me!" Mindy cheered herself with a mini cheerleading formation of a round off into the splits.

"And it's not just all about me, me, me," she added quickly noticing that no one had joined her in the celebration of herself. "Tomorrow I'm going to swap places with Cindy so she can experience how great it is to be me."

Just then Cindy synched in, "Oh, my. I just got off work. What did I miss?"

"Nothing Twinny, just Kid, trying to put a downer on TEN, which she can't because it's so totally awesome!"

"Yay!" The Twins chimed in unison.

"It's not a downer, but we are all being brainwashed to think, buy and even love in a way that the Upper Worlds tells us to." I defended my position.

"We're all so different, but we all listen to the same music. Watch the same movies and consume the same way everyone else at school does. Jet doesn't do any of that, and he rarely watches screens."

"It's a shaky hypothesis basing what's regular and irregular on Jet," Max said.

"Skye's just like me, and she doesn't watch the screens either." Jet said proudly.

"And I rest my case," Max said taking off his spectacles, signalling the end of the conversation.

I had to win him over. I needed his help.

"Just look at all of our bedrooms." The Twins, Wain and Max looked around. Yes, they did differ in that Wain and Max had tech related things and The Twins had pink glittery stuff, but there were common themes that we all shared.

"For instance, why do we all like the Allstars?" I asked, "We all have their images on the walls and saved on all our screens."

"Because DJ Dan is so good-looking. They are the greatest, and we must play their music, buy their records and all of their merch at all times." Mindy gushed.

"And they're all fully fashioned forward. They are the greatest, and we must play their music, buy their records and all of their merch at all times." Cindy informed.

"Their music has a funky beat." Max said snapping his fingers offbeat to a rhythm inside his head. "They are the greatest, and we must play their music, buy their records and all of their merch at all times."

"They're just generally awesome the best band on the planet. They are the greatest, and we must play their music, buy their records and all of their merch at all times." Wain threw his hands over his mouth, panic-stricken, as if confused by what he had just said.

Jet and I slowly turned to face each other.

"Why do you like the Allstars Kid?" Jet asked.

"I just do," I said my voice trembling. I pursed my lips not wanting to say anymore, but somehow the words flew out of my mouth. "They are the greatest, and we must play their music, buy their records and all of their merch at all times."

"Oh, my days!" Jet jumped up, "You *are* all being brainwashed!"

"Like total buzz kill," Mindy whined.

"So what do we do about it?" I asked shocked that I was right.

"If you are sure that TEN is controlling us with messages put in their broadcasts then why don't we just find a way to stop it." Jet said.

"How? I wouldn't know where to begin."

"You mentioned that a mixing desk runs the whole subliminal system," Max said trying to regain his logical composure after sounding as brain dead as the rest of us. "There must be a mainframe, and if you can get the coordinates, I can crack the coding. We could interrupt the signal and change the frequency, modify the encoded message to whatever we want it to say."

"Really? Could it be that easy?" I asked.

"Anything is possible; it's just a matter of figuring out a way," Jet said. "We'll take our cue from you," he nodded with a newfound respect for his sister.

***

"Like, oh, my, gosh! It's even better than Mindy said it was." Cindy squealed enchanted by the underwater scene beneath our feet and the Vir Sim celebrities along the corridor.

"Nice to see you lay-deez." DJ Dan greeted us just like he had done the day before. Unlike yesterday, I was not impressed by the gadgetry. Today I was on a mission.

"Yeah, yeah, heard it all before," I said dragging a starry eyed Cindy down the hall.

Cindy and I walked into the busy, reception area where Ivan was waiting for Cindy, who he thought was Mindy.

"Dah-ling!" Ivan trilled air-kissing Cindy on both cheeks.

"Okay," Cindy responded confused. I elbowed her in the ribs.

"That's Ivan, Mindy's friend," I whispered.

"Oh yeah. Hiiiii!" Cindy chirped.

Ivan took two dramatic steps backwards and looked Cindy up and down. "You look different today. I liked your coiffure better yesterday."

Cindy self-consciously touched her hair. She could never get it as perfect as Mindy always seemed to.

"But that's okay girlfriend, one of the stylists will fix it for you in the studio."

"Ok, like yeah, sure."

"Have we got an exhilarating day in store for you little lady," Ivan told Cindy linking her arm.

" 'Kay, and what about my friend?" Cindy asked pointing to me.

"Oh?" Ivan responded doing his infamous up and down look.

"I'm all right; you go ahead," I said sizing up the TX door that led to Sector Seven.

"Fab." Ivan chirped relieved that he didn't have to take me, the hoody-wearing, pony-tailed girl, with him to the studio.

Before she could say another word, Ivan grabbed Cindy and dragged her off towards the glass tower.

I skipped through the foyer and turned the handle of the heavy door leading to Sector Seven, but it was locked. I swiped my finger on the print recognition system.

'Access Denied.' it stated loudly.

"Can I help you?" A sleek Guardian caught me struggling with the door.

"I'm meant to be working in there." I insisted.

"Transmission is out of bounds. No one is granted access." The Guardian said firmly.

"But yesterday I was - "

"But nothing. Move away from the door."
The Guardian scanned my router. Within seconds
my details flashed before us.

"You are work experience from
Falconbrook High. You must join your fellow
student in the studio. Now come with me."

The Guardian forcefully pushed me
towards the glass elevator while radioing
instructions to the studio staff on his IM. I took one
more wistful glance at the door to Sector Seven
and then sullenly walked off to join Cindy.

***

"That was so awesome." I chattered
excitedly to Cindy on our way to the lunch zone. "I
can't believe we got to watch a real life taping of
Go Fish that's like my favourite show ever! And did
you see Lance Lavern wave at me!"

The glitz and glamour of the star-studded
studio had put my earlier mission to get the
mainframe digits from Sector Seven way out of my
mind.

"And they're going to use you as a
background feature in the next taping for sure." I
gushed.

"Yeah, I know." Cindy smiled, but she had
been quiet all day.

Her hair was now fashioned into a new
cutting edge asymmetrical style worthy of being in
Centrale, and her outfit had been changed by a
studio stylist.

183

"It's even better than Mindy described," I said.

"Yeah," Cindy agreed, way off her usual super excited self.

"I can't wait to tell everyone at school," I added sounding more like Mindy than Cindy did.

I continued to chatter as we picked up our food groups for lunch. I opted for the nutri granules with a dash of essential fatty acids, a fruct-a-lite and koko desert. Cindy just took a vacuum of 02 infused with nutrients. We took a seat on the trendy levitating chairs and rested our food mid air on the space trays. Cindy inhaled her 02 deeply.

"Yum." She smiled feigning enthusiasm.

"Is that all you're going to have? You should try some of this koko; it's so tasty. My ma says it's a synthetic derivative of the cocoa bean, which makes real chocolate. She tasted it when she was on National Service in Freeca. That's where she and my dad met as part of the Youth Corps. Ma says that chocolate has the best taste in the world, a hundred times better than this koko. I can't even begin to imagine how good it must be.

"You know most AEs are not designed to consume more than a minimum daily calorie intake, so I doubt I'd ever be able to taste such a treat."

Even though Cindy was smiling, as she always did, I could sense something was up.

"Are you alright Cinds? You don't seem like yourself today."

"It's nothing really. It's just ironic. Here I am only consuming air, which makes me an airhead, which everyone thinks I am anyway."

"No, who would ever say such a thing?" I said not wanting to hurt her feelings.

Cindy attempted to roll her eyes but looked cute instead of irritated, "Of course they do. Just because I'm beauty personified, everyone thinks I'm stupid."

"You are extraordinarily beautiful." I agreed.

"Oh, I'm not boasting. If truth be told, I hate my Code Type." Cindy said flatly.

"What?" I couldn't believe what I was hearing. "You're more than just beautiful. You're kind, funny and a good friend. I would love to have one ounce of what you and Mindy have. Do you know how many hours I've spent in the mirror trying to smile like you?" I confessed. "You two are adorable. What's there to not like about your Type?"

"That's just it," Cindy tried, and failed, at sounding cross. "People always lump us together. I'm an individual you know. I have my own thoughts and feelings, but no one cares about that. It's the Twins this and the Twins that. And, if that wasn't bad enough, everyone prefers Mindy to me anyway."

"Don't say that Cinds, that's not true."

"Yes, it is. Even here at TEN all anyone has said to me all day is that I looked better yesterday, my clothes were more on trend yesterday, and I was way funnier yesterday. And yesterday Mindy was here and not me. I was born second, and ever since then I've been the runner up to everything Mindy does."

"It's not like that," I said, knowing full well it was. "And we, your friends don't think of one of you as better than the other."

"It's ok. You don't have to lie. We all know Mindy is way more on point than me. She loves all of the attention. I don't. I just do it because I don't know any other way. I'd rather blend in with the crowd and not care about my appearance, like you Kid."

"Thanks, I think that's a compliment."

"It is, the biggest you can get. There's nothing great about being stunning. You may not have your Type yet, but we all have our issues, believe me."

I hugged Cindy tightly. No one's life was as straightforward as it seemed.

"Excuse me while I powder my nose. I don't want Ivan to see me red and puffy." Cindy hopped from her chair.

I watched her walk across to the restroom. As she did, I spotted Techy James leaving the canteen. I jumped off the chair and dashed off after him.

"Hey James, how's it going?" I tried to sound casual as I cornered him by the exit.

James looked at me blankly, "Do I know you?"

"Yes, I'm Kid, I worked with you yesterday, and I need to get back into Sector Seven."

"That area is top secret. I must not discuss what goes on in Sector Seven." James said hostilely.

"Erm okay, but it's just that I left something there that I need, so can I pop by and get it?" I asked.

"No!" James snapped loudly as he left the canteen. "And please do not speak of this again."

I edged out of the room embarrassed. Cindy ran after me.

"Like what was that about?" Cindy squealed.

"I don't know," I said.

James overreaction had me certain that what happened yesterday was not an elaborate figment of my overactive imagination. The thrilling time in the studio had almost blinded me to my mission, but now I was refocused.

"All I know is that there's much more going on at TEN than meets the eye."

***

Back in my bedroom that evening the crew had gathered, physically and virtually.

"There's no way I'll get back inside Sector Seven. It was pure luck last time." I told my friends.

"You make your own luck." Jet said, sounding like The Res.

That one meeting with the leader of the underworld had left a serious impression on him.

"It's not that simple. I won't be able to get the coordinates for Max to hack into the mainframe."

"Yes, you can, through me," Wain said.

I turned to look at him. "What?"

"You've been to Sector Seven before, right?" Wain said

"Yes."

"And you saw the digits on the mixing desk." Wain continued.

"Yeah, briefly but it was a long number, and I don't remember it."

"But it's somewhere in your memory bank, right?"

"I'm not sure; I didn't pay attention."

"Well maybe if you let me in your mind, I can find it." Wain concluded.

"Whoa!" Philippe said. "You know you shouldn't use ESP for that, we're warned against using our powers on Code Types. We don't know what might happen."

"I know yo, but do you have another solution? Kid has seen the coordinates; they're stored somewhere in her memory. I'll find it if she lets me."

Wain turned to me, "You know I'd never let you come to any harm. If it felt like you were at risk, I would stop the process immediately. Last night at the TL Movement meeting we were discussing a direct assault on the Upper Worlds and now Kid here you are bringing it to the crew. You're a revolutionary, just like your ma."

Philippe shifted uncomfortably at the mention of TL. He didn't understand the Tachion Liberation Movement's fight for freedom against the Upper Worlds.

"I really cannot entertain any talk of revolution. Why anybody would want to harm another is illogical to me." Max said pushing his specs up his nose.

"Well let's not talk about revolution brother. Let's just act on it yo," Wain said, "starting with TEN."

Revolution was the last thing on my mind. That wasn't why I was stalling. I didn't want Wain, or anyone else, reading my thoughts. My mind was private. It housed my insecurities and my fears. I didn't want even my closest friends knowing those.

"Don't worry, I promise I won't look for anything else but the digits," Wain reassured me.

"Well - "

"Well, I wouldn't encourage it," Max interjected. "Naturally it would be a fascinating first-hand study, but I wouldn't want you to be the guinea pig. I care about you too much Kid. Your mind is already screwy from everything that has been going on. To have someone else in your brainwaves could short circuit it, send you haywire. It's too dangerous. If your father knew you were even considering this, he'd have you re-engineered for sure."

I looked into the TV screen and zoned out, thinking about all of the events that had taken place recently. The Harlequin in the schoolyard, my intense dreams, the expedition to UC, Mr Grimm, The Arcadians, The Res, the Soul Survivor Prophecy, work experience at TEN, seeing all of my favourite stars, encoded messages in media transmissions. It had been the most intense period of my life, and finally, I was living for a purpose. I knew what I had to do.

"Thanks for the concern Max, but it's a chance that I have to take."

Max pushed his specs up nervously.

I turned to Wain sure of my decision, "Let's find those digits."

***

The whole crew watched in awe as Wain begun the process of entering my mind.

Jet and Skye perched nervously on my bed.

"Be cool, Sis. You'll be just fine." Jet said.

"Thanks." I gave him a thumbs up and tried to put on a brave face before Wain attempted to put me under.

I lay on the floor in the middle of my room and Wain levitated above me staring directly into my eyes.

"I'm gonna do this properly." Wain announced clearing his throat.

"Ok." I'd never seen him act so seriously before.

"Keziah Monrova do you give me permission to enter your mind?" Wain asked.

Mindy stifled a giggle; the formal request sounded funny coming from him. Philippe winked

190

at her. Mindy smiled broadly back. Brad looked from one to the other and sulked. Romance was budding between Mindy and Philippe, and there was nothing he could do about it.

Max tutted at their silly flirting. He was on tenterhooks. Was he the only one worried about how dangerous this was?

"Yes, I do," I nodded.

"Good. Then let's begin. Kid, inhale deeply, hold for three counts then exhale deeply."

"Ok," I said and followed his instructions.

I began to breathe in and out slowly. As I exhaled, Wain inhaled my breath. As he exhaled, he breathed his air into my face.

"Ewww, that's really gross!" The Twins chimed in unison.

"Yeah." Sal agreed, "I hope you've brushed your teeth."

"Totally. Bad breath would be the worst!" The Twins giggled.

"I'm joining our life force together yo, so we become one," Wain explained.

"Still gross." Sal murmured.

"Wanna join our life force Minds?" Brad said blowing air in her direction.

"You're so silly, Braddy!" Mindy said coyly twirling a golden lock around her finger.

Brad shot a dazzler. Mindy beamed back. Philippe looked away feigning interest on a loose bit of stitching on the lace of his shoe. Brad smiled triumphantly. The competition for Mindy's affections had no clear winner just yet.

Usually, I would feel very silly breathing into someone's face, especially with all my friends watching. But something was coming over me. I was beginning to feel relaxed. I yawned.

"That's it, Kid, just go with it," Wain said.

My eyelids began to droop. Wain opened his wide, concentrating intensely. A small silver smoke like cord rose from my forehead into Wains. I closed my eyes.

"I don't like this," Max said. "I don't like this one little bit."

"It's ok." Jet tried to calm Max. "Wain knows what he's doing." He said, protectively pulling Skye closer.

The smoke became thicker and thicker, swirled faster and faster filling the entire room and then,

BANG!

"Aaaa!" Mindy and Cindy threw their arms over one another.

"Jeez!" Brad jumped out of his skin.

"Is everyone ok?" Philippe jumped, his muscles rippling underneath his face.

"Oh man," Sal cracked her knuckles, "what's happened to Kid?"

***

Wain and I had been transported to a hazy space, like the attic room of an ancient house like you see in the history books. It was filled with old style paper boxes with documents strewn everywhere.

"We're in," Wain said gently. "This is your mind, Kid."

"Wow." I spun around to take it all in, "It's beautiful."

The mind space led off in so many different directions and to so many other places. In the distance, I saw a rushing river, a mountain range and a constellation of stars.

"There's a lot going on here. Sorry." I said.

"Don't worry about that. Let's just find the mixing desk digits and be on our way. Try not to tamper with anything though yo, we don't want to put anything out of place and mess you up." Wain said carefully treading over loose thoughts scattered all over the floor and ducking words suspended in the air.

Toot Toot!

A miniature old-fashioned steam train carrying a cargo of thoughts chugged through Wain's legs. It smoke signalled the message,

'What must Wain be thinking of me?' before speeding off into the distance.

Wain glanced over at me.

"I know you're worried about me reading everything in your mind, but I promise I won't. Let's just look and find the digits quickly."

"Ok." I agreed relieved, and a warm yellow glow of relief flooded the space.

I strolled towards the back of my mind and picked up an orange memory. The scene was of Jet and me as small children playing ball together. We were laughing and joking and looked so happy. Our dad was with us, monitoring our behaviour.

He always used to write reports about whatever we did when we were little. Back then he was so interested in us. He never made time for us now.

Jet threw a ball, and it bounced on the table and hit Dad on the head. Dad made a silly face and pretended to be knocked out. We all fell about laughing until our sides ached.

"I forgot Jet and I used to have fun together." I smiled reminiscing.

Under a pile of happy images of friends, Wain picked up a pink thought about Max. It had tiny hearts dotted all over it. He quickly put it back under the rubble. He didn't want to pry into subconscious thoughts that Kid didn't even realise she had.

I continued down memory lane and picked up an old blue image from when I was ten. I was with dad, Jet and Max camping at a spot near Ethereal Bridge. We would go every summer for fact-finding missions. It all stopped when I started at FB, and my dad got promoted in his job.

Wain was at the front of my mind, and a green thought caught his eye. He picked it up, and it displayed an image of Kid being jealous when Mindy was given special treatment by Ivan.

"I was a little upset about that," I marched up to Wain. I felt I needed to explain. "I'm not often jealous of my friends, but I just couldn't help it."

"Don't worry. These are your first day at TEN thoughts. The digits must be somewhere around here."

Wain and I looked around at the scattered thoughts; Ivan and the glass tower, the long corridor, Sector Seven and Techy James. The earplug patches, hundreds of TV screens, the mixing desk and then, *the digits*.

"Here it is!" I yelled.

"Ha! I knew it would work."

I read out the mainframe number, "5791236875."

"Right, you remember the first five digits, and I'll remember the last five," Wain said. "Now let's get out of here."

SNAP!

Wain opened his eyes. He was back in Kid's smoke filled bedroom looking down on her from his levitated position above. He clicked his fingers, but Kid didn't stir. She was still in her mind. Wain clicked his fingers again. Kid didn't move a muscle. Panic gripped him.

"Keziah Monrova, I command you to leave your mind." Wain's voice was shaky and fearful.

He had only ever tried this on other Tachions before. He hadn't thought about how the process might affect a non-Tachion. Kid continued to lay asleep.

"Like, why isn't she responding?" The Twins howled.

"This is why the First Truth exists. Tachions should never use their powers on Code Types." Max reprimanded Wain.

"Yeah. You really shouldn't have done that." Brad agreed.

"Well, what was he supposed to do? Kid wanted the digits, and Wain was the only one who knew how to get it." Sal defended Wain.

"Yeah." Wain agreed, "I only used my abilities because Kid agreed to it."

"But she didn't know what she was letting herself in for. She's a Code Type. She has no understanding of how your Tachion abilities work." Max argued.

"Look, this is not a Code Type versus Tachion debate. We're all here for Kid. She's the important one, not our personal views." Philippe tried to squash the rising tension.

"It's just not right." Brad shook his head.

"Please Kid, please come back to us NOW!" Wain clapped loudly.

Kid did not stir.

Jet turned to Skye. "Do you think you can do that thing we practised?"

"I'll try my best," she rasped.

Skye sprung to her feet and crouched beside Kid.

"What are you doing?" Max asked nervously.

"Trust me." Skye took charge. "You must all remain completely still. I need your energies, no matter how far away you are. You must give me your full attention. I'm charging from your life force."

Gone was her shy demeanour. Skye acted with a maturity well beyond her thirteen years.

"Be cool Skye. Just like we've practised a million times," Jet said reassuringly. "Only this time it's with a real person."

"Man! You've never done this on actual people?" Brad threw his arms up in defeat.

"Only to knock them out, not to bring them back." Jet said with attitude, agitated that they were questioning Skye's abilities.

Skye, eyes a blue blaze, turned her back on the crew.

"Cover your ears." She commanded.

"How will she revive Kid if she's not even looking?" Brad moaned.

"Cover your ears!" Skye roared so loudly everyone did exactly as they were told.

"Ready," Jet said softly, guiding Skye. "Steady. Now!"

Skye reached out her palm in the crew's direction, and an ionised silver force field engulfed them. The waves of light travelled all the way across town and into each one of their bedrooms.

Skye clenched her fists, took a deep breath and sang an almighty one-note melody.

"Zeeeeeeeeeeeeeeeeeeeeeeeeeeeeeeeeeeee!"

The sound was barely audible to the human ear, but its sharpness affected the brainwaves.

SMASH.

The glass on all of the screens in Kid's room shattered. Max's spectacles cracked. He, Wain and Jet fell to the ground shielding their ears in agony.

Sal, Philippe, Brad and The Twins holograms fuzzed in and out as the high-pitched frequency from Skye's wail interrupted the signal.

Kid juddered. The mind-altering sound pulled her back to this dimension. The room full of smoke turned into a small whirlwind and dissipated back into Kid's forehead.

SNAP!

197

I awoke coughing and spluttering.

"Are you okay Sis?" Jet ran to my side.

I touched my head. "Absolutely fine, I had the best time getting lost in my mind."

"Way to go Skye!" Jet hugged her.

Skye hid by his side, her shy demeanour returning.

"Phew." Wain wiped his brow with the back of his hands.

"That was frightening." Max wailed. "Don't ever do anything like that again!"

"Impressive force field Skye. I felt it all the way out here." Philippe said.

Skye was a little Tachion. Her tremendous ability made him wonder for the first time what he, a hulking Tachion, could do.

"Yo! You're a Tachion sensation. You have proper skills!" Wain high-fived Skye with his three palms. "No one I know can do what you just did. How'd you learn to do that?"

Skye stepped behind Jet and let him speak for her.

"It's taken practice. We've been working on it for a while now."

"Fascinating." Max said, moving away from Wain and towards Skye.

Wain was no longer his muse. He now had a more extraordinary Tachion to study.

"I thought I would have to wait until advanced biology before I started to explore Tachion genetics. And here you've been, all the time, right next door."

Skye backed further behind Jet for safety.

"Skye would be fuzzed if the Authorities knew she uses her Tachion abilities," Brad said. "Even being a witness to what just happened put's us all in trouble."

"But no one's going to tell anyone Brad." The Twins said.

"This is crew business; we'll keep it just between us," Sal added.

"Thank you." Jet said glaring at Brad.

"Did you find what you were looking for?" Philippe asked feeling uncomfortable with the whole situation. Most Code Types had an innate fear of Tachions, and he didn't want to give his friends a reason to be frightened of him.

"We found it alright, 57912," I said my bit.

"36875," Wain said his.

Max typed it into his aero pad. He wasn't happy with Wain's methodology, but they had retrieved the data he needed. He pushed his now broken specs up his nose.

"Give me some time. I'll see what I can do."

***

"Where's Sal?" I asked.

It was an hour later, and we were once again virtually gathered in my room.

"Preparing more put downs for Madeleine Stone at the music emporium tomorrow." Philippe laughed, trying to keep everyone's spirits light, "She wished you good luck though."

"And Brad?"

"He said he would prefer to sit this one out
- " Mindy began,

"- I think he's got training anyways." Cindy
interrupted.

Mindy looked over at her Twin with her
nose scrunched up, which was her confused face.

"No, he said - " Mindy started.

"- That he is busy." Cindy interrupted again
returning her sisters stare.

They blinked at each other a few times
before Mindy backed down from the
standoff.

"Okay," Mindy said.

The Twins were acting weird, and Brad
didn't usually train this late, but I didn't dwell on
it.

"So what have you got for us, Max?" I asked
eagerly.

"TEN has special encrypted security on the
sequence you gave me. There is no way to hack
into the system externally, and I tried several
different ways."

"Why don't we just go to TEN and blast our
way in?" Jet said.

"Yeah." Skye agreed.

"Because you would get annihilated on the
spot," Max said dismissing their childish
comments.

"And the whole point of the exercise is that
we want to disable the messages without them
noticing," I said agreeing with Max.

"There must be another way to change the
signal yo," Wain said.

"There is. I've formulated a plan using these microsensors." Max said holding up microchips on his fingertips. "If you can get back into Sector Seven with these on your person, these bugs will temporarily disable any system, and I can guide you on how to hack the mainframe from my lab.

"It sounds great, but there is absolutely no way back in. I tried, but it's a restricted zone." I said.

"But Ivan has an access all areas pass." Mindy piped in.

"Do you think you can get it?" I asked.

"We can try." The Twins said together.

"Good. Mindy and Cindy, your role will be to get Kid into Sector Seven without anyone noticing."

Max liked taking charge and giving orders. He was beginning to get into the swing of it.

The Twins nodded in unison without question. I had no idea AEs could be so brave.

"Kid, if what you say is true and there are subliminal messages in the TEN broadcasts, then you can delete them and there will be no more mind control. And if there aren't any hidden messages, there will be nothing to erase, and nothing will change. Either way, we won't be harming anyone, so I'm ethically able to assist you.

"However I do insist that you talk to your parents, because if this is a delusional spin off from *you-know-where* they need to know so they can help you."

"You get me into the mainframe to erase the hidden messages Max, and I will tell my folks everything," I said.

"Then, pal of mine, you have a deal." We shook on it.

***

Mindy and I shifted nervously on the chic floating chairs in the canteen.

"This is like so-oo exciting," Mindy yelped, "I feel like a spy on a secret mission."

I was so glad to have her with me. Some would say that she was too airheaded to recognise real danger, but her confidence was contagious and made me feel braver.

I checked the digital display.

"It's noon. We better get this show on the road." I whispered conspiratorially.

"Yes. Cinds is already over there with Ivan," Mindy motioned, "He thinks she's me," she giggled.

"How did you get in?" I asked.

"You know I'm friendly with Bert on security. I just chatted with him and finessed him for a while before I waltzed in with no worries. He didn't even scan me."

"Ok great. So are you cool with what you have to do?"

"Sure." Mindy chirped revelling in the secret mission. She wasn't afraid at all.

"I was made for this, don't sweat it." Mindy sashayed off towards James who was eating his lunch with a bunch of other Techies.

I looked anxiously from one corner of the busy lunch zone to the other. Cindy was at one end chatting to Ivan, Mindy was charming James at the other. Both were trying to get the pass card to Sector Seven. If anyone spotted that there were two people with the exact same face, in the exact same place, then it would be curtains. Luckily the lunchroom was bustling with people, too obsessed with themselves to notice three teenagers.

My ear buzzed. It was Max on the line.

"I've hacked into the central security hub and disabled all recording devices. What's going on your end?

"Cindy is giggling with Ivan and Mindy has cornered James. All parties are talking, but that's about it," I said looking around.

"Ok, keep me posted. Over and out," Max said like a military sergeant.

I suspected his involvement with my latest scheme was not just because I had asked him to, it was also a great opportunity for Max to test out all of his homemade gadgets.

Mindy tottered back over to our table.

"Well?" I asked, expectantly.

"Oh my like gosh!" Mindy was miffed. "That Techy guy is like so much hard work, he was having none of it. He point blank refused me entry to Sector Seven. What a dork!" Mindy folded her arms and sulked.

She had never experienced this kind of rejection before. Guys always did what she asked of them.

"Okay, don't sweat it," I said downheartedly.

I knew it couldn't be that easy. There was no way a regened jobsworth like James would give up his pass, no matter how charming Mindy was.

"Oh my. Cinds is coming over. I'll make myself scarce." Mindy mingled into the lunchtime canteen rush.

Cindy hot-stepped it to my table.

"So how'd it go?" I asked despondently. If Mindy couldn't get the pass, then the plan was probably futile.

Cindy smiled, wider than usual and dangled the access all areas pass triumphantly.

"Cinds!" I gasped in disbelief.

For once Cindy had outdone her sister.

"Ivan's gone to top up his lippy, he doesn't know I took his pass, so let's be quick."

"You pick-pocketed his ID key?"

"Yes, why? Did you think I couldn't do it?" Cindy asked.

"No, it's not that. I just didn't think being a master of deception was your Type."

"You don't get to be the current holder of twenty-seven Miss Teen beauty queen titles and not be able to out smart your opposition," Cindy said with a mischievous twinkle in her eye. "Now let's go."

I jumped off the chair, placing a quick call to Mindy and Max.

"Cindy got the ID pass, and we're going in. Minds, you lay low."

"Yay, go Twinny!" Mindy cheered.

"Affirmative," Max said.

"Over and out." I signed off.

***

"It was like so-oo sick." Cindy chattered. "Ivan was like twittering on, and I was nodding and pretending to listen, and when I took the pass, he didn't even notice."

"You did great, now swipe the system," I said looking around nervously by the TX door.

Cindy swiped it. Nothing happened. I was so on edge I could feel my heart thundering in my ears,

"It's not -"

"Access Granted." The security system announced as the TX door flew open.

"Yes!" I said as my racing heart sunk back into my chest. "Just one more door."

Cindy and I bolted down the darkened corridor. I looked frantically left and right trying to identify the right room.

"How can you tell where to go? It all looks the same." Cindy said.

"It's this one," I said speaking into the audio receiver, "Max we're here."

Cindy swiped the door to Sector Seven, and it flew open.

"You did it! You're a star!" I hugged her.

"Are you like going to be okay?" Cindy asked. "I can stay with you if you like."

This mission had released the risk taker in her.

"I'm good. I don't want you to get into any trouble. You've done so much for me already. Now go and give Ivan back his pass before he realises it's missing." I said. "Go. Go."

"Who me?" Max came through on the audio receiver.

"No, Max you stay, Cindy you go."

"Good luck." Cindy tottered back down the corridor.

"Put on your IM so I can see what you see," Max instructed.

I clipped my IM to my collar giving Max a full view.

"Good job. Got you on the aero pad."

In front of us were standard issue protective lab wear, white coats and safety goggles.

"Put them on. Look like you fit in." Max said.

"Good idea." I quickly put on a lab coat.

Rows of decoder sticks were charging in a bank. I shoved one into my pocket.

"What's that?" Max asked.

"It's the thing they use to erase your memory at the end of the day," I explained.

"Wow! A real life nebuliser," Max marvelled, "nice work, it could come in handy."

As I walked further into the room, Max could see the frequing area, the walls filled with hundreds of screens and the mixing desk.

"See, this is where they freq," I said.

"Fascinating." If Max hadn't seen it with his own eyes, he would never have believed it.

My head began to hurt immediately, and I quickly popped the patches on my ears and turned the dial to block out the signal.

"Get to the mainframe pronto," Max said. "I'll process the freq room data at a more convenient time. Right now we have more pressing issues at hand."

A group of Techies walked in. I bowed my head and made myself look busy by James' empty mixing desk. The Techies walked past chattering amongst themselves.

"Phew." I breathed a sigh of relief.

"This is too close for comfort, get to the mainframe as soon as." Max barked into my ear.

I hurried past many other rooms set up identically to James' with a mixing desk and hundreds of screens.

"It looks as if the individual rooms are in a formation." Max deduced. "From what I can see the rooms are set in a spiral pattern. Logically the mainframe would be placed in the centre, each room feeding into the core."

"So I need to get to the middle?"

"Affirmative," Max said.

I ran around each room until I finally reached a room full of monitors and sensors. It was the hub of activity. The mainframe.

"Bingo." Max said.

"What shall I do next?" I asked.

Before Max could respond, a state of the art robotic Guardian seized me.

"Halt! This is a restricted area. State your business?" Demanded the Guardian.

I froze in panic.

"I should have guessed that they wouldn't leave something so crucial unguarded. Silly me, I should have been one step ahead." Max cursed himself.

"State your business." The Guardian ordered again, scanning my router.

Max typed furiously into his aero pad. "Stay cool Kid. He's only running an ID check on your eye scan."

"You are work experience. You are in the wrong sector. Leave immediately, or I will annihilate you."

I knew his talk of annihilation was not an idle threat, but I was in touching distance of the mainframe. I would never get another opportunity like this again. I had to complete what I came to do.

"I'm going for it, Max."

"What! Have you taken leave of your senses?

"I've got to try."

"Give me a second!" Max insisted.

I reached out for the mainframe. The Guardian harnessed his weapon. He had given me ample warning and was now well within his rights to end my life.

Before the pop con fired, the Guardian slumped to the ground and shut down, as did all of the other android personnel in the building.

In the canteen, the automated waitress collapsed into the protein pills she was serving. The robotic receptionists at the front desk ground to a halt mid greeting visitors.

"What did you do Max?" I gasped.

"I shut the Guardian down from the serial number on its neck. I've sent all tech at TEN into sleep mode, similarly to the way I did with your Auto Nan. But there's no time for chit-chat. You've got less than sixty seconds before all systems reboot."

I ran to the mainframe and administered Max's bug. Thousands of subliminal messages scrolled across the computer screen.

'Buy this...'
'Believe that...'
'Eat this...'
'Hate that...'

I began to delete each line one by one.

"Come on, come on." I panted.

"Just press delete all!" Max wailed, "There's no time to waste, twenty-five seconds."

I pushed delete all, and the screen went blank.

"Get out of there! Twenty seconds."

My fingers trembled as I typed in the new message, which from now on would be encoded into all of TEN broadcasts across all media worldwide.

I didn't have time to think of anything clever or witty, so I wrote the first thing that came into my head,

FREE YOUR MIND.

I jumped over the Guardian and fled from the mainframe. There was utter chaos outside as the Techies struggled with their failed robotic companions and computers. Amidst the confusion, I kept my head down and rushed past them until I reached the first room and threw off my lab coat and goggles. I ran out the door into the darkened corridor.

"*Reboot successful.*"

I overheard as the door swung shut behind me.

"Phew!" I breathed out hard, "that was close! But the Guardian read my router. He knows who I am."

"Just like with Auto Nan. He won't recall anything that happened just before the shutdown. He did not have time to save the data. Your whole encounter will be lost."

"You're a genius, Max." I sighed, relieved.

"I know." He said.

"You don't belong here!" Techy James startled me, appearing out of the darkness in the corridor.

"Erm, James, fancy seeing you here."

"How do you know me? I don't know you. I'm going to report you to security."

I whipped out the eraser from my pocket and blasted him between the eyes.

"Aaah!" James screamed, slumping to the ground.

"Sorry," I whispered stepping over him, "but at least you won't remember."

I fled from transmission and fell in line with all the other workers in the foyer. Everyone was abuzz with news of the power failure.

Nothing like that had ever happened before at The Eye.

"We did it, Max." I whispered before leaving the building.

My work here was done and what an experience it had been.

Write the lyrics to your own song,

Sing it loud and proud.

Dance to the beat of your own drum,

Stand out from the crowd.

TEN

Dot Pac

Jets hands trembled as he looked up at the crowd gathered in our backyard. He bit the corner of his lip nervously. All eyes were on him. The small makeshift stage he stood on was a replica of the one in the Barracoon amusement Arcade. Max, Wain, Sal and Philippe had done a good job constructing it. Jet knew they had done it to impress Kid rather than for him, but he was grateful all the same.

"Erm, is this thing on?" Jet spoke into the microphone.

"Yes!" The crowd cheered.

"Oh, ok." Jet looked bashfully at the audience he had drawn for his first ever live performance.

"Well, thanks for coming. On the drums is Nevaeh Skye and I'm Jet Monrova, and together we are Dot Pac."

Jet turned to Skye, who as ever, was by his side. She gave him the thumbs up bouncing on the spot. Jet smiled back, this time he was the one feeding off of her energy.

"We hope you enjoy," Jet said and with a confident motion strummed the strings of his guitar.

Skye banged the drums and sang a raspy, soul filled tune. Her voice was mesmerising. The melodic sound was like nothing the crowd had ever heard before, and they cheered loudly in appreciation.

The hairs on my arm stood up, and I got goosebumps like I always did whenever Skye sang. I grinned full of pride. It was only meant to be gathering for a few friends, but the word had gotten out, and people had travelled from far and wide to hear Jet and Skye play.

"It's funny," I said to Sal, "It used to annoy me when Jet twanged that string thing, but it sounds different to me now."

"It's cool. What's that music they're playing?" Sal asked.

"It's some old timers groove that Jet just kind of picked up naturally, without even being taught."

"This is like so much better than The Allstars nonsense," Mindy said.

"Ha! I thought you loved The Allstars," Wain laughed.

"So did you." Sal reminded him with a smirk. "We all did."

"They're like so-oo passé," Cindy said.

"Yeah, I deleted them from all my screen savers." Mindy said.

So had I, the rest of the crew and everyone at school. Their music had lost its appeal since I had erased the subliminal messages at TEN.

"What about DJ Dan? I asked.

"Eeww he's like so not my Type anymore," Mindy said. "But Jet looks cute playing that music machine."

"Yuck!" I gagged.

The Twins giggled. I made a puke face and turned to walk into my house. I needed to cover the outdoor sector. The noise from the cheering crowd was rising, and I didn't want to get a decibel warning or violate any more Truths. I had already broken enough laws to last a lifetime.

More importantly, I had promised my parents that I would be responsible and monitor this gathering while they were out. I guess there was some advantages of having a Compassionate Type mother. She was so thrilled that Jet wanted to have friends over, she had fully supported his gig and even convinced my dad to leave the house so we could have our 'privacy.'

"It's a great turnout," Max said.

"Yep, I can't believe my folks agreed to it."

"Indeed and not even Auto Nan here to watch over you."

"Exactly!" I laughed.

"But you will tell your parents everything won't you Kid?"

"I said I would. The whole unedited truth from venturing to UC to hacking TEN. I'll tell all, after the concert."

Max had said it a hundred times, and he was right. I needed to tell my parents, well my ma anyway, about everything that was going. After all, that's what grownups were for; they guided you to make the right decisions. And I knew ma could be trusted with any of my secrets, although I doubt she'd ever let me or Jet out of her sight again.

"Good to hear. I'm proud of you Kid," Max said. "You're doing the right thing."

"Got any refreshments yo?" Wain interrupted us.

"Yep. Give me a sec," I said giving Max a thumbs up before dashing into my house.

I made my way into the kitchen and pushed the button for a roof to cover the backyard. The mechanical outer shell moved automatically over the outside perimeter. The transparent enclosure would soundproof the yard and prevent a neighbourhood disturbance.

I stuck my head in the fridge looking for the H_2O pouches for my friends. I located them crudely wedged between two vegetation test-tubed matters my dad was cultivating for a home project. I placed the cooled substance carefully on a tray. I was so happy the crew had come to support Jet and Skye. I hadn't seen Brad yet, but I was hoping he would make an appearance later. I actually missed him as he hadn't been around a lot lately. I guess he had a lot of ball practice.

"Be a diamond and give me one of those. I'm parched," a wheezy voice said from behind me.

Startled, I whizzed around. A woman with a mass of frazzled black hair and a long wart ridden nose was standing in my kitchen, so close she was nearly perched on my shoulder.

"The concert's outside. This is private property." I informed the golden oldie.

Without invitation, the woman took a drink from the tray, gulped it down in one glug, burped loudly and then wiped her mouth with the back of her hand.

"Aaah that's better," she said smacking her lips together. "I'm not here for the music."

I looked at her in disbelief.

"Then how can I help you?" I was irritated but tried not to sound rude.

I recognised her from somewhere. Maybe she was one of the neighbours who had come to complain about the noisy gathering.

"Well I hope you can help me," the witchy looking woman said sitting at our dining room table and making herself comfortable. "I'm sincerely hoping you can help us all."

This woman had to go. Dad had made it very clear that no one was allowed into the house and I didn't want to disobey him.

"This is a private function, but you're welcome to enjoy the music, *outside*," I said trying to be cordial.

The old woman leisurely put her feet up on the dining table. "I'm perfectly cosy here thank you. I believe you have something of mine."

I looked at her blankly.

"A crystal ball. Shattered I'm told."

"What The Res gave me?" I whispered instantly on high alert.

"Yes, Keziah. I'm Lady Zono, and I want my property back."

"Oh, my days." Just like The Res, I now recognised Lady Zono from my dreams.

"Nice to meet you," I said shaking her bony hand.

"Congratulations Keziah, you completed your first mission. You took out the first eye of the beast, The Eye Network. By taking down TEN, they'll no longer be able to push garbage into everyone's brains with their broadcasts. You have liberated minds. Free will reigns."

I blushed. I couldn't believe it. I had achieved the first eye – just like the Arcadians believed I would. Maybe there was something in this Prophecy. Could I really be the Soul Survivor? Put on the planet to save all souls?

"Your brother is playing a rocking set. I haven't heard anything like this for aeons." Lady Zono said as she bopped her head to the music. "Jet is excellent on the guitar. Let's hope he's able to develop skills quickly in other departments too eh?"

"Pardon?"

"Oops!" Lady Zono covered her mouth as if she had said something she shouldn't have. "Don't mind me. I'm just an old gal, speaking out of turn. Let's not run before we can walk."

Lady Zono jumped up, and half dragged me out of my kitchen and further into my own house.

"Now down to business, where is my glass rock?" Lady Zono clumsily changed the subject.

"I've kept it safe in my room," I said.

"Righty-O." She said as she led the way upstairs.

***

The shattered crystal was hidden from Jet, my parents and the rest of the world, in a sock underneath my bed. I fetched it and carefully poured the gemstone into Lady Zono's palm. The jagged pieces reflected the light creating a kaleidoscope of colour. She cast her hand over the fragments and the crystal magically reformed into one solid ball.

"Oh I have missed you dear one," Lady Zono said puckering up and kissing the ball. "I have my babies strewn all around the world for safe keeping. Far too dangerous to have them all in one place, don't you think?"

"Er, I guess so."

"Thank you for looking after her for me."

"You're welcome," I was pleased to be of service.

"You know why I keep the crystals away from each other don't you?" Lady Zono asked, peering at me intently.

"Er, no."

"So Zyclon can't get his hands on them. They've got far too much juice, tell too many truths. Who knows what he would do if he could see the secrets the crystal balls tell me."

"Ok."

"You know who Zyclon is don't you?"

"Er, no."

"He's the one behind the scenes trying to control this world. He's wicked and cruel, and there's nothing he wouldn't do to get what he wants. You know what he wants, don't you?"

"Not a clue."

"For this world and everyone in it to belong to him. If that happens all souls will be lost, and the world will cease."

"I'm not sure I follow," I said not understanding a word Lady Zono was saying.

But she continued anyway, "He already has a stranglehold on this place, the Upper Worlds. Everything is holographic simulation this and virtual reality that. One, zero, one, zero, zero, ones, binary code all over the place. No actual authentic reality in sight. But as long as Mother Nature reigns in the land of Freeca and even our very own little Commania, we may have a chance. Not everything is going exactly according to his plan. Haaa ha Haaa!" Lady Zono cackled startling me.

"Alrighty then," I said, not sure whether to be frightened or enlightened by this woman.

"Each one of my balls is a very rare and precious crystal. They know many things. Now let's see what this one wants to tell me about you." Lady Zono peered deeply into the crystal; her eyeballs magnified in the glass.

Bright rainbow colours shot out from the ball and surrounded me. I watched in awe as the colours began to paint a scene in my bedroom as if an invisible artist was creating a masterpiece. I found myself amidst an illustrated forest, with bright flowers, a vivid lake and hut houses.

"Wow." I was amazed as the natural woodland scene enveloped me.

"I see leafy green trees and a nation at ease," Lady Zono narrated the drawing.

"Pardon?" I said, revelling in the luminous, vibrant scenery.

"The future has revealed itself. You will discover the next eye with Dr Stoneway and the Saps in Commania."

"Commania?" I echoed. "But from what I know that place is hidden in real nature! All of the greenery in the Upper Worlds is either GM or a virtual simulation. I have never stepped foot in real, living nature before. Why do I have to go there? How would I get there? What will I do there?" I asked panicking.

This was all moving so fast. I was just about ready to 'fess up all to my parents and now this. My next mission was presenting itself.

"Do not be afraid Keziah, you are the Alpha, you will figure out what you need to do. I will give you all the guidance I can.

"Yes, Commania is in the heart of wild nature, which can be a perilous foe or a precious friend. I would suggest that you befriend it.

"The road to Commania is long and winding. You'll need a helping hand."

Max immediately sprung to my mind. I knew I could rely on him. He would never let me down. But to convince him to journey with me to Commania could be too much to ask of him.

No, it wouldn't be Max this time. For this mission I would need someone who wouldn't question what we were doing, someone fearless, someone tough.

"It's got to be Sal," I said looking out into the backyard at my friends.

Sal rhythmically nodded to the music Dot Pac played, unwittingly accepting the challenge ahead.

"Something told me you might choose her," Lady Zono said knowingly.

CRASH!

She smashed her crystal ball onto the floor, shattering it into a million pieces. Brightly coloured glitter flew into the air. One small piece of iridescent gemstone remained which she swiftly swept into her hand.

"No missile or bullet or gun can harm, as long as your field is strong. Add to your energies every day, and it will protect you all life long," sung Lady Zono.

"What's that?" I coughed as the multicoloured glitter landed all over me.

"It's a spell. You will need protection to your physical being and as long as you do what I said you'll have it. Your energy field will be strong."

"My what?" I asked.

"Your energy field. Don't worry; they'll teach you in Commania."

Lady Zono whipped the long black leather lace from her well-worn boot, tied it around the last remaining part of the crystal ball and attached it swiftly around my neck. The gem hung down by my heart. A light blue ray emitted from the crystal and stung my cheeks, rattling my teeth.

"Ow!" It felt like Lady Zono had stung me with static. "What on earth are you doing?"

She ignored me.

"This crystal will protect you when times get sticky. Never take it off."

"Erm, no offence but I don't think the shoelace thing is really my look. Thanks all the same."

"Never take it off. Promise me."

I pulled a face. I didn't really want dingy old boot strappings hanging around my neck.

"Promise me." She said again sternly.

"Alright. Ok. I promise you. I'll wear it if it means that much to you."

"It does," Lady Zono said seriously. "The Res set the wheels in motion, before time I may add. The Res is many things, but a patient man he is not. I told him I didn't think you were ready, but you've done marvellously so far, so I guess you are."

Lady Zono kicked off her shoes and flopped onto my bed. Long knobbly big toes poked out of the holes in her striped socks.

"We are here now. You are in action, and The Prophecy cannot be stopped," she said motioning for me to sit next to her. "Now come along Keziah, there is much you should know."

I sat beside the eccentric old woman, covered in glitter, with a crystal hanging from my neck, to hear what the second eye could be.

One Heart.

One Nation.

One Community.

Commania,

The land of unity.

ELEVEN

Commania

"...It'll be totally fine Ma. We have so much planned for the school holiday." I tried to sound casual as I squashed my PJ's into my backpack. I had already packed so many gadgets for this mission; I was going to be more prepared than even Max.

Ma hovered in my room.

"But you've never stayed away from home for an entire week. Will it just be you and Sal?"

"Yeah, why?"

"Perhaps Auto Nan could go with you," Milan suggested.

"Ma, that is so humiliating." I protested. "What other fifteen year-olds do you know take their Nan to a sleepover?"

I sweated. Perhaps ma knew I was planning a trip to try and find Commania.

"Well, it's just that Sal is a tough little cookie and I don't know her parents. Auto Nan could look after the both of you, keep you safe. I'll program Nan to give you manicures, facials anything you want."

I breathed a silent sigh of relief. Ma wasn't onto me; she was just being super concerned like she always was.

"Ma, you know I'm not into all of that girly stuff. I think I'll pass on the Auto Nan offer, but thanks anyway." I said stuffing my favourite blue fleece hoody into my already crammed bag.

Ma crossed the room and lounged on my bed. Whenever she did that, I knew she wanted to talk.

"You know I always knew you would be special."

"What ma?" I asked distractedly shoving my sneakers into my backpack and zipping it shut.

"My mother told me." Milan continued, "She said she was told by a mystic to have a compassionate daughter, even though it was such an old-fashioned Type to request. The mystic told her that her child would need to have a big loving heart as the children that her daughter bore would need careful nurturing as they had important work to do."

"Ok, ma." I did have important work to do, and right now she was holding me up from it.

"So, in essence, your Grandma made me, so that I could make you. And Jet too of course." Milan smiled.

She rose and placed her warm hands on either side of my face,

"If I haven't told you recently, you are truly wonderful Kid, and I love you and always will with every beat of my heart. And even when my heart stops beating I will still love you. As the bond of love stretches from here till forever and nothing trumps true love. Absolutely nothing. Not even the end of time."

Her soft afro curls framed her beautiful dark brown face, and for that moment all that mattered in the world was my ma and me.

"Thank you." I smiled.

"So shall I call Sal's mother and arrange a scheduled time so we can synch in every day?"

"No don't do that!" I panicked.

I wasn't staying at Sal's, and I'm not sure what she had told her mother to buy us a few days of freedom.

"Sal's home communication centre is out of service." I lied. "I'll call you from my IM," I said heading for the door.

"Ok. Love you, Angel." Milan called out.

"Love you too ma," I yelled bounding down the steps and out of the door.

***

Sal opened up her garage door and threw both our bags into the trunk of her aero bike, which she affectionately named The Speedster.

"Commania," Sal said rubbing her hands in glee. She had been a perfect pick for this mission, enthusiastic from the word go. "So we're really going to do this?"

"Yep," I said. "I've been doing my research. Well getting Max to download all his knowledge to me anyway. Commania is a secret community and well hidden from the Upper Worlds. Luckily Lady Zono gave me this map. The problem is the directions are not detailed. We've just got to keep our wits about us."

I handed Sal the chip containing the map, and she input the data into her guidance system.

"This ride is awesome," I said saddling up on Sal's vibrant red aero bike.

"It's my baby." Sal beamed proudly. "It's omni coloured, look," Sal said as the bike changed to a shiny metallic green right underneath me.

"Amazing." I marvelled.

Jet and I were never allowed these kinds of cool gadgets, just boring science ones.

"Put this on." Sal handed me a transparent helmet made from oxy-chronon, so was as tough as nails.

She put on her red protective gear and revved up the engine. The bike immediately sprung into action, and we shot straight into the air with her first manoeuvre.

"Whoa!" I yelled. I wasn't used to the aero gliding system of The Speedster.

"Be cool. I've got you." Sal smirked.

I held on tightly, and The Speedster flew out of Sal's garage and down the intersection.

***

On The Speedster, we glided down the busy highway with ease. Many other sleek solar and nuclear vehicles were also leaving the city, taking advantage of the holiday period. The roads were gridlocked, but Sal was a natural sky rider and drifted smoothly in the air.

So far the ride had been comfortable, but there was something niggling me. I looked behind us to double-check before speaking through the inbuilt helmet mic to Sal.

"Have you noticed that blue bike has been behind us since we left your house."

Sal looked in the rear view mirror and spotted the blue bike.

"You reckon so? Let's see."

Sal made a sharp, unexpected left turn and checked her side mirror. Sure enough, the blue bike, with two passengers, followed suit.

"Yep, they're definitely tailing us," Sal said coolly.

I panicked. Perhaps the Techies at TEN somehow found out that I had changed their subliminal messages and were now after me. Or worse still, maybe ma had sent Auto Nan to babysit us.

"Hold tight," Sal said and pressed her foot hard on the accelerator.

The Speedster took off higher into the sky vertically, crossing lanes of traffic at top speed.

"Aaah!" I screamed.

I couldn't look as Sal dodged a barrage of oncoming bikes. The blue bike followed suit just as daringly. Other vehicles braked sharply and beeped their horns to avoid a collision. Sal's Speedster zigzagged across the skyway and off the beaten path. My stomach flipped nauseously as I held on for dear life.

"I think we lost them." I gulped.

Sal slowed down the bike, and I released my grip relieved that we had reached the desolate wasteland of the Outer Limits in one piece.

Just then the blue bike hurtled over us, pulled a triple somersault mid air before breaking sharply in front of us and cutting off our path. The Speedster skidded to a halt.

Only one person I knew could be that reckless.

"Jet!" I shouted, taking my helmet off. Sure enough Jet flipped up his visor, and Skye stopped the blue bike.

Sal switched off her engine and shook her head, "Your little brother is nuts."

"I couldn't agree more," I said hopping off The Speedster and steaming up to Jet.

"What in the world do you two think you're doing? You could have killed us all."

"Sorry, Kid." Skye apologised, casting her big blue eyes downwards shyly.

"Where did you get that bike from and how'd you learn to ride like that?"

"I borrowed it," Skye said sheepishly, "aero biking is part of our training."

"Training for what?"

"Something like this," Jet jumped in, "you didn't think you could go off on another mission without me. I know you're up to something. Where are you going?"

I was fuming.

"Where I'm going, I'm going without you, so just go home and Skye, stop riding like a crazy person."

"We were gutted not to be part of the action at TEN, that sounded icy. We want to help you with this mission." Skye said in her raspy tones.

"It's not a mission okay. I'm just hanging out with Sal, staying over at her house."

"So why did you take dad's old camping gear and re-route Sal's home phone to your IM?" Jet asked.

"What are you like some kind of spy?" I said irritated by my brother's efficiency.

"Ok fine, don't tell me what you're up to. Ma thinks I'm staying at Skye's for the week, but I'll just go straight home and tell her what's been happening – and I mean *all* of it."

I narrowed my eyes. Jet knew way too much about everything, and now he was holding me to ransom. I turned to Sal.

"Do you think they can be trusted?" I asked.

"Like, whatever." Sal shrugged unimpressed by the sibling's spat. "Let's get going; we've still got a long way to go before we are anywhere near Commania."

"*Commania.*" Jet gasped.

"That's the ultimate!" Skye bounced hyperactively on the spot.

"Great," I muttered. Now Sal had let the cat out of the bag there would be no way to get rid of Jet and Skye.

I decided on damage limitation.

"Okay, here's how it's going to be. You two can come but only if you promise to behave, stay out of trouble and do exactly what I say at all times."

Jet and Skye nodded in enthusiastic agreement.

"Of course." Jet said.

"Any fooling around, we all go home," I added calling his bluff.

"Yeah whatever you say, you're the boss. Boss." He said excitedly running back to the blue aero bike.

"Ok," I said reluctantly walking back to The Speedster, "Well follow us, stay close and no speeding or crazy stunts," I warned.

"No problem," Skye said, popping a wheelie.

I shook my head. It was going to be near impossible controlling those two.

I saddled up next to Sal, and our newly formed quartet rode off out of the city in search of the hidden land of Commania.

***

After riding through the dusty wasteland of the Outer Limits for what felt like hours, Sal finally pulled The Speedster to a halt. Skye followed suit. We jumped off the bikes, and all took in the impressive sight in front of us, Ethereal Bridge.

Ethereal Bridge was an engineering marvel, a famous landmark of the Upper Worlds. It was intricately designed with iron sculpted into an ornate pattern that depicted the scene of a great battle between the fabled underwater dwellers of Mermen and the winged sky people. I remembered the tale of the water and the sky's stormy relationship from a third-grade storybook.

Many moons ago Ethereal Bridge was the main way in and out of the Upper Worlds. The other side of the bridge led across the ocean, out of our world into the Great Unknown.

"Look at those." Jet said, pointing to the sky.

A flock of strangely shaped birds noisily squawked as they circled overhead. The largest bird led and the others followed. As soon as we stopped to look at them, the birds changed course and began to fly south. All except one little bird who continued flying straight at us.

The little bird landed atop Jet's head and pecked him on the forehead.

"Cheep, cheep, cheeeeeeeep," it twittered sweetly.

"Hey! Get off of me." Jet waved his hands. But the little bird stayed put and nestled further into his hair.

"Cheep, cheep, cheeeeeeeep," it twittered again.

"This little guy is way cute." Skye said, carefully stroking the bird's blue, white and brown feathers.

"Really?" Jet said.

"Yes." Skye assured him, "He's the coolest aren't you Little Cheep Cheep?"

The bird chirped as if in agreement.

"Ok." Jet said unsure but allowed the little bird to stay on his head because Skye liked him. "Just don't do any funny business up there."

Little Cheep Cheep stopped pecking Jet's head as if responding to his request.

"Now that you and your feathered friend have an understanding," Sal mocked Jet, "the map's directions stop here, and it doesn't indicate which way to go."

"Maybe it's across the water?" Skye rasped.

"That's just too far; we would end up out of Pangaea. And The Speedster hasn't got enough juice to go all that way."

"Well, maybe you're not reading the map right." Jet said.

Sal looked deeply at Jet.

"Why don't you just pipe down." She suggested.

Jet was instantly quiet.

And that's when I heard it.

"Hee, hee hee, hee, hee."

I could hear children's laughter, and it was coming from the thick forestry by the side of the bridge.

"Do you hear that?" I said.

"Hear what?" Sal asked.

"The laughing from the forest."

We were all silent and then it started again.

"Hee, hee hee, hee, hee."

"Yes I do!" Skye heard it too.

"Look, what's that?" Jet asked.

A dash of bright multicoloured ribbons danced through the trees.

"Let's go after them." Jet dashed off.

"Jet, slow your row," I shouted annoyed.

I had told him to do what I said, and at the first chance he got he was already breaking the rules.

"You can't just run off."

"Sorry. But it must be a sign, we should follow them."

The ribbons bobbed further into the distance.

"We're losing them." Jet urged.

"Lady Zono said Commania was well hidden in the trees and she warned that real life nature could be treacherous. So let's proceed with caution, ok?"

Everyone agreed, and we rode carefully into the forest.

***

Max scooted through the air on his homemade hover board while replaying his IM. He shook his head contemptuously. Kid had left a message to say she had gone off on another mission without him when he'd expressly told her to tell her parents everything.

He rounded the corner leading into a heavily guarded upscale neighbourhood. Max had already been to Sal's house to complain but she had also disappeared, so it was logical to him that they had gone off together. How could Kid have gone away with Sal and not him? Surely he would have been more helpful. Hadn't he proven himself to her? He was always there when she needed him. Yet, once again, she had ditched him in favour of somcone else.

Max glided past a troop of stern looking Guardians, further hunching his already unassuming demeanour. In this exclusive neighboured it wouldn't take much for an overzealous Guardian to fuzz a teenager without warning. Max kept his head down and zoomed towards his destination, The Twins house.

***

Sal and Skye's bikes edged slowly forward, this way and that way, following the ribbons, but the twisted, thorny foliage made it too difficult to keep up the pursuit. Sal powered down The Speedster.

"I don't think we can go any further. We're not going to be able to bring our bikes through the dense undergrowth."

"But if we stop now we'll lose them." Jet said. "Let's ditch the bikes and go after them on foot."

Sal wasn't blown away by that idea. "The Speedster's my pride and joy. I don't want to abandon her here."

"Look they've stopped," Skye said. "It's as if they're waiting for us to catch up."

Sure enough, the ribbons bobbed in the same spot.

"Well? It's your call, Kid. What shall we do?"

"Sal, I promise we'll come back for the bikes, but for now let's continue on foot."

"If we must." Sal reluctantly agreed.

We scrambled off the bikes, took the backpacks from the boot and ran carefully through the undergrowth towards the ribbons, which were on the move again

Max rang the doorbell of the Twins palatial home. His eyes were scanned before Ms Lush, opened the door.

"Oh, hello Max," she said through horse like teeth.

Unlike the Twins, Ms Lush, The Twins mother, was not genetically beautiful; in fact, she was far from it. And because this was her greatest sorrow, she lived her life vicariously through her daughters.

"The girls are in their rooms." Ms Lush said.

She was happy that her daughters were associating with such well-bred company. It was no secret that she was snooty and only wanted her girls associating with other Gold Star Types. Max was a leading brain of his generation, which made him perfect company for her daughters in her eyes.

"Thanks, ma'am," Max said.

"But before you go to see Mindy and Cindy, please do talk me through your latest work on the evolution of the Tachion."

"Certainly ma'am." Max was chuffed.

He loved talking about his essays and lately he had collected a lot of first-hand data on the subject.

"Let's converse in the study." Ms Lush walked Max through the plush marble hallway and into the huge mansion.

***

A leafy branch slapped me in the face, and I stumbled on the knotted roots beneath my feet.

"Ow." I moaned rubbing my cheek with one hand and battling the thick vines with the other.

"It's a struggle to keep up with the ribbons, they're moving so fast." Jet panted.

We were not used to being surrounded by so much of this nature stuff. It was damp, rocky, squelchy and smelly.

"Oh, my days! I've had enough of all of these creatures!" Sal cried out, swatting away the bulbous flies that buzzed around us.

"Nature stinks! This real grass and tree stuff, it's so alive! The holograms are much better. It doesn't come with bugs. All the beauty without the hassle. No wonder His Excellency, William Admiral called for it to be eradicated from the Upper Worlds."

Skye shook her head disappointed at Sal's attitude.

"It's typical of a Code Type to prefer a pretty fake illusion rather than the gritty real thing. Everything has a place in the world you know, even gnats. I think it's a shame what The Admiral is doing, wiping out animal species, outlawing nature just because he thinks it looks messy in *your* environment. We cultivate nature in Zero." Skye rasped.

Skye's venom made Sal feel bad. But trekking on foot through dirt was not her idea of fun. And worse still what Skye had said about her couldn't be further from the truth.

"It's nothing to do with being a Code Type; it's just that - Oh, forget it," Sal said staring down Skye.

"The ribbons have disappeared." I wheezed, collapsing to the ground out of breath.

"We lost them." Sal said stamping mud from her feet.

"How could we. They were just there!" Jet said.

Skye looked around. Their path was completely obscured by wild flowers and thick bushes.

"We won't be able to find our way back to the bikes. We're the ultimate in lost."

"To follow on foot was such a dumb idea." Sal fumed scratching her back.

All this nature made her feel incredibly itchy and irritable.

"I didn't see you come up with a better plan, big shot!" Jet snapped back.

Sal narrowed her eyes. This little boy was getting on her last nerve.

Jet and Sal started bickering again. Skye defended Jet, and even Little Cheep Cheep twittered as if chiming in. I couldn't take the arguing. I walked away and sat underneath the largest tree.

"This way." A little voice said.

I looked upwards.

The ribbons bobbed way up in the treetops. I could not see who was holding the strings, but once again they were patiently waiting for us.

"Look." I pointed.

They all stopped squabbling and came over.

"What's this?" Jet said touching the tree bark.

A ladder made from twisted vine leaves wound itself all the way up the side of the tree.

"Climb." The child's voice instructed us before the colourful ribbons ascended further up the tree and out of sight.

I gripped the ladder and eagerly pulled myself up in pursuit of the ribbons. Sal followed behind me with Jet and Skye.

I was the first to scramble to the top of the vine and belly flopped clumsily onto the plateau. What I thought was a tree opened up to a whole other level. It was foggy at the top, but I could still make out the colourful ribbons bobbing in front of me.

Three small children, the bearers of the ribbons, appeared from the mist. They wore long material garments with scarves covering their heads. They eyeballed me without saying a word.

Sal, Jet and Skye clambered to the top, shoving and pushing each other as they did so.

"You're so slow." Jet complained.

"Pipe down irritant." Sal tutted.

"Leave Jet alone." Skye rasped.

Upon seeing the children, they stopped arguing. No one spoke, and the children silently stared at us.

"They're scaring me," Sal whispered nudging me in my ribs, "say something."

"Hello," I said cautiously walking towards the small children. "Have you been leading us here?"

The children nodded.

"Where are we?" I asked.

"This is Commania." The smallest child answered, taking my hand. "I'm Poppy, your guide. Come with me."

The other two children followed her lead. One took Jet and Skye by the hand and the other held onto Sal.

"Er, ok," Sal said. "You're confident little people, aren't you?"

The children walked us beyond the haze, revealing a thriving, bustling land. Trees as tall as tower blocks, stood proudly displaying their dark green and burgundy leaves. Brightly coloured flowers bloomed abundantly. Fluffy little animals ran around playfully with each other. There were hordes of people jovially busying themselves doing all manner of things from washing clothes by hand outside their wooden hut homes to cooking the ancient way with pots on fires.

"Wow! So this is Commania." I had never seen anything so vibrant and full of life.

The picture the crystal ball had drawn in my room paled in comparison to the real thing.

Through the bustling crowd a small man, leaning heavily on a twisted cane, scuttled right up to us.

"Aha! Keziah Monrova et al. Welcome, one and all."

"Do you know him?" Sal said from the side of her mouth.

"Yes, I think I do." I smiled recognising the small man from my dreams.

"I am Dr Stoneway." He greeted me taking my hand in his. "Nice to see you again." He smiled warmly.

"And you too." I smiled back. "How did you know we were coming? Did Lady Zono tell you?"

"No, no. I didn't, I didn't know at all, but we always send a band of our young uns to wait for you, just in case." Dr Stoneway said.

He had kind eyes and a cheerful face with heavily wrinkled tanned skin. His receding hairline sprouted an impressive silver ponytail that trailed down his back. His hunched shoulders and bow legs made him seem way shorter than he was and tiny round glasses swung from a cord around his neck.

"And who else do we have here?" Dr Stoneway asked.

"Sal."

"Skye."

"Jet, sir." They all answered one by one, with an instant respect for the noble looking man.

"Aha!" Dr Stoneway exclaimed again. "You don't look very much like a Sal. And you Skye are truly as remarkable as the heavens above that provide us with all we need. And Jetsir," Dr Stoneway paused to think, leaning heavily on his cane before he continued, "You, my boy, are pivotal."

We all smiled politely not understanding what he was saying but liking him instantly all the same. Dr Stoneway beamed back a knowing smile.

"Now come, come. I'm glad our young uns led you here in good time." Dr Stoneway looked to the sky. "It's just after five in the PM, and we're about to eat."

***

Mindy sat regally on her magenta pink recliner in her pale pink room, with rose pink walls which were filled with metallic pink screens displaying her face. Since deleting all of her Allstar posters, she had to replace them with something else she loved. And what could be more fitting than herself?

Mindy twiddled her golden tresses around her finger. Her smile was even wider than usual because Philippe sat opposite her. He awkwardly tried to relax his bulky frame on a cotton candy coloured beanbag. He was also grinning like a Cheshire cat. Mindy's dimples became even rounder as Philippe looked down shyly and then back to the main screen. A movie he had selected was playing. He had viewed at least twenty other films before their date, to pick the right one.

Mindy was super excited to be alone with Philippe. She thought he was perfect in every way. He was strong, sensitive and funny. She wasn't bothered about his appearance. His personality was way more important.

The melodramatic music signalled the end of the movie.

"That was like uber emosh," Mindy said not sure what to say as she was only half paying attention. She had spent most of the film stealing glances at Philippe.

"I'm glad you liked it," Philippe said.

There was an awkward silence as they looked at each other. Both smiled goofily.

"So. Where's Cindy then?" Philippe asked for asking sake.

"Like, I don't know. Since what went down at TEN Cindy seems a little like distant, wants her own space."

"That's a shame," Philippe said. But if truth be told he was enjoying this rare occasion of being alone with Mindy.

"So, like, we've watched a movie, and you've eaten all the corned pop."Mindy play punched Philippe as if upset that he had eaten all of the sugary food she was genetically forbidden from consuming. "What shall we do next?"

Philippe took Mindy's delicate hand and held it gently in his massive palm. He leant forward and Mindy drew closer. They faced each other nervously. Philippe's double hearts skipped two beats. Mindy's perfect pout and Philippe's chapped lips were about to come together when all of a sudden Mindy's bedroom door flew open.

"Yuck!" Max said, ruining the fledgling lovebird's special moment.

***

We were all seated in the centre of Commania around an enormous oak tree stump made into a communal table. A large gathering of Saps were chattering amongst themselves while they dined.

I was enthralled by the sights, sounds and smells of this strange land. From my research, Saps were portrayed as a decaying, lifeless, inferior species. But that didn't coincide with what I saw before me. Some of the Saps were grey in skin colour, but they were mostly different shades of white, pink, beige, yellow, red, brown and black, just like Code Types.

I had learned at school that Saps needed breathing apparatus, as their lungs were not modified to process the carbon filled air. But only a few were breathing with an aid and the ribbon-bearing children that had led us here were much fitter than me, Jet, Skye or Sal. It simply wasn't true that the Saps were weak. Seeing it with my own eyes made me question what other untruths I'd been taught at FB.

"I thought all Saps needed help to breathe?" I asked a cheery faced woman in flowing material garments who sat next to me.

"Some of us do, but that's why we live here in the trees, above the smog of your world. The trees are our friends, our life force. They give us oxygen in the day that provides us with breath, our lifeline. Here, in Commania we work with nature, not against it or try to control it like they do in the Upper Worlds. We plant, grow and rear all of our food with the one essence we all have. Love."

"Oh, right," I said trying to take it all in.

The Saps didn't talk in riddles as everyone in the Upper Worlds thought, but their softly spoken speech pattern and their sing-song accents still made them hard to understand.

"Now please eat, this meal is in honour of your arrival."

I looked at the table but didn't know where to begin. I was not familiar with this kind of food and Poppy had to explain to me what it all was. Freshly baked bread, bountiful fruits, rice, pulses, beans and stews.

"A meal fit for a king, or a Keziah," Poppy said before she patted my hand and walked away.

Dr Stoneway munched noisily next to me.

"Aha! I know it must look a bit intimidating to your palette if you're not used to this kind of thing," he said, between mouthfuls.

"That's right," Sal nodded, "where we're from we mostly eat nutri- granules and vacuum packed sustainable liquids."

"May I suggest you begin with this." Dr Stoneway passed a platter to us. "This is warm bread with cheese and fruit. Try it."

We all took a piece and looked at it for a while. Jet was the first to tuck in. He nibbled on what they called a grape, and the flesh broke between his teeth.

"Ooh! This is sweet." He licked his lips.

Sal sniffed the cheese and pulled a face, "It smells funny."

Skye chewed happily on a piece of bread.

"My family can never afford to buy the store manufactured nutrients, so we grow and prepare this kind of solid food all the time."

I wasn't sure about the food, but there was something I was longing to taste.

"Dr Stoneway, do you have any chocolate?"

"Aha!" Dr Stoneway said and reached into a bowl.

"We usually reserve that for after the main meal, but we can make an exception on this one occasion."

He handed me a small brown square, which didn't look at all appetising.

"Try it." Dr Stoneway said.

I sniffed the hard substance then quickly took a bite. The chocolate melted instantly and what felt like every taste bud in my mouth came alive. The velvet texture coated my tongue, and the sweetness gave my head a rush, the sensation was incredible.

"Now that is good!" I zinged.

"Aha! Everyone eat and drink to your hearts content. After dinner, we take a nap." Dr Stoneway announced for our benefit.

"You sleep after you've eaten?" Sal asked.

"Yes, we're mammals we enjoy our sleep, it is essential." Dr Stoneway said.

I thought back to our trip to UC and Max saying that Saps believed their dream world was as important as when they were awake. He was right and full of so much helpful knowledge. I missed Max and was sad to have left him behind.

He would have loved it here in Commania. It would have been a fantastic field trip for him. I made a promise to myself to make sure Max got to experience Commania one day.

"We wake up early grateful to the sun for rising. We eat, dance, sing, exercise, educate or work, dinner, nap and then Kimetic." Dr Stoneway informed us of their daily activities.

"What's Kimetic?" I asked scoffing mouthfuls of chocolate.

Dr Stoneway smiled again, "You'll see."

***

"What's the commotion?" Cindy asked, walking into her sister's parlour.

"I caught them getting it on," Max said scornfully.

"Way to go Minds. Good for you."

"Thanks, Twinny," Mindy smiled coyly, thankful for the support.

"Shall we call your mother to see how *good for you* she thinks it is?" Max said.

"Oh like, that's true, mother would be like so-oo against you two having a relationship. You know she doesn't trust Tachions. Sorry, Philippe, that's just the way she is."

Ms Lush only allowed Philippe into the house because she pitied him. She could understand that his Code Type parents had tried to create the perfect athletic child, but it went wrong, and Philippe had turned out to be a rare genetic mistake. The Twins hadn't told their

250

mother about knowing Wain. His family were Tachions through and through and had been so for generations. There would be no way the Twins could explain their new friendship with him to their mother.

"Maybe it would be a good idea not to tell mother," Cindy said.

Philippe shifted uncomfortably, the muscles in his face rippled, "I don't want to be anybody's dirty secret."

"Like that's her problem, not mine." Mindy said defensively.

"It's not just your mother, that's a big no-no on the Upper Worlds. Code Types and Tachions can be friends but reproducing is not fair to your children. Genetically they could be anything." Max said.

"Then we should change the way things are." Philippe seethed.

"Yeah who made those rules anyway?" Cindy asked.

"It's like so-oo out of date." The Twins said together.

"Yeah. In UC all different people were together romantically. Their Code Type status didn't even matter." Philippe held Mindy's hand.

"Well that's why they live underground, in *you-know-where*, so that they can get away with that sort of dangerous behaviour."

"What!" Philippe strode towards Max outraged, pulling Mindy behind him.

"So you think it's justified that Mindy and I be banished to a forbidden place so that we can be together?" Philippe asked towering over Max.

Max nervously took off his spectacles. His aim wasn't to upset his friend.

"It's nothing personal Philippe. You're a great guy. It's just the social order of things. There are many arguments that I could present about cross Type relationships that make for a fascinating conversation. I was just telling Ms Lush - "

" - This isn't debate class. Just answer the question, Max. If Mindy and I were together would that be abominable to you?" Philippe said through gritted teeth.

"One could argue yes," Max said, sticking to his principles. "If you're not prepared to listen to what I have to say, then it would be illogical to keep up the discussion."

Philippe's fist curled into a ball.

Max cowered.

"Don't do it!" Cindy called out in horror.

Philippe threw an almighty punch purposely landing his fist on the wall, instead of Max's face. The wall smashed as if it were hit by a bulldozer. Instinctively his grip tightened on Mindy.

"You're hurting me, Philippe," Mindy whispered frightened by his temper. She had never seen him act this way before.

"Sorry Minds," Philippe said immediately releasing her.

He was instantly remorseful, the last thing in the world he would ever want to do was hurt Mindy.

Ms Lush stormed into the room, "What is going on here? What happened to my bespoke Diamonique wall?"

The room fell silent. Nobody made an attempt to answer. Mindy and Cindy turned to stare at Philippe. He hunched his shoulders feeling awful.

"I think you should leave now," Max said apportioning blame.

Philippe's face muscles trembled. He couldn't imagine his precious first date with Mindy would end up like this.

"It's not up to you Max!" Philippe barked, then turned and spoke more softly, "Mindy, do you want me to go?"

Mindy looked from Philippe to a wide-eyed Cindy, to a disapproving Max to her angry mother and fled from the room.

"Mindy - " Philippe started after her.

"Leave her be!" Ms Lush commanded, angrily. "I should have known better than to let a Tachion into my house, no matter what your sob story is. I've always said Tachions are dangerous."

Philippe cowered as every word from Ms Lush's mouth felt like it was ripping away a part of his soul.

"Security, I need your assistance." She radioed on the intercom.

"I apologise ma'am; my parents will foot the bill for any damage I've caused."

"Yes they certainly will, and you can tell them that I said you must stay away from my daughters. Your Type is not welcome in this house."

"Mother!" Cindy squeaked. "That is just so-oo out of order; you can't say that."

Two state of the art platinum Guardians marched into the room and seized Philippe. He could have overpowered them easily if he wanted to, but he didn't struggle. The sensation of his two hearts breaking made him feel powerless.

"I'm so-oo sorry Philippe. So sorry," Cindy said.

Ms Lush didn't share her daughter's sentiments and commanded the Guardians,

"Take him out via the back door. I don't want the neighbours to see."

Mindy bounded out of her house, down the steps and ran straight into Brad who had just gotten out of his cruiser.

"Whoa, there little lady. Where's the fire."

"It's worse than that," Mindy gulped, "Max said that if Philippe and I kissed it would be wrong because he's a Tachion and Philippe got so-oo mad -"

"You kissed Philippe?" Brad said, more upset by the prospect that Mindy had kissed someone other than him, rather than the fact that it might have been a Tachion.

"Is that so wrong?" Mindy asked desperately.

Brad's brawn for a brain whirled into action. Philippe had outdone him on so many occasions recently where Mindy was concerned, and he had to get back on level pegging.

"Yeah, it's wrong. All Code Types frown on that sort of behaviour." Brad lied, pulling Mindy close. "I mean what would Madeline Stone, and the Pretties think if you dated someone like Philippe?" Brad snorted as if the very idea was ridiculous. "I mean come on."

"Why are you being so mean? I thought you and Philippe were good friends."

"We are. Big P is awesome, but he's not right for you. You're so gorgeous Minds. I mean you're a ten out of ten. The cream of the crop." Brad whispered into her ear. "You need someone in your league. A Gold Star Code Type to match you. Bring out the best in you. Perhaps a superior athletic being. Hey, that's someone like me."

Before Mindy could say another word, Brad kissed her.

"That was amazing," he smiled victoriously.

Mindy smiled back, but only because that was the only expression her face could genetically pull.

"Let's get out of here," Brad said ushering Mindy into his cruiser.

She looked back at her house and saw Philippe being ejected by security. Then a strange feeling she had never felt before overwhelmed her. A tickle fell from her eye. She touched her cheek and felt that it was wet. It was something she had never experienced before. A solitary tear rolled down her face.

***

255

It was after dark, and all was quiet in Commania. The Saps were sleeping on the feather down beds, small wisps of smoke burned out from the campfires, and the animals frolicked in the front yards in wooden pens.

Sal, Jet, Skye and I were lounging in long pieces of materials tied between trees that the Saps called hammocks. The night was warm and peaceful as we gazed up at the twinkling stars.

"Ahh. This is the life." Jet said.

I wanted to agree with him, but my eyes felt so heavy I could barely keep them open.

All of a sudden I was in a vivid green field heading towards a fresh pasture, my friends surrounded me as I bid them farewell.

"Don't leave me, Kid." Jet begged, holding my hand.

"I can't stay."

"We need you," Skye rasped.

"You two both know you only need each other."

"What will we, like, do without you?" The Twins asked linking my arms.

"You'll all be fine, just please stick together."

"Why would you want to leave us?" Philippe asked hugging me gently.

"This is just the way it has to be."

"Why? What have you seen yo?" Wain asked.

"How it all ends."

"But this is just the beginning," Sal said.

"It is for you. You have a bright future."

"What about me?" Brad flashed a dazzler.

"If you play fairly, you'll always be a winner, so never cheat, or you'll lose badly."

"You can't go, you can't leave me," Max said betraying that he had deeper feelings for me than just friendship.

"I have to go now. Please let me be."

One by one my friends slowly released their grip and allowed me to escape to freedom. I elevated into the air, carefree, soaring high into the sky.

Suddenly someone tackled me to the ground.

"Let me go." I wailed.

But the assailant gripped me and wouldn't let me leave. I turned to see who was trapping me. Surely my eyes deceived me.

"I never thought you of all people would do this to me." I wept. "I never imagined that you would betray me."

"Keziah. Keziah. Keziah."

I opened my eyes to see Sal, Jet, Skye and a stranger, a very handsome Sap, peering over me.

"What? What did I miss?" I said, wiping the drool from my mouth.

"I think you were having a nightmare." The handsome Sap with dark brown hair and bright green eyes smiled holding out his hand.

"Here, let me help you. I'm Deschanel."

"You Saps sure do have some funny names." Jet chuckled.

I gave him a sharp look then turned back to Deschanel. He was quite possibly the best-looking person I had ever seen in my life.

"I'm Keziah, but you already know that because you were calling my name, but everyone calls me Kid for short because Keziah is a long name, well not that long just a bit long." I rambled.

Deschanel smiled.

Sal rolled her eyes, "Shall we get going to this Kismet thing or whatever?"

"Yes, let's go and join the rest in *Kimetic*." Deschanel corrected her gently, leading the way.

"What is this Kimetic thing all about?" I whispered to Sal not wanting to sound ignorant in front of Deschanel.

"I don't know." Sal shrugged, "All I know is that the whole of Commania is into it."

We followed Deschanel from the sleeping quarters, past a row of wooden houses, to a clearing.

"This place is so peaceful," I said as we walked through the star lit village.

"I just want to explore." Jet bounced.

"Me too," Skye agreed.

"Jet, you're not going anywhere, you stay with me," I instructed, grabbing him roughly by his t-shirt.

Deschanel looked at me puzzled by my sharp attitude.

"He is his own person, has his own mind, as long as he's not hurting anyone else why can't Jet do what he feels?"

"Because he's always getting into trouble, and he wasn't even meant to be here, and he'll probably run off and get lost."

"No, I won't run away." Jet protested. "I like it here."

"Trust him," Deschanel said easily. "If Jet lets you down, he lets himself down, and if he doesn't care, he will feel the consequences. Either way, it's on Jet, not you."

I didn't even need to think about it, Deschanel was right, and he had made it all sound so simple.

"Well go then." I released Jet from my grip. "But the two of you stick together and be careful," I warned.

Jet straightened his collar, "Thanks, Deschanel," he said before bounding off with Skye.

Deschanel smiled at me instantly alleviating my fears.

"Your brother will be fine. Let us continue on our way."

Sal looked at Deschanel and was about to crack her knuckles but then stopped.

In the clearing, the Saps were sitting with their eyes closed. They were grouped in small circles and sung a soft HUUU sound.

"What are they doing?" I whispered.

"That's it. That's Kimetic." Deschanel said. "They're in contemplation, purifying their energy fields and getting in touch with their inner selves."

"And that's what you want us to do?" Sal asked, screwing up her face.

"If you want to you'd be most welcome to join us, but there's no pressure," Deschanel said.

I thought the Saps looked rather odd.

"I think I'll sit this one out," I said taking a seat underneath an oak tree.

"Whenever you're ready Kid." Deschanel smiled. "And what about you Sal?"

I expected Sal to be having none of this strange behaviour either so was utterly surprised, and a little bit jealous, when she took Deschanel's hand, and he led her off to join one of the smaller Kimetic circles.

I sat under the tree and watched them in their group. Deschanel began swaying calmly, and Sal mirrored his movements moving in perfect unison.

"What is this hocus pocus?" I said bitterly.

The circles continued to chant peacefully. There was a big turn out; it looked as if the whole of Commania was into this *Kimetic*.

I kept staring at the group and from where I was seated, it looked as if Sal was glowing a green colour, but it couldn't be. I rubbed my eyes. I was obviously tired, and the nap hadn't driven the snoozy feelings away.

I heard the wood of his cane scrapping the ground before I saw him. Dr Stoneway stood in front of me.

"Ahhh. It's so nice to look up at the stars and listen to the wind rustle through the trees, isn't it?"

I scrunched up my face, "What? Why?"

"Because sometimes it's nice just to *be*." Dr Stoneway smiled.

"Be what?" I asked.

"Still."

I shook my head; these earthy Types were such strange people.

"Not going to take part and join in with Kimetic, young Keziah?" Dr Stoneway asked taking a seat next to me.

"Nah, not my thing," I said flippantly.

"Aha. Not into trying new things then?" He asked.

"I'm just here to get the mission and go," I said full of self-importance.

"Right, right. Sure, sure. And what mission would that be?" Dr Stoneway asked.

"The one you're going to give me. I thought you knew all about The Prophecy?"

"Aha, well let's see now." Dr Stoneway said tapping his cane on the floor, "I'm not going to give you a mission."

"But Lady Zono said that I'd find the second eye at Commania with you."

"Yes, ahem, that's quite correct. Zono is a stupendously spectacular woman, magnificent indeed." He said, taking off his glasses and breathing hot air onto them and then wiping them with the material of his cloak before returning them to his face. Every movement was slow, deliberate.

"But, I thought - "

"You thought wrong." He cut me off. "I'm not going to assign anything to you as I cannot give you something you already have."

"What? So, if you're not going to help me, what am I doing here?"

"Aah aah ahhh." Dr Stoneway waggled his finger. "I never said I wasn't going to help you. I haven't lived all of this time, for many, many sunrises and sunsets, to meet you and not assist you."

"So start assisting," I said folding my arms.

"Well ok, if you insist that I assist, I insist that you assist yourself with Kimetic."

I looked towards the circular groups of Saps whose buzzing circles were now levitating a metre from the ground.

"Whoa! How are they doing that?"

"You can do anything when you know your true self." Dr Stoneway said with a glint in his eye.

The choreographed whirling would have taken years of practice. It wasn't for me. I shook my head.

"I'm ok here thanks."

Dr Stoneway smiled and nodded once, "I've lived a long time on this Earth plane, and I'm far too long in the tooth to help those who won't help themselves."

"I don't know how to help myself or what to do. I haven't exactly been given instructions you know. Some Urbanite dressed as a Harlequin turns up at my school, tells me I have to act quickly. I follow my troublesome brother to UC. I meet The Res, the world's most dangerous man, he tells me

I'm pivotal in some Prophecy, people honour me, I go back to school and work experience, and I'm back to being treated like a nobody. I relatively shut down TEN, a witch gives me a map, and I wind up here. No other citizen on the Upper Worlds would have done any of that for fear of being fuzzed. If that's not helping myself, then what is?" I said, crossly.

"Aha! That's right, the road of the Soul Survivor is the path less travelled; you have to find your footing, blaze a trail for others to follow behind you. Always be an innovator, be bold, try new things."

"What, like Kimetic?" I scoffed. "I don't think I can get into it. Maybe it's because I'm Human, certain things do not appeal to me."

"Aha yes, Humans." Dr Stoneway shook his head, "I remember the last ones. Their arrogance, ignorance and fear led to them justifying their actions in despising many things, mostly each other. Too scared to embrace one another for fear of being hurt or rejected. They covered it up well enough though. Made themselves believe someone else was always wrong and they were always right. No matter what they did, no matter the cost, they lived for being right. Even if that meant their ultimate destruction, which it did, they died, in their own minds, being right! Not happy, not at peace, not with love, but right. Keek keek kee." Dr Stoneway chuckled heartily unable to contain his own laughter.

I didn't see anything at all funny in what he was saying. I eyed him deadpan as he continued.

"Humans had the capacity for so many positive actions; it's such a pity that they fed the negative ones."

"But The Res said by being Human I was special." I blurted out.

"Yes, yes you are. Don't get me wrong; for all of their trouble and their strife Humans were beautiful beings. Extraordinary works of art. As a Human, you're far superior to any other walk of life. Not that the Code Types would let you believe it. Contrary to popular belief Code Types are far from perfect. They are as flawed as the Tachions and all of the other life forms they berate and subjugate. Take your friends for instance."

"What do you know about my friends?"

"A lot actually. I've studied The Prophecy in detail for many, many moons. Mindy and Cindy are Code Type AE – Aesthetically Beautiful. But aesthetics are often vain and airheaded. Ain't got much going on up here in the noggin." Dr Stoneway said tapping the side of his forehead.

"Then there's Brad, he's Code Type SA – Superior Athleticism; a marvellous athlete for sure, but they are usually conceited egomaniacs. Then there's Max. His Code Type is IE, Intellectual and Scientific, a Brainiac. They usually can't sway from logic. No matter how hard they try, they always fall in line and stick to the rules, paradoxically even when the rules don't make any sense."

For all of his hundreds of years studying The Prophecy, Dr Stoneway wasn't even a master of it. Here he was criticising all of my Code Type friends, and he hadn't even mentioned Sal, who he had met. He couldn't be that well versed in The Prophecy. I didn't have to listen to him.

"You have no right to bad mouth my friends. Without them, I wouldn't have gotten this far, and made it here."

"Aha, good, good, so good. I'm so glad you realise that. I was just giving an example. Apologies if I upset you and you took my words to heart. But that's what makes you so wonderfully Human, your heart. You can unlock any one of your abilities, bring them into being and excel in them. But with passion comes emotion, and the emotion is a distraction that you will have to learn to conquer."

I was agitated to the maximum. Dr Stoneway was giving me a lecture that I didn't want to hear. My ma was always going on about respecting my elders, and he was probably the oldest man alive, but I didn't ask for his advice, I only wanted my mission. Dr Stoneway carried on talking unperturbed by my sulky face.

"You must keep an open mind, try new things, dare to dream thoughts full of wishes, high hopes and aspirations."

"I don't have time to dream." I snapped back, "I'm too busy trying to save the entire universe, remember?"

"You can never be too busy to dream my girl. It's one of life's pleasures and sometimes the only thing you can do in this hectic world." Dr Stoneway stood up, leaning heavily on his cane.

"Yeah, whatever," I answered quietly.

265

The conversation had got my back up. Why couldn't he just give me a mission and let me be on my way? I wanted to be back home in the clean, pristine, regimented Upper Worlds. I didn't belong here.

"Remember your humanity; your Human-*kindness* is what makes you so unique. It's that individual quality you have that is magnificent. You are free to have more artistic flair than any Artisan Code Type, have more psychic ability than any Tachion and be more versatile than any Lappion.

"Being Human is to be celebrated. The only thing all other life forms have going for them is that tiny bit of humanity in their DNA, without that we would have all been doomed a long time ago." With that Dr Stoneway turned to leave, but not before adding,

"Don't look on the outer for what you can only find on the inner. It will come together young un, I promise you, it will all come together. It always does." Dr Stoneway chuckled as he scuttled off into the distance, leaving me alone.

Everyone was enjoying Kimetic without me. The circles had now elevated and in a perfect cross-legged pose, were whizzing around way up in the air. It was quite a sight to behold. I tried to spot Sal, Jet or Skye but they had blended in with the mass of Saps, and I couldn't make out one from the other. I looked on feeling sad, lonely and insignificant. If this was what it meant to be Human, the ancestors could keep it.

***

Philippe ran through Sub Zero, the beaten down Tachion part of town. He had wanted to talk to Kid, but couldn't get her so he used his ESP to locate Wain instead, even though he knew he shouldn't. If the Orbs detected him, he would be fuzzed by the Guardians. But right now he didn't care if they terminated him.

Philippe spotted Wain in a crowd wearing a blue band on each of his three wrists and holding a placard that read, *Tachion Power.* He had never been to a TL rally before. Wain, on the other hand, was a regular. They had been communicating telepathically about the day's events, as Philippe approached he began to speak aloud,

"...So then the Guardian threw me out, and Mindy sped off with Brad, she didn't even see me, doesn't know I saw her kiss him."

Wain shook his head, "Man, that's why I'm an activist, yo. You can never trust those Code Types, no matter how nice they seem, they always backstab you in the end."

"You know I don't like when you say things like that Wain. My parents are Code Types. I was born a Tachion because of the mutation in my DNA. Your family have always been Tachions. Our situations are different."

"Nevertheless Bro, you're one of us and we have to stick together. Look around at how the Code Types treat us, keep us fenced in Zero, away from them, like animals."

Philippe looked at all of the Tachions around him. Some had apparent mutations like he did, but others could pass for Code Types, and on occasion probably did.

He read some of the placards held by the Tachion protesters. One stated, *More food*. Another said, *Desent edukayshun*. One placard held by a small one- eyed girl simply said, *Equality*.

Philippe shook his head. He felt like a fraud here; these were not his issues. His mum prepared nutritious meals daily. He attended FB, one of the best schools in the state. He lived and thrived in Upper Worldian luxury, not in Sub Zero squalor. He accepted the Tachion struggle, but it was not his. Just because he looked like them, didn't make him one of them. His parents had taught him that. But his parents didn't understand what he had to go through to fit in. He didn't understand the Tachion community and was made to feel like a freak amongst the Code Types. Only Mindy had taken the time to try to understand him, and now everything was ruined.

"That's why I don't mess with the mainstream yo." Wain said, snapping Philippe out of his thoughts, "I'd rather stay here, in Zero amongst my own. I feel safe here."

"I used to feel safe in the Upper Worlds, but I'm not so sure now. I never knew people like Max felt so strongly against us." Philippe pounded his fist into his hand.

"Max is a trip! And I was just beginning to like that guy. Look, I don't expect you to be as deep into this as I am. But read the TL literature; you have to take a stand. Otherwise, the Upper Worlds will crush you, they'll crush all of us and won't even bother to look at the sole of their shoe and the mess they've made."

Philippe didn't like when Wain did his fighting talk, he wasn't sure how involved Wain was with the TL movement, but he knew it went deeper than misspelt placards at freedom rallies.

"Wait till Kid hears this. She'll have words with Max and talk to Mindy for you. Kid is just like her mother. She cares about *all* people. I'm certain her compassionate Type will kick in any day now."

"I don't know if I even want Kid to smooth anything over for me." Philippe lied to hide his dented pride.

"Well, Kid will do it if you ask her to or not, you know how she is, the backbone of the whole crew. I'm not even surprised she's this prophet or whatever she's meant to be. She's different from the rest. She's the only Code Type I trust."

"Yeah." Philippe agreed, "Kid is special."

"Here, take this," Wain said transferring data from his IM to Philippe's. "It's information about the TL, the real deal, not what they tell you on the Upper Worlds. The movement could do with a hulking Tachion like you."

"Sure." Philippe replied despondently.

Both his hearts felt heavy. He needed to talk to Kid. She always looked out for him, she would know what to do. Where was she?

Energy is neither created nor destroyed.

So embrace your spark and light up the void.

TWELVE

Kimetic

"...And then we picked fruit from the trees, real circular fruit! Not like the fruct-a-lite stuff we get in tubes." Jet chattered excitedly.

"Yeah, apples are crunchy and kind of flaky but juicy and shiny." Skye hopped from one foot to the other as she explained.

Even the little bird that nestled in Jet's hair constantly chirped in as if giving me an account of the wonderful time everyone was having.

"Yeah, whatever," I said, trying to hide my interest as I swung lazily in the hammock.

We had been in Commania for three days now, and while the others had been practising Kimetic and going off to explore this new and strange land, I had chosen to spend my time alone. I didn't want to be here; I wanted to get my mission and go.

"So when are you going to stop sulking?" Jet asked, hand on hip.

His stance and tone reminded me of our dad. I rolled my eyes and turned over.

"It's great here. Why are you being so anti-social?"

"Why don't you just go away and be all happy clappy somewhere else."

Even though he irked me, I knew Jet was right. I had kept to myself since the first night and

Dr Stoneway's lecture. I only joined everyone at meal times because Dr Stoneway insisted. He had this hang up that we should all eat together. I wouldn't have even bothered to obey his instructions if there wasn't any chocolate. That was the best thing about this place. The food. I didn't get why everyone else, especially Sal, was acting like this was the greatest place on earth.

Sure, the Saps couldn't do enough for us like plait our hair or wash our clothes or invite us to join in the games they seemed to play endlessly. But all that freaked me out. I didn't get why they were all so friendly. There had to be something wrong with them. They were just *too* nice.

"So are you going to join us today?" Sal asked with an actual teeth-baring smile. Gone was her usual scowl.

I looked her up and down. She was wearing a long multi-coloured, knitted garment Deschanels' mother had made for her. Sal was getting into this way of life. She looked like a proper Sap.

"Nah. It's not my thing." I said.

Ever since Dr Stoneway had spoken to me, I couldn't shake my bad mood. He had talked about, 'conquering my emotions' but I didn't feel like taking his advice. I didn't even understand what he meant.

"Kimetic is good. It's changing me." Sal offered quietly.

I looked her over again. She was right, Sal was even beginning to look different, and it wasn't just her clothes. Maybe it was because she was smiling so effortlessly.

"There's a lot I've been keeping to myself and being in Commania is helping me bring it to the surface so I can deal with it. I can show you some things I've learned if you like," she said.

I could tell she wanted to talk, but I didn't.

"Nah thanks, I'll pass."

"What's wrong Kid?" Sal asked, cracking her knuckles. "Have I done something to upset you?"

"No, I'm fine." I lied. "Did Deschanel go with you fruit picking?" I asked, trying to change the subject.

Apart from eating chocolate, staring at Deschanel was the only thing that made being in this muddy, mossy, itchy, irritating place worthwhile.

"Yeah, he's an excellent guide. In fact, I'm going to meet him now. See you at lunch." Sal stomped off towards the bustling village where the Saps were undertaking their morning chores.

"Sayonara!" I threw over my shoulder and rolled back over.

"You're such a loser." Jet said.

"What?" I reared myself angrily over the hammock.

"The Prophecy must be wrong. There's no way you could be the Soul Survivor."

"I'll leave you two to talk." Skye unlinked Jets arm and sauntered off.

"Catch you up." Jet said, then turned to face me. "You're lazy, moody, miserable but most of all a scaredy cat."

"What's your problem!" I shouted; he had touched a raw nerve. "If I were such a scaredy cat, you wouldn't even be here! You're lucky I even brought you to Commania."

"No, you're the lucky one. You've only gotten this far because of all of your friends and here you are sulking like a brat because you're jealous of Sal and Deschanel's friendship."

"No, I'm not." I protested weakly. Was it that transparent that I liked Deschanel? I hoped not.

"Yes, you are. I see the way you look at them. And because Dr Stoneway didn't tell you what you wanted to hear, you're putting a downer on it for everyone. We should be making the most of our time here until you complete the mission. But no, not Kid, she's so great, she's better than everyone!"

"Seventy-two hours in Commania and all of a sudden you're some wise guy." I snapped.

"At least I'm trying to learn new things. But don't mind me. You just keep on doing what you're doing, laying about and moping all day. And when The Prophecy fails, be proud of the fact that it was solely down to you!"

"Why you - " I fumed, scrambling after him. I fell out of the hammock and landed sprawled out on the floor.

"Pathetic." Jet turned and walked off.

I watched him amble into the distance teary-eyed with my knees and ego both badly bruised.

Jet was right. I had been acting like a loser, but it annoyed me that he had pointed it out. He was like my walking, talking conscious all of a sudden. When did he get so smart anyway?

"Hee, hee, hee."

The sound of giggling crept up behind me. Poppy and the other children, who had led us to Commania, looked down on me, laughing. Great! All I needed was little kids mocking me. I wished I had never followed them here in the first place.

Poppy, held out her small chubby beige hand. The other two, one brown, one pink, helped me up from the ground and they led me away from my hammock.

The further we walked, the denser the terrain became. But Poppy read the vines, and undergrowth like a keen adventurer read a map. For a little person, she had perfect footing and didn't miss a step. I tripped a few times.

"Let's sit here besides this Kapok tree." Poppy said.

The three children sat cross-legged underneath it.

"You young'uns are extraordinary." I marvelled.

"Takes one to know one," Poppy looked me dead in the eye before she patted the ground next to her. "Sit."

I slowly sat down next to the extremely capable child.

"Close your eyes and still your mind," Poppy commanded in a manner that sounded as if she had not long learned how to talk.

I laughed to myself. I hadn't taken on board anything Dr Stoneway, the oldest wisest man on the planet, had said and here I was being given instructions by a five-year-old. Somehow it was easier than following anyone else's orders, so I did what I was told. I shut my eyes.

"Good. Now focus slightly above and between your eyebrows and gently concentrate, but not too hard. Look with a manner of effortless effort. That's your door to your inner worlds. Do you see it? Do you see it?" Poppy asked expectantly.

"No," I didn't see anything but a black space with squiggly colours swimming around.

"Breathe. Look deeper, past the noise in your head, past your worries, fears, doubts and concerns. Do you see it now?" Poppy said encouragingly.

I pulled a face; I couldn't hear any noise. Then I realised she wasn't talking about sound. Beyond the noisy images of my mind, there was something, but I didn't know what it was.

"Don't strain, relax." Poppy said.

I relaxed my face, my brain and my body. My breathing became deeper. Thoughts of the past day, week, month ran through my head. I sat watching it all pass until it emptied from my mind. Now I felt calmer.

The children began to softly chant and I found myself joining in. Soon I felt a tingling sensation, it started in the centre of my forehead and rushed all over my body.

The soles of my feet rooted into the soil as if I was one with the mighty tree beside me and we both grew from the earth below. Every strand of my hair connected with the sky, receiving transmitted waves from the ether that tuned into every soul on the planet. I could feel everything far and wide. A sound of rushing water flooded my ears as if I were in the depths of the sea and the blue-skied heavens danced in my mind. Simultaneously I felt a billion sorrows and a billion joys which gave me a sensation of complete balance and an understanding of everything and everyone. I had never experienced such a feeling in my entire life. There was no space or time, yesterday or tomorrow. I was one with this present moment, and it was magical.

I didn't need to open my eyes to know that I had elevated and was whizzing above the ground in a circular motion. I watched my internal screen, and a brilliant blue light blazed while a soothing humming filled my ears. I was drifting, flying fast within me, but at the same time, I felt outside of myself. I could see my physical body atop the tree, eyes closed, in a circle with the little children, but another part of me was floating, going elsewhere.

I opened my eyes and was sitting beneath the Kapok tree. It was no longer made of wood but rather constructed of binary data, a mass of dots and ones creating a virtual holographic picture, like the ones all over the Upper Worlds.

The whole scene was a crude digital replica of Commania. Gone were the wooden houses and campfires. No longer did birds soar, lush vegetation grow or playful animals frolic. Every element of life was missing. In its place were burnt out tree stumps and frazzled earth, hidden just beneath the surface by pretty simulations, which sketchily fuzzed in and out.

Something terrible had occurred here, and Commania had been destroyed. Whoever had created this fake version didn't have an eye for detail or simply didn't care.

"Oh no! What had happened to this thriving, loving, sweet place?"

I got up from the tree and walked gingerly through what would have been the bustling village full of Saps. Not a soul was in sight. As I took each step, the binary code parted and then regenerated. I reached the clearing where the Saps would usually eat their meals together. Instead of the Sap population, I saw a committee of people in white coats gathered around the long communal table. At the centre stood a man covered from head to toe in red. His form looked like no Code Type, Tachion, Lappion, animal or creature I had ever seen.

I dropped to my belly and slid along the undergrowth to hide. This wasn't the mud that squelched underneath my feet that I complained about but secretly loved its soft feeling. This was dry arid land, unsuitable for any being on Earth to live in.

The committee toasted as the figure dressed in red spoke. His sinister voice sounded as if he was underwater gasping for air.

"We have finally entered the Maya stage, the final illusory phase. This was the last stand, and we have eradicated Mother Nature and all of her life forms from The Upper Worlds."

One White Coat began to laugh, and the others followed suit.

"Yes, my faithful followers. The world is mine!" The man raised a silver goblet and displayed long talons on each finger.

I watched in horror. I couldn't see his face, but the man's hands alone were so vile it made the hairs on my head prickle.

"Yuck," I whispered.

The bush simulation cut in and out, revealing my hiding place.

"No-oo! how can this be, how did you survive?" The man wailed in his distorted voice.

The entire congregation of White Coats turned to look at me. They began to chatter amongst themselves rapidly.

"It's the Human!" Someone announced, and the White Coats shook in fear.

"Seize her now!" The man in red demanded.

I hopped to my feet and turned to run. Then I realized that the White Coats looked more afraid of me than I was of them. I turned to face them and folded my arms.

"Noooo!" Several White Coats trembled, scared stiff.

Others backed away and ran from me.

"You fools!" The man in red shrieked. "I should have dealt with this myself a long time ago."

His body ghosted towards me. His eyes flashed red beams, "Kneel before me and surrender!"

My knees buckled. I was scared, but I stood my ground.

"Never!" I yelled back.

"I said *KNEEL!*"

"I said *NEVER!*" My heart thumped, "You'll never win. As long as there are people like me who refuse to be frightened by you and your kind, you've lost!"

"Aaaahhhhhrrrrghhhhh!" The man in red lunged at me and grabbed me with his long talons.

"Ha-Uh."

I opened my eyes and sharply inhaled a lungful of clean fresh air. I whizzed to look around, but the man in red and the White Coats were gone. It was just another bad dream. I was alone under the Kapok tree. I touched it and felt the rough bark on my palm. I grabbed handfuls of real green grass growing out of the actual brown soil. The squelch got underneath my fingernails. I smelled the grass and rubbed it to my face in joy. I was back in the real Commania. The one where people sang at the tops of their voices and laughed when nothing was even funny. It was a place of real nature and was muddy and mucky and oh so wonderful! I hadn't appreciated its beauty until now.

I must have been asleep for a long time as daylight had faded and fires burned to keep camp warm and bright. There weren't any digital displays to check the time, but I was beginning to realise which part of the day it was just by the colour of the sky and the activities of the Saps. I pulled myself to my feet. The sweet aroma of the Sap food filled my nostrils and an unspeakable joy filled my heart.

The dream had made me realise how truly adorable Commania was. How heartbreaking it would be if it were ever destroyed. That was something I would never let happen. With a new positive attitude, I skipped towards the clearing and the communal dining table.

Like clockwork, the Saps were seated together at the huge oak table ready to eat. I sheepishly sat in my usual seat opposite Jet and Skye, and next to Mrs Winterbottom, a hardy, plump Sap. Her eyes shone as soon as I sat down.

"Glad you're joining us. Have some of this."

She ladled a delicious smelling sweet potatoe stew in a bowl and placed it in front of me.

"Thank you," I replied ravenously and now embarrassed about my previous bad behaviour. "You're too kind."

"Hey." Jet nodded.

"Hey." I nodded back.

"Are we cool?" He asked.

Skye fidgeted beside him looking anxiously from one of us to the other.

"Icy." I replied.

No more words needed to be spoken. He was right. I had been moping. I would apologise to Dr Stoneway and Sal and everyone else affected by the way I had been acting.

A fluorescent green Tachion with flaming hair took a seat next to me. I gasped between a spoonful of stew. This Tachion stood out vastly amongst all of the Saps but somehow didn't look at all out of place. She was easily the most unusual Tachion I had ever seen.

"Please don't be afraid." She said.

I wasn't afraid at all. In fact, I was in awe of how spectacular she looked.

"Do I know you?" I said.

The green Tachion cracked her knuckles, "Yes. I told you I was changing."

***

Plates, set on the great oak table, were filled with stews, pulses, and vegetables. Most of the Sap diners were eating heartily. But our four meals had gotten cold. Jet, Skye and I couldn't take our eyes off the green skinned and flame haired Sal.

Dr Stoneway looked on from the head of the table satisfied that all was unfolding as it should.

Sal spoke timidly, "For me to be born perfect was my parents only wish. They are both Type Pn, genetically modified solely to parent.

"And they had an ideal family with their first daughter, Sal - mark one. She was bright, cute, their own little ray of sunshine. When she was six, she began to get sick, due to an oversight in her molecular structure, a heart defect that couldn't be repaired. Sal died aged seven. Their ray of light obliterated.

"Two years later, cloned from my sister's DNA, I was born. Sal - mark two. My parents were delighted, they had their perfect little family back. That was until they realised something was different about me. The DNA that they tampered with to correct the heart defect made my genes mutate. When I cried, I glowed green.

"Mum was inconsolable. I was not her precious child reborn. I was a defective version of the real thing. They tried to make me normal by covering my skin with makeup and sending me to school in the Upper Worlds. No one need know I wasn't a Code Type as long as they could fake it and let me pass as one.

"They loved me the best they could, but I would never replace the first Sal, the daughter they had loved and lost. It's not their fault they rejected me, it's just their Type."

Sal stopped talking and looked around pensively. She had finally mustered the courage to be her real self and assume her true identity, which was a very brave thing to do.

"Please don't be afraid, you're safe with us." I said gently.

She took a deep breath and continued to relay her story.

"My parents would never look me in the eyes, but that was okay because when they did I could read their minds and it hurt too much to know what they thought about me. So I hid my special power away. It's hard when you know what people are thinking. What I didn't know then was that I also had the power to corrupt a brain wave, in essence, change someone's mind, to influence what they think. If I knew that then I would have probably used it on my parents - "

"So you can read minds!" Jet said excitedly. "What am I thinking right now?"

"Jet! It's not a party trick." I said.

"It's ok." Sal smiled. "Jet's thinking I look way cooler green."

"Wow! You do. So much better!"

"What am I thinking?" Skye rasped.

She was used to other Tachions having a certain level of psychic ability but didn't know any who could change someone's mind.

"That you wish I had come out as Tachion sooner."

Skye nodded.

"What am I thinking?" I asked nervously.

I wasn't even sure myself. Today's events had my mind completely blown.

"I don't know Kid. I truthfully have never been able to read your thoughts. And as a rule, I try not to read anyone's, unless I want to change it." Sal stopped nervously. She didn't want her friends to judge her.

"It's an awesome talent. Please continue with what you were saying." I nodded encouragingly.

"Ok. My parents had another child, my little brother, Solzeberg. He's so academically gifted, and he makes them so proud and happy. Everything was right in their world, apart from one small problem. Me.

"My parents decided their family was complete without me. So, I struck out on my own and ever since I've fended for myself. I had my router destroyed and, all my ID's are fake. I got myself a top of the range Auto Nan. It's a good cover; everyone thinks she's my actual mum. My parents never see me or call. I'm the genetic mistake which could have spoiled their happiness, and they would rather forget I existed."

The whole campsite was now listening as Sal talked. She was so brave and speaking so openly. I spotted Deschanel with his family. He listened intently, hanging on Sal's every word.

"I had all the freedom in the world, so I took my Auto Nan, programmed it myself and went anywhere I wanted. It's quite easy to convince people you're allowed to be in places you shouldn't be when you have a grown-up with you. Adults don't like to question the rules; they just go along with them. That's how I got to UC for the first time. I went to UC in search of the pills and makeup that my dad had given me to keep me looking 'normal.' That's where it started and ever since I've been Capsing to maintain this Code Type identity of Sal. It's extremely painful to Caps, and I have to do it so often. I'm tired of pretending and lying to everyone."

I bit down hard on my bottom lip to stop myself from crying. I felt so stupid about my moodiness. I had been so self-absorbed since we got to Commania that I had forgotten The Res' wise words of The Prophecy being a journey for all of us. Sal had been going through all of this pain since I've known her, and I had never even noticed.

Sal slowly looked up at all the sets of eyes looking at her.

"This is the first place that I have experienced what it feels like to be loved, so much so that I want you all to meet the real me," she took a deep breath, "so please let me introduce myself. My name is Dai. I am Tachion. I look a little bit different, but I am a very nice person." Tears rolled from her eyes and splashed onto her luminous cheeks.

I jumped up from my seat and led the charge as all of the Saps flocked to Dai.

"You're incredible and brave. I wouldn't want you any other way," I whispered, hugging her tightly.

Others joined our embrace holding onto her until we were a big circle of love with Dai in the centre.

***

The clickety-clack of ceramic and wooden plates being cleared away echoed throughout Commania as the Saps went about their evening chores. Some washed dishes; some read bedtime stories to the children and others napped before Kimetic.

A small group remained gathered at the table. I sat with them and scoffed chocolate. I looked on as Dai talked with Deschanel in hushed tones further along the table. She smiled coyly and smoothed down her hair as he spoke to her. I smiled at them. Dai deserved this happiness.

I heard the scrape of his cane before Dr Stoneway appeared before me.

"I'm proud of you." He said.

"Me? For what?" I asked. It should be Dai he was proud of, certainly not me. I had been acting like a petulant child.

"For Kimetic. The young uns told me you had an experience.

"Yes, yes. I did actually." With everything that had happened this evening I had almost forgotten all about it.

"Dai has set an excellent example. Perhaps you'd like to share a little too?"

"Well," I felt shy, "I'm not sure I know what to say."

"Just speak from your heart." Dr Stoneway said.

"Ok, erm well Kimetic itself was phenomenal. I'm not really sure how to explain it, but I felt a connection to all life, the flowers, the trees, the roaring seas and all people. Does that sound crazy?"

"Not at all Keziah, not at all." Dr Stoneway did a happy jig, throwing his hip to the side like a young man.

"That's why in Commania we practice Kimetic every day. Whether in a group or alone. It guides us. Allows us to experience Oneness. In that I mean I am you, you are me, and we are one. If every being on the planet actually, I mean truly, I mean profoundly realised this, we would have none of the problems we currently face."

I nodded in agreement.

"But after Kimetic I had one of my dreams."

Some Saps gathered around and sat on the ground by Dr Stoneway, intrigued by what I had to say.

"Aha. What did you see?"

"A very different Commania," I said gravely, "One where the trees and houses were burnt out and replaced by rubbish simulations."

Frightened murmurs came from the Saps as they whispered amongst themselves.

Dr Stoneway nodded his head, "We've kept a stronghold here for so long. This is our home, and we will never flee from it. But we know Zyclon is coming for us. Doom and destruction await us unless The Prophecy is fulfilled."

Dr Stoneway drew closer, "So with that being said, what did you learn today?"

"Well, I realised that I've been terribly self-centred, not only here in Commania but back home as well. You see I've been so insecure for so long about not having a Code Type that it has clouded everything I do."

"Yes, when the go rears it's head it can colour everything one does." Dr Stoneway encouraged me.

"I guess my ego ran wild, and my emotions spiralled out of control when I heard about The Prophecy from The Res."

The Saps gasped at my mention of The Res. He was as feared in Commania as he was on the Upper Worlds.

"Now, Now." Dr Stoneway reassured the Saps with a smile. "The Res is, shall we say, rather direct but he wants The Prophecy fulfilled as much as you and I. Please continue, Keziah."

More Saps flocked to the table to listen to me speak. Usually, in such public circumstances, I would rather cease to breathe than talk openly about myself. But this warm environment, with kind people, took away my fears.

"I'm sorry I didn't give any of you a chance to get to know me. I've kept to myself because things didn't happen how I expected them to. And when things don't go my way I become moody and shut myself off. My brother Jet taught me that."

I looked up and the whole table, including Jet, was staring at me.

"So I'm just realising right now, that my over sensitive emotions are one of my greatest flaws."

"There is nothing wrong, we all continuously unfold. Even I learn something new about myself all of the time. And I've been around forever!

So now you've identified these things about yourself what are you going to do about it?" Dr Stoneway asked.

I thought for a while.

"Work on them, conquer my self-defeating thoughts. I don't have to give in to them. As you said, Dr Stoneway I can control my negative emotions."

Dr Stoneway broke into laughter, "Aha. I see congratulations are in order."

"For what?" I asked. I didn't see my failings as a cause to celebrate.

"For opening your mind's eye. By mastering this, you now have the ability of *Knowingness.*

"This Knowingness is beyond the mind and its trickery of vanity, jealousy, anger and greed. Your Knowingness, call it intuition if you may, will give you access to all wisdom, knowledge and truth, which is already buried deep inside of you.

"In this high state, you will be guided by the universe illuminating every step of the way. You will never have to walk alone. And it is here that you access your Inner Greatness. Your *Inner G.*

"Inner G comes when you truly know yourself, and no one and no thing can influence you or affect the way you think, act and be. It takes practice but once you get to grips with your Inner G and live it every day, then guess what?"

"What?" I asked.

"You become the best version of you that you can be, your highest self, your *True Self.* And guess what happens when you are your True Self?"

"What?" the crowd of Saps sang in a chorus along with me.

"Then you will impact positively on all of those around you, which will impact those around them and those around them until you have positively affected the entire planet, solar system and the cosmos." Dr Stoneway clapped his hands gleefully.

The Saps clapped along with him.

Dr Stoneway whispered in my ear, "That's how we all win in this game called life if we all choose to be the best player. Realise yourself as Great and Great you will be."

He turned and addressed the excited crowd.

"So three cheers for Keziah. You've done it. You've completed your mission!"

"What?" I was shocked. "I didn't think you were giving me a mission."

"I didn't. You have captured the second eye by opening your third eye, your mind's eye." Dr Stoneway tapped his finger to his forehead.

"Trust in it. Believe in yourself. You are the source of all things in your life. What you have learned from Kimetic, keep connected, and the universe will guide you."

I nodded trying to retain all of the information. Dr Stoneway was a wise man and this time I wanted his advice.

"So the mission is completed?" Dai asked. "I'm not ready to go home yet."

"I don't want to leave either." Jet said.

"Yes, you've done it! Done it indeed. You have all grown in consciousness. And now you must continue along your way. When the time is right, it will be our honour to host you again, Dai, Skye and Jetsir."

Dr Stoneway turned to face the Saps.

"My land of Commania. Tonight we dance and sing merrily in honour of the Soul Survivor."

I blushed as The Saps cheered jubilantly.

"The dawning of a new day, a great day, one filled with hope is upon us."

293

Two steps forward,

Three steps back.

When fear is triggered,

Prepare for an attack.

THIRTEEN

No Retreat, No Surrender

Brad stepped out of his cruiser when he saw us pull up outside my house on the aero bikes. I hopped off The Speedster and ran to greet him.

"It's so good to see you!" I hugged him, burying my face into his broad chest.

I was full of high spirits since completing the second mission in Commania, and I had learned a lot from my time spent with the Saps. But coming home and being able to see my parents and all of my friends, including this sweet doofus, gave me a joy that filled my whole heart.

"Good to have you home Kiddie-Girl." Brad hugged me strongly lifting me off my feet.

I looked back at Sal in her full Tachion form as Dai.

"I've got something to tell you - " Brad, and I said at the same time.

"Look at us acting like the Twins." Brad guffawed.

"For real!" I laughed beckoning Dai over.

"Who's that?" Brad said without trying to hide his disgust at the fluorescent green Tachion in front of him.

"I'll let her explain," I noted his frosty attitude, which immediately turned our sweet reunion sour.

"We haven't got time for intros. What I've got to say is private, for your ears only." Brad said, totally ignoring Dai.

"Whatever you have to say you can say in front of Dai, who this is by the way," I said pulling her closer.

Brad turned to look at Dai for a moment then turned back to face me.

"I'm not sure that's a good idea." He said.

The old Sal would have told Brad exactly where to go, but as Dai, was vulnerable and stayed silent.

"Just say it," I said, trying to keep on top of my rising emotions as Dr Stoneway had advised.

"Well ok. There's a divide in the crew, Code Types against Tachions. It happened when Philippe went wild and flipped out at the Twins house. Ms Lush had him thrown out because he hurt Mindy."

"What? I don't believe that!" Dai shouted unable to hold her tongue any longer.

Brad looked at her suspiciously, "Hey, don't I know you?"

Dai stared deeply into his eyes and then Brad lost recollection of his recollection.

"What was I saying? Oh yeah. Me, Max and the Twins have decided to stay away from Philippe and Wain. Ever since he did that mind thing on you, it freaked me out. You know he seriously violated The First Truth. I suggest you, Sal and you little bro stay away from Tachions too."

Brad glared coldly at Skye, "I know Jet and her are close and all, but I wouldn't encourage their friendship if I were you."

"Brad, this is ridiculous, Jet and me - "

" - I know you guys haven't officially got your Code Types yet, but it's obvious you're a Compassionate Type, like your mother. Stick to your own kind, trust me."

Brad brushed passed Dai, totally ignoring her, and jumped back into his cruiser.

"I'll bell you later." He said as he sped off almost knocking Skye's bike over.

"Where's the fire knucklehead!" Jet hollered as Brad cruised away.

"I never knew Brad hated Tachions so much." Dai trembled with anger.

Riding home from Commania Dai had wavered and wanted to take a Capsing pill, to turn back into Sal. I had convinced her not to by assuring her that the crew would accept her no matter how she looked. How wrong could I have been.

"I can't believe he warned you to stay away from your Tachion friends."

"What? Why?" Skye rasped.

"I'm sure it's a misunderstanding, something pretty big must have gone on while we were away," I said, trying to make sense of Brad's rant.

"Don't defend him." Jet spat. "I don't want to hear that numbskull's stupid opinions. That's why I don't like hanging out with your friends, it's much better when it's just me and Skye."

"I'm not making excuses. I've known Brad since kindergarten, and I've never seen him act like that."

"I'm changing back." Dai cracked her knuckles. "I don't want to have to mess with your minds and erase what you know about me, so I swear you all to secrecy. You cannot tell anyone my real identity."

"Don't do this Dai. You've come so far." I said.

"That's easy for you to say. This world is yours for the taking, designed for you, the Code Types. I can't live on the Upper Worlds as a Tachion!" Dai said, her flame like hair blazing.

Skye hung her head. She had seen too many Tachions deny their true identity. It was a shame.

"There must be another way. You're so much happier in your natural state, Dai."

"I'm Sal, not Dai. Get it?"

"Ok, jeez! Got it." Jet said, not wanting this uncomfortable situation to go on any longer.

Skye kept her eyes downcast and nodded her head. Dai turned to me for the final agreement to keep her secret. Her desperation made my resistance crumble.

"Whatever you want D – er - Sal," I mumbled.

"Good." She popped an emergency Capsing pill, which she kept in a wrist bracelet.

"Aaagh." Instantly she doubled over in pain as the bitter pill took immediate effect.

I rushed to her side.

"Don't touch me," she yelled, dropping to the floor.

We stood back and watched unnerved as Dai's body convulsed on the ground. Her eyes bulged out of their sockets and her body contorted before her bright red frizzy mane softened into ringlets. A pale green being, a cross between Tachion Dai and Code Type Sal, rose to her feet.

"I need to get another dose," she said, weakly stumbling to The Speedster.

"You can't ride like that."

Sal-Dai shook me off, "I can't let anyone see me like this," she whispered as she climbed on her bike.

With one flick of a switch, she glided off leaving us in total shock of what we had just witnessed.

After a long pause, Skye was the first to speak. "Why can't anyone just be happy with who they are?"

I nodded slowly in agreement. Knots twisted in my stomach. Something bad was coming, I could feel it. The happy, peaceful tranquillity of Commania was long gone.

***

I lay in bed, eyes darting around in the darkness, trying to make sense of everything that was happening. I hadn't spoken to any of my other friends about what Brad had said. Right now I didn't want to. I was just happy to be back home. I was even glad that Jet had gone to stay at Skye's. It

299

gave me time alone with my parents, and I couldn't believe that I had missed them so much.

Time away had made me realise just how lucky I was to have my ma and dad, the odd couple. For all of their genetic differences, they were good people who loved each other. Jet and I had not always been the perfect children, especially of late, but our parents would do anything for us. They had provided us with a loving home and kept us safe from harm. I now realised not everyone was afforded that start in life. I was grateful for my parents.

I closed my eyes, but sleep still evaded me, so I looked at my inner screen, focusing my attention on the place just above and between my eyebrows. I started Kimetic. Before long I felt light as a feather. I left my physical body and looked down at myself asleep on my bed. The fantastic feeling of being in my inner world, yet outside of my body, was not one I would ever tire of.

'Max.'

I was so enjoying floating around outside of myself I wondered why Max had popped into my head.

'Go to Max,' the soft voice, my own voice, whispered within me.

Just like that I was back in my body.

Why would I tell myself to go and see Max now? I knew he would be upset with me for going to Commania without him, but surely he would understand. Plus I knew he would find what I had to tell him about it fascinating.

300

I checked the time display. It read 2 in the AM. Max would be sleeping for sure, but that had never stopped me in the past. I jumped out of bed, crept down the stairs, shoved on Jet's rocket sneaks and flew across the yard.

***

"...I'm telling you, Philippe completely lost it. But if you were here, instead of Commania, you would have seen it for yourself, so I wouldn't have to tell you for the eighth time." Max wearily pushed his specs up his nose.

"I said I was sorry for going off without you. And don't exaggerate it's not the eighth time." I was curled up on the foot of his bed, happy to be in his company.

"It was eight times, I counted."

"Still there was no reason for Brad to act like that. It was horrible, in front of Dai and Skye too. He was heartless."

"Yes. Perhaps Brad didn't choose the right time, but what he said was accurate. We have to be careful of Tachions. They're volatile, able to change at any given moment."

"How can you say that Max?"

How would he be with me if he knew that I wasn't a Code Type after all? How could I explain to him that I was Human? The Res and Dr Stoneway had spoken about it like my humanness was an awesome tool to be harnessed. I doubt Max would agree with that.

"We've had Tachion friends all our lives."

"No. You've had Tachion friends all of your life because your mother is a care worker in Sub Zero. If it weren't for you, I probably wouldn't know any."

"You wouldn't be friends with Philippe, Wain, Skye or Sal if it weren't for me?"

"What are you talking about, Sal's not a Tachion."

"Oh yeah, what am I saying?" I almost let Sal's secret out. I faked a Twin-esque giggle to try and cover it up.

"Skye is intriguing, but she's your little brother's friend. Your little brother who despises me."

"Jet doesn't despise you," I said defensively. "He's off-ish with everyone."

"Anyway back to what you were asking. Wain is fine. The fact that his two brains work simultaneously is a biological marvel. I thought I had bonded with Philippe, but I guess not, since he turned on me. I'm a thinker, not a fighter. I can't comprehend that macho stuff."

"I just can't believe Philippe would do something like that. He hasn't got an aggressive bone in his body. I need to speak to him myself."

"Well, perhaps you'll be able to make sense of his actions. I couldn't. Without you here, everything just fell apart. You're the glue that bonds us together Kid. I missed you when you were away."

Max looked at me squarely for the first time. In his eyes, I saw behind his neekiness, his gadgets and his intellect. I saw the very essence of who he was. That part of a person that is timeless and true. At that moment my heart opened. At that moment I felt love.

"I missed you too Max."

WAHE, WAHE, WAHE!

Sirens wailed, and red lights flashed from across the lawn. Max and I rushed to the window.

"What's happening?!"

A horde of White Coats dragged my parents, into an awaiting Officials car while high tech Guardians swarmed my house. Sheer terror gripped me like a vice.

"I am trying to deduce what is happening in your home. My first supposition is that they're looking for you. Perhaps it has something to do with Commania, or more likely the Authorities have traced TEN interference signal back to you. I did tell you it was only a matter of time before... "

I was not listening to Max; I was running on automatic. I jumped into my rocket sneaks.

"Thanks for everything Max. You're the greatest."

I kissed his cheek before flying out of his bedroom window. I needed to put as much distance between myself and the Officials. But first I needed to get Jet before they did.

***

"...So what about ma and dad?" Jet asked sinking further into the feather filled cushions in Skye's living room sofa. Right now he needed all of the comfort he could get.

303

"They have no knowledge of what we've been up to. Even if they get questioned they'll be fine." I tried to reassure Jet as well as myself.

Skye rested a steaming beverage in a glass mug on a coaster for me and fidgeted nervously at the edge of the sofa.

"So if you can't go home, where are you going to go?"

"Maybe we should head straight back to Commania." Jet said.

I thought for a moment. Commania was far too much of a peaceful fairy-tale to be dragged into this nightmare.

"I can't risk the Authorities looking for us there. They would wreck the place."

"Well let's head to UC, the Authorities will never find us there."

"It's kind of risky," I said.

"And like the ultimate in dangerous, the PGs will be on high alert looking out for you."

"True." Jet agreed with Skye.

"You can stay here," Skye said. "That's if you don't mind being surrounded by Tachions."

I noticed the resentment in her tone but decided to ignore it. It wasn't my fault my friends were acting like morons, and I had more pressing issues right now than to have a Code Type versus Tachion debate.

"Thank you for the offer Skye, but we can't stay here," I said.

"Why not? What are you trying to say?" Jet got his back up defending Skye's feelings.

I sighed loudly. Why did even the simplest things have to be a fight with Jet?

"Because Skye's your best friend, and everyone knows it. It's only a matter of time before the Officials find their way here. In fact, we'd better get going."

"That's true." Skye agreed. "So where are you going to go?"

"We need to go deeper into the Tachion community, somewhere we won't be detected. Somewhere that's so far off the mainstream radar that no one can find us.

"We need to stay somewhere that has no ties with the Upper Worlds with someone who is willing to hide us."

"Well that doesn't leave many options," Skye rasped.

"But it leaves us with one option, the best one," I answered with the sudden realisation.

"Who?"

"Wain." Jet and I nodded. Finally, we agreed on something.

***

"...You cannot be serious!" Jonsey, a big red Tachion with flowing dreadlocks, barked furiously at Wain.

Jet and I backed further into the shadows in the corner of the room. Wain's two brains worked overtime trying to figure out a solution. He thought this would be the best course of action. Obviously, he was wrong.

305

"Well, I propose - "

Jonsey cut him off, "The TL is already top of the Authorities most wanted list. Hiding two Code Type fugitives is just going to bring us more heat."

"But they are for the movement, and they're against the Upper Worlds system too," Wain said.

I squinched my nose, that wasn't entirely accurate and to be honest, I wasn't even sure how I had gotten myself into this predicament. This so-called Prophecy had started a course of action and a chain reaction that had led us here. I didn't want to be part of the TL - in many ways they were the same as the Authorities, but at the complete other end of the scale. I wanted to walk the middle path. I didn't dare open my mouth though to voice that. Jonsey was far too fierce.

"I can't believe you bought them here!" Jonsey shouted.

"It's the only place I know where you've disabled all signals so their routers can't be tracked," Wain said meekly.

"Whatever little game they're playing has nothing to do with our cause. And you've brought them right into the nucleus of the operation. They could be Code Type spies for all we know." Jonsey raged.

"But they're not even Code Types. Yet." Wain protested.

A smatter of laughter filled the air as the other Tachions in the room scrutinised Jet and I harder. I blushed. How embarrassing, that the stigma of my puberty was about to be discussed in a room full of volatile Tachions.

"What?" Jonsey half barked, half smiled.

"They haven't got their Code Type yet. They're late bloomers." Wain continued with more gumption.

Jonsey belly-laughed. I kept my eyes on the floor hoping that at any minute now the ground would open up and swallow me. Jet, on the other hand, balled up his fist and unleashed his hot temper,

"What's so funny about that?" Jet fumed.

"Jet," I called quietly from the corner of my mouth, "this is not the time to get bright."

But he ignored me.

"So we haven't got a Code Type, big deal! At least we don't claim to be some big bad militants who actually creep around in a dusty, old library.

"Our little crew single-handedly took down the whole of The Eye Network. What has the *great* TL – the so called Tachion Liberation Movement ever done?"

"Why you - " Jonsey stomped forward.

I jumped in front of Jet protectively and prepared for the worst. I always knew my brother's survival would be the death of me.

Jonsey stopped in his tracks when he saw the display of bravery and unity.

"So we have a live one here, hunh?" Jonsey growled in a softer tone. "I wish more Tachions had your spirit."

Wain ran to his friend's side, "Yes full of heart. These are good peoples yo. I've known them all of my life. Their mother is a Compassionate

Type and works at the orphanage where I grew up."

"One of those patronising do-gooders!" A voice from the mob of Tachions said, unimpressed.

"It's not like that. She's a good person who cares for everyone." I heard the words tumble from my mouth before I could stop them.

I had never defended what I considered my ma's weak will before. But here and now, more than ever, I realised my mother's intent.

"My ma wants a peaceful way of life for everyone, and she tries to achieve it the best way she knows how - by being nice. It doesn't always work, and people often take advantage of her kindness, but at least she's trying to make a difference."

All I wanted more than anything right now was to be safe at home with my parents, wrapped up in all of my ma's kindness, my dad's practicality and Jets impulsiveness. But that little voice of intuition, that I had finally begun to understand, was telling me that those days were gone, and it would never be that way again.

"So you two both have heart, hey?" Jonsey said. "Well let's put your fearlessness to the test. Let's see if you really are Code Types or not. Macadamia! Get the circuitry."

With that, an orange Tachion wheeled in a rusty, squeaky electronic unit.

Wain's eyes grew wider and began to spin, "Oh no. It's the dreaded CTT."

I tried my best not to flinch. I knew exactly what the unit was. I had heard how painful the

Code Type test was, that's why my ma had never let my dad or any doctors perform the procedure. Now here I was in a rundown building, nowhere near a hospital, about to have the test performed.

"If you aren't Code Types, you can stay here with us in safety. I swear my life on it." Jonsey said in pleasant tones, putting his hands across his chest in an oath.

"But if you are Code Types you're probably spies and you Wain are a traitor," Jonsey growled.

Wain swallowed hard. I stared petrified at the amateur machinery. Jet's scowl deepened.

"And if you're spies, and you a traitor Wain, we'll personally deliver you all to the Authorities ourselves. Now hit it!"

Macadamia plugged in the CTT unit and a huge electric buzz filled the dusty, paper book filled room. Jet and I clutched our ears. The loud zinging infiltrated my mind and drowned out my internal screams for help.

***

"...I still can't believe she's with the Tachions." Max, perched rigidly on the cotton candy beanbag in Mindy's room, said fretfully.

"I can't believe she took sides like that," Brad said, wrapping an arm around his new girlfriend for comfort.

"Well. It's not like they had much of a choice." Mindy defended Kid and Jet, wriggling free of Brad's grip.

Since she had agreed to make it official and Brad was now her boyfriend, he hugged her at every given opportunity. It made Mindy's skin crawl, but no one would understand that if she told them. The likes of Madeleine Stone would have given their left arm to be Brad's girl.

"But I would have figured out a way, somewhere safe for Kid and Jet to go. I'd never let her down, and she chose to hide out with them, the Tachions." Max said.

He was particularly upset because Kid had kissed him before she left. He was happy she had done so but logically couldn't work her out. Did she have romantic feelings for him? She knew his stance, he wasn't even going to think about dating until after graduating from college, but Kid had sent his world into a tailspin. And now she was gone.

"And to think we had to find out about our best friend's whereabouts from that freaky little Tachion, like she's better than us," Brad said, playing with Mindy's hair.

"Don't say that," Cindy said, "Skye was just relaying what Kid had asked her to tell us."

"Yeah." Sal agreed, annoyed at Brad and Mindy's loved up behaviour at a time of such trouble. "Don't call her *Tachion* like that."

"Like what?" Max asked.

Sal didn't like the heat. She felt as if Max had been looking at her suspiciously all day. She knew how close he and Kid were. She could only hope that Kid had stuck to her word and not told him that she Capsed.

"Like, horribly -" Sal trailed off, uncharacteristically meekly.

"You weren't there Sal, Philippe completely lost control of himself and flipped out. Wain is openly vocal about his involvement with the TL and Skye has no comprehension of her fearsome powers, which she's not afraid to use. That scares me. They could turn on us at any moment." Max said.

"Yeah. It's not like we can't be friends with Tachions, but let's just keep the inner circle of the crew pure, just us Code Types. Who's with me?" Brad said as if giving a halftime pep talk to the football team.

Mindy nodded to keep up her pretence of adoring Brad.

Cindy nodded to mirror her sister, like she always did.

Max nodded reluctantly as he deduced which way the vote was going and logically he wanted to keep in line with the majority.

Sal nodded not wanting to be the odd one out.

"And what about Kid?" Cindy asked.

Charged up with everyone agreeing with him Brad carried on the fighting talk, "She's chosen which side of the fence she wants to be on, and it's not here with us."

Max nodded woefully, "You're right, I suppose she has."

Everyone grew silent. The divide in the crew deepened.

***

"Ow!" I grumbled in pain as a sensation shot through my entire body as I turned over on the thin mattress on the cold concrete floor.

My eyes hurt so much even blinking felt like a chore. I slowly attempted to adjust my vision to the dimly lit room.

Across the way, lay Jet. His eyes were shut, his neck crooked and his tongue lolled out of the side of his mouth.

"Jet, Jet," I called out hoarsely.

He didn't move. I stumbled to my feet and felt the imprint of the hot pins which had been stuck into the pores of my skin. I staggered forward to my brother.

"Jet!" I screamed.

"What?" He mumbled, wiping his dry mouth.

"Thank goodness." I cried, "I thought you were…" I trailed off. I didn't want to entertain the dark imaginings that swept through my mind.

I gently wiped the grazes on my brother's forehead with my fingertips. The CTT process had been an excruciating ordeal. Tiny metal probes had been placed down the nail bed of each one of our fingers and toenails. The probe was attached to a unit, which sent a laser through the pores into the body, blasting nanotechnology gatherers into the stem cells to collect our DNA. The pain was so immense that I had blacked out after the third wave of volts rocked through my body.

Jet and I had gotten through this traumatic experience together. We looked at each other in silent acknowledgement of each other's bravery.

A crack appeared in the door, and a bright artificial light filled the room. I shielded my painful eyes and saw two hands push the heavy door open. Wain entered the room carrying a tray of food in his third hand.

"I brought you some nourishment," he offered softly with a tight-lipped smile. "Good to see you're finally up."

Wain walked gingerly towards us and placed the tray gently on the ground.

"How was the test yo?" Wain asked not knowing what else to say.

"It was great! Go Tachion Liberation!" Jet spat sarcastically as he turned his back on Wain.

This time I didn't excuse his rude behaviour, it was justified.

I rose to my feet and returned to my mattress.

"Ow, ow, ow!" I moaned as each step I took sent pain rocketing through me.

I flopped onto the bed and beckoned for Wain to join me. He sat next to me looking more shocked than usual.

"It was like nothing I've ever experienced," I said in a rough voice that didn't sound like my own, "the pain was immense. I didn't think we would survive it."

"Well, you did. One advantage of the test is that it destroyed your routers. The Authorities will never be able to find you." Wain offered. "And also, no further harm will come to you while you're here."

"How can you be so sure?" I asked, the loud fuzzing noise of the CTT still ringing in my ears. "The TL might turn on us at any moment."

"They won't. The results are in." Wain said tapping on an old style hand held computer. "You two are officially not Code Types."

"Given half the chance we could have told you that." Jet snapped.

"We're Human. The Res told us that in UC." I told Wain. "I did try to explain - "

Wain cut me off, "Yes indeed you are! Your genealogy is so advanced, in a throwback kinda way. It's a scientific wonder!"

"So what does it mean?" Jet asked as he sat up with the greatest of difficulty.

Wain cleared his throat, "You two can harness whatever specialist area you choose. There is no end to your potentiality. On a larger scale, I am now totally convinced that you are here for some special reason. The Prophecy must be true. On a smaller scale, you have the allegiance of the TL. The Movement will protect you until the ends of the earth."

With that news, the whirling pain in my head began to ease. Jet half smiled and laid back, his head cradled in his hands.

"Maybe now we'll have time to kick back and figure a way out -" Jet began.

Wain rose to his feet and glided to the door, "I'm afraid not; you have a visitor."

Jet and I looked at each other, again on high alert. I sat up rigidly expecting the worst. Wain opened the door and beckoned. Quick steps approached the room.

"Who is it?" I hissed.

Before Wain could answer, Sal entered the room. Her lips were pursed, her face wrought. She didn't waste time with niceties.

"Kid, the word on the street is the crew have been arrested by the Authorities. Max, Brad, Mindy and Cindy, alongside your parents are in custody. And you are big news. Look!"

Sal projected a news pod. The digital readout showed a breaking story with an image of me in high school with the by-line, *Most Wanted*. The story went on to say that alongside The Res; I was the singular most dangerous person known to the Upper Worlds.

"Oh my days," I was dumbstruck. "All of this because of me?"

Jet jumped across the room to get a closer look.

"What about Skye?" He panicked.

"I think she's alright, no word of her being implicated," Sal said.

"And I got a psychic call last night from Philippe," Wain said. "That boy is working his powers yo. The Authorities haven't got him yet, some of the TL are hiding him in Zero."

"They're hauling us all in. The Authorities are coming, and they won't stop till they get you." Sal cracked her knuckles loudly.

The news story about me was as big as you could get. Now, I had the Authorities after me, the Tachions torturing me and what felt like the world against me.

"Woah!" Jet said as the news report showed an image of his face.

"Also on the run is Keziah's brother, thirteen-year-old Jet Saint Monrova. The Monrova siblings are agents of terror, enemies of the state and a danger to your personal safety..." The newscaster reported.

The News on TEN was a distortion of the truth. But the citizens of the Upper Worlds would believe it. I had put everyone I loved in grave danger for what exactly? To save the world? Get real Kid! The Prophecy, or whatever was going on here, was nothing more than raggedy bits of information given to me by strange strangers from weird worlds. And I had trusted them.

"I've got to hand myself in," I said.

"No way Kid! You can't do that."

"Read the headlines Jet. This isn't a childish game. I'm big news, and this has gotten way out of control."

"You're the real deal yo. The tests prove it."

"You can't give up now; we've come this far."

"Enough." I held up my hands for silence, my head pounded.

I closed my eyes to ease the pain. I had to end this here; it's wasn't fun anymore. I didn't want any of my friends hurt. Because of me, they were in prison. Here, in a dusty spare room of the

TL headquarters, I was powerless. And if on a small scale I couldn't even help my friends, how was I meant to save the world?

I realised the room was silent and opened my eyes to see Jet, Wain and Sal staring at me.

"No one knows you're here, *yet*." Sal tried to sound upbeat.

"We, the Tachions, will protect you." Wain said.

"We can do this sis. We can make the difference. We *are* the difference." Jet rose shakily to his feet in steely determination. "We must fulfil The Prophecy."

"If I don't surrender what about the rest of the crew? Their safety is more important than mine."

"Look, their parents are all powerful players on the Upper Worlds. I'm sure things will work out fine for them. It always does for their Type."

"Wain's right," Sal said. "Aside from their parents, they're all Gold Star Code Types on their own merits. The cream of the crop. They won't be senselessly fuzzed or regened. Their valued DNA affords them that privilege."

"I know you're right but we still have to formulate a plan to get the crew off the hook." I sprang into action.

"Wain, I'll need you to use your telepathic powers. Tap into their brainwaves, track them, do whatever it takes to assure me that they are well. Then go to the Authorities and clear their name."

Wain nodded, "Whatever you say, I'm down with it."

"And keep yourself safe too."

"Always yo."

Next, I turned to Sal, "Please find Skye. I'm going to need both of your help to make sure nothing like this ever happens again."

"Whatever you need, I'm here for you." Sal cracked her knuckles.

"Good."

It was time for me to take control and embrace the endless possibilities of my Human potential. The Prophecy and saving the world would have to wait because my nearest and dearest came first.

They make the laws,

Which reign over the
dominion,

But certain rules need to be
broken,

In my humble opinion.

FOURTEEN

Lock Down

"I'm certain this is a childish prank. Nothing more than a dare or a silly game that's gotten out of hand." Bibi said walking down the glass corridor.

His explanation was met with silence from his esteemed colleagues. He knew most of the White Coats who surrounded him. They were from Techno Corp where he worked as a head researcher of biotech.

Along the hallway were four glass cubicles, which were tinted so you couldn't see from the inside out. Isolated in each cell was Mindy, Cindy, Brad and Max.

Mindy had the broadest smile on her face but visibly shook with fear. Bibi stopped to look at her.

"She's no good," Mr Moogs, the leader of the group of White Coats, finally spoke, "we've got all we can from the Lush Twins. They're unable to string a coherent sentence together."

Bibi and The White Coats walked passed Cindy's cubicle but didn't stop. Cindy was rocking from side to side. A smile transfixed on her face.

"Exactly the same as her sister, naturally." Mr Moogs said.

Bibi and the White Coats approached Brad's cubicle. He paced around the small steel table in the room like a caged animal.

"He won't give her up to us. None of them will tell us where she is. Brad, however, did fill us in on Keziah's Tachion friends that have evaded capture, Philippe and Wain, he said they're dangerous. They're being hauled in as we speak."

Bibi nodded in concurrence, but he had never known either Philippe or Wain to be a problem. Philippe was a gentle soul and Wain polite and courteous, despite his upbringing in Sub Zero.

"What about him?" Bibi pointed to Max in the last cubicle. "He must have some information; he's my daughter's closest friend."

"Is that so?" Mr Moogs said surprised. "Maxwell Schneider has been the most resilient, refuses to talk at all. And as long as we don't get any answers on the whereabouts of your offspring, you will all remain imprisoned."

"I am a lead scientist at the Institute. This lunacy has gone too far." Bibi cried outraged.

The mass of White Coats turned sharply to air their disapproval.

Bibi lowered his voice to a less confrontational octave, "My wife can't take the sleep deprivation. We don't know who or what has made our children display such deviant behaviour."

"You have failed in your parenting duties to prepare them as full grown Upper Worldians." Mr Moogs said spitefully.

"It's my wife," Bibi sighed, "she's a Compassionate Type; she wouldn't allow for our children to be Code Type tested. Keziah may have a defective gene. If she needs to be modified, I will override my wife and sign all consent for regeneration. Jet idolises his sister – he has probably just been dragged along by her."

"Very well. But what if modification fails and the only answer is termination?"

Bibi was astounded by such fierce talk.

"Well, I hope it won't have to come to that. I can regen my children, rewire their brains to think and do whatever you want them to." Bibi tried to sound casual, but he was panicking. "I don't think a childish prank of hacking into the state broadcasting system warrants such a harsh sentence."

"Your offspring have proven that they cannot be trusted to fall in line with the laws of the Upper World. What if total annihilation is the only answer? Would you be with us or against us?" Mr Moogs asked vengefully.

Bibi shook his head sorrowfully, "I hope it never comes to that, but if it does you have my permission, permission to annihilate them," he whispered barely audibly. *"The will of the state must be upheld,"* Bibi said, quoting the constitution like the dutiful citizen he was.

"Correct answer, Dr Monrova. Thumbprint this agreement of consent for termination and you and your wife will be released effective immediately."

A White Coat pushed an electronic declaration towards Bibi.

Bibi slowly raised his thumb, hesitating for a moment, before leaving an imprint on the screen.

"Good, very good." Mr Moogs said contentedly.

He turned to face the cubicle in which Max sat very still, staring into space.

"Now before you leave, you have one last duty. Talk to the boy, maybe you can get something out of him."

***

"Stop that!" The Guardian instructed Wain and Philippe as they rode shackled like convicts in the Authoritarian van. "We can detect your brainwave patterns and know you are communicating telepathically. Any more of that illegal activity and you will be annihilated on the spot."

Wain and Philippe took the guard's threat very seriously. This particular model of Guardian was known to be particularly ruthless. And in any case, Wain had communicated to Philippe all that he needed to know.

Their capture was inevitable, and now they had to work with the plan Kid had set. She had given them a script of what to tell the Authorities to exonerate her friends. Now that Wain had informed Philippe of what Kid's wishes were, they both knew what they had to do.

***

"This is not a game Maxwell," Bibi hissed, "we're dealing with extremist behaviour here. The

Authorities deem this as a major threat. You're lucky you weren't all annihilated."

Max kept his head bowed but peered through his brown fringe at the man he revered most in the world, Dr Bibi Monrova. Not only because it was his best friend's father, but also because he was a well-respected, visionary biochemist whose discoveries were heralded.

When the White Coats interrogated him, he dared not utter a word. Even though Kid had sided with the Tachions, he would never betray her friendship. But now it was not that easy. His hero, was putting pressure on him and Max's logical brain ticked over time.

"Kid is unwell. She requires modification if she is to survive. Your silence and misguided loyalty are not helping her."

Max stared over his specs, chewing the insides of his cheeks, willing his brain to stop screaming what he knew was the obvious, logical thing to do.

"What person in their right mind would re-configure The Eye Network signal with the message of *'Free your mind'*? Tampering with official state property is forbidden. Kid could receive years in exile because of such a prank, or worse."

Bibi wiped the beads of sweat from his forehead with a handkerchief and sat to look Max directly in the eye. He loosened his tie and unbuttoned his collar. Why wouldn't the boy talk? He was behaving way out of his Code Type status.

Had this been him twenty years ago he would have confessed immediately.

The Code Type species was evolving, Bibi thought, he always knew it would. One of the main reasons why he had offspring in the first place was to track the evolution process. His own children were variables that he should have been researching more closely, but he had lost sight of his study, and now this.

"My wife and I, who are pillars of the community, have to hang our heads in shame because of Kid's silliness, I mean what else - "

"She's hiding out with the Tachion Liberation Movement." Max's mouth moved so fast that the speed of the speech startled Bibi into silence.

Before Max could zip his lips, his logic gripped him.

"And that's not all she's been up to."

Bibi leant in closer.

"Since her time in Underground City, I believe Kid's been having an ongoing delusional episode."

"Underground City?" Bibi exclaimed in disbelief.

"Yes, we all went there. I have serious doubts about the validity of the experience, but Kid believes we met The Res and he told her that she was the Soul Survivor and about a Prophecy which states that she was put on this earth to save all kind. She has three missions to complete. Kid figured that the first task was to interrupt the broadcast signal at TEN."

"When? Where?" Bibi spluttered. He hadn't been expecting this.

"Then she left me and went to Commania where she said she completed the second mission. She is trying to evade capture to finish the third."

"I don't believe this. How could I not have realised that my own daughter is a defective Type."

Max continued to tell all.

"We routed TEN's signal to my aero pad. Kid had the coordinates stored in her memory bank, but she couldn't remember it, so Wain had to enter her mind to retrieve it."

Bibi held his head in his hands. Why hadn't he paid more attention to his children? How had he allowed it to come to this?

Max was now in full swing, "I can write a more detailed account of all nuances so far, like how I rewired your Auto Nan and re-routed the Guardians at TEN and caused them to shut down. But I will need my aero pad to do so. I've saved all of the data on there."

Bibi choked. If there had been any chance of saving his daughter's life from termination it had certainly been lost the minute Max's logic kicked in.

Bibi slowly rose to his feet and patted Max on the shoulder. He wished he had never pushed the boy to speak.

"You'll go a long way in this system young man." He looked towards the blacked out glass wall. He couldn't see out, but he knew that all the White Coats were looking in.

"Are you happy now?" Bibi said regretfully.

The congregation of White Coats on the other side of the wall nodded their heads in unison. They had finally gotten the answers to everything they needed to know.

***

Wain sat tentatively on the cold glass seat. He tried to get the story straight in his head before the interrogation. He ran the scenario through both his minds,

'Against his will he was forced to house Kid for two days, she robbed him, fought with Jet, clearly insane. Stole aero bike from Sal, left the Upper Worlds, heading to the wilderness of Freeca.'

Wain knew Philippe would reiterate the same lines. He only hoped in a different order; he didn't want it to sound too rehearsed.

Just then four Guardians stomped into the room followed by Mr Moogs. The robotic guards stood in each corner of the room and faced him, pop con guns poised.

Wain gulped loudly, but he was used to this kind of threatening behaviour from living in Sub Zero. The Guardians always intimidated people there.

Mr Moogs sat in front of Wain with a weird smirk on his face. He looked happy, but not friendly.

The White Coat peered at Wain in silence for a while. Wain's eyes darted nervously around the room trying to avoid direct contact with the lab-coated man. His presence was so cold it sent a chill up Wain's spine.

Mr Moogs revelled in Wain's discomfort and after a long drawn out pause, he spoke in an odd voice that had a tin like quality.

"So why do you think you are here?"

"I'm here, Sir, because Kid is a lunatic, she held us hostage with crazy ideas that we were all forced to go along with. She stole an aero bike and is on her way to Freeca. She - "

Mr Moogs held up his latex gloved hand to stop Wain from speaking,

"We know all about Keziah Monrova, caught up in her own fantasy world. The so-called *Prophecy* is a childish myth, a fairy tale that's been recycled for centuries. There's always someone who claims to be the saviour of all kind. When will those of a lower IQ realise that there is no saviour. This is it. We decided their destiny many moons ago. Their miserable little lives are all they have and will ever have. They should fall in line with their genetic disposition and stop believing in delusions of grandeur."

Wain's eyes bugged out.

Mr Moogs smiled smugly.

"Now that Maxwell has fully informed us of all that has been happening, we've sent the rest of your cohorts home with slapped wrists, a penalty fine and the reality that they have been caught up in a silly game. The next time they get bored I'm sure they will find something more patriotic to do, rather than interfere with government signals and venture down to the Underworld."

"Oh, well alright then," Wain said somewhat relieved.

The Authorities didn't believe The Prophecy anyway, that was good, the only good thing he thought about Code Types. They were all so arrogant about their superiority they would never believe the concept of something like the Soul Survivor, a being greater than themselves.

"So am I free to go?" Wain smiled sheepishly, relaxing a little.

"No." Mr Moogs answered quickly, before reclining in his chair.

"Two questions," Mr Moogs announced holding up two fingers. "Where is Jonsey Kerpowski hiding out?"

"I - I - I -" Wain stuttered nervously. "I thought you thought - "

"Ok, question two," Mr Moogs snapped before Wain could answer.

"When are the Tachion Liberation planning their next attack on the Upper Worlds?"

Wain's eyes opened as wide as saucers. Sweat beads sprung from his temples, which he wiped away frantically with the backs of his hands.

"What do you mean?"

"We have been watching you for years. We know who you are Wain Levi, a high-ranking officer in the Tachion Liberation Movement. The brains behind the outfit some say." Mr Moogs said disgustedly.

"No, I'm not, you have it wrong," Wain said unsteadily.

"What we can't believe is that you walked into this, allowed yourself to be captured so easily, all for a *friend*. What would your fellow TL lowlifes make of this? Tut, tut, tut." Mr Moogs laughed mirthlessly.

"Friendship is the only thing I've got yo, and I cherish my friends."

Incensed by his backchat, Mr Moog's rounded on Wain,

"Where is your leader Jonsey hiding out?" He barked.

"I won't tell you!"

"When is the next TL strike on the Upper Worlds?" Mr Moogs slammed his fist on the desk.

Wain shook his head, tears in his eyes, committed to the cause till the end, just like his mother had been.

"I'll never betray my Tachion brothers and sisters."

"On guard!" Mr Moogs instructed.

The Guardians took aim. Wain clenched his three fists and pushed them proudly high into the air. A sky blue band, the Tachion Liberation secret dress code, adorned each wrist.

"Tachion Liberation *forever*!" Wain declared as he closed his eyes, he knew what was coming next.

"Fire!"

On command the Guardians blasted controlled gamma rays at Wain. The fuzzing sound from the pop con lazer filled the air, muting his screams of terror. When it ceased, an ear-piercing silence mingled pungently with the scent of a terminated life.

"Clean this mess up." Mr Moogs ordered as he looked over the heap of smoking ashes. "Even the smell of them makes me sick!"

Wain was gone. And all that was left to honour his fifteen years on the planet were three metallic wristbands.

Cold hearted,

Frosty attitude,

Deemed sub, so you think
less of thee.

Ice cold,

Zero chill,

Those with an ego led
mentality.

FIFTEEN

Sub Zero

Skye sprinted down a grey cobbled street through the devastated area of downtown Sub Zero. Diverse Tachions flanked her on either side.

The inhumane living conditions coupled with the current Authoritarian occupation had made an already unbearable situation totally unliveable. No stone had been left unturned in the Authoritarian search for Kid. Vehicles had been flipped over callously like defenceless beetle bugs. Hollow shop fronts smouldered as the fires that had raged within them from the mass annihilations burnt out. The contents of burst rubbish bags messily littered the pavement; sanitation was the last concern of the terrorised Tachion community.

Across the street, a congregation of military Officials, who worshipped the art of war, prepared to launch their next attack. Skye and the group who ran with her were the targets.

Zzzzzzaaaap!

A series of pop con missiles fired. Skye instinctively created a glowing blue force field of protection. Her face contorted revealing the strain she was under in doing so. The bullets exploded on impact, and everyone remained safe inside.

"Thank you, thank you Little Missy," cried out the people around her.

Skye kept on running. She was exhausted and needed to conserve all of the energy she had left to hold tightly onto her backpack. Its contents were more important to her than anything else in the world.

Across the road, a family of Tachions stood cowering in front of two Guardians. Skye reached out her hand to them, but they were too far away for her to protect. The father and mother cradled their children. Skye kept it moving and didn't look back, blocking out the painful sounds of the entire family being fuzzed.

Finally, Skye reached her destination at the top of C Junction; an area that used to be a bustling shopping district was now derelict.

"This is me," she said to the group under her protection. "Head south. You'll find safe shelter there."

Where Skye was going, she knew she couldn't take them with her. It was far too dangerous.

The adult Tachions were reluctant to leave the security of her remarkable junior talents. They couldn't believe she knew how to harness them.

"Bless your bones." A chubby burgundy Tachion said sincerely as he took leadership of the group.

Skye left the crowd and hopped through a brown wooden latch door covered by garbage bags. She jogged down the spiral staircase leading to the old library, which to the initiated eye was the Tachion Liberation's secret HQ.

Skye rapped six times on the door in the sound sequence Wain had taught her. The door opened almost immediately, and she was hastily pulled into the interior darkness.

"Did you get it?"

"I got everything you asked for Kid, and I spoke with Seymour, the Arcadians will come and help us." Skye rasped, breathless.

Jet wasn't concerned about anything apart from Skye. He pulled her in close, and she collapsed in his arms. This solo mission had been a tough one and using her powers continuously had exhausted her.

Jet hugged Skye tightly allowing her to rejuvenate by feeding off his Human warmth and energy.

"Thank you, Skye. I knew you wouldn't let us down."

***

A mass of White Coats marched down a harsh tungsten lit hallway and entered a clinically white room. The room was empty and soulless with the exception of one wall made entirely from coding script and a huge desk at the far end. The digital data scrolled incessantly with dots and ones. Seated at the desk with his back turned to the entourage was His Excellency, William Admiral, the leader of the Upper Worlds.

"Your Excellency, General Grey has reported that the search for the Monrova child is relentless in Sub Zero. Every home, every institution, everyone is being searched and questioned. Tachions with known anti – Upper World ideologies and those failing to comply are being annihilated. By terminating any Tachion resistance, under the guise of rooting out the girl, we are killing two birds with one stone. Fear reigns. No one will dare rise against us again." The chief White Coat, Mr Moogs, said.

"Hmmm." The Admiral murmured, without turning to face the group. He removed the leather gloves from his hands and interlaced his fingers to reveal sharp yellowing talons. He tapped them together loudly signalling for Mr Moogs to continue.

"Everyone on the Upper Worlds is completely captivated by this childish mythology. We should have disseminated this 'Soul Survivor Prophecy' nonsense years ago. It's amazing how people will believe anything." Mr Moogs chuckled.

"We will find Keziah and have her publicly terminated to put an end to this silly national obsession."

"It will take more than her annihilation to bring the masses to order." The Admiral spoke in a low, timid voice.

The White Coats looked at each other quizzically before Mr Moogs spoke up.
"Your Excellency, what knowledge do you have to share with us on this matter?"
The Admiral spoke into a device he used whenever he addressed the nation, which turned his feeble tone into a forceful timbre full of gusto.

"For centuries mankind has been waiting for its saviour." The Admiral said shortly.

"But Your Excellency, we are *Code Types*, genetically superior beings who determine our own existence and are masters of our, and everyone else's, destiny. Surely this *Prophecy* is fictitious. It goes against all our beliefs and principles. I, alongside my esteemed colleagues, believed that the search for this child was just a smokescreen, a scapegoat for tearing down those who have attempted to rise against us and all that we stand for, without a public outcry from the peaceful and rebellious Types."

The mass of White Coats nodded and murmured in agreement. Mr Moogs gained confidence in his colleagues' concurrence and continued,

"This so-called Prophecy is just a nonsense concocted by desperate underground dwellers."

The Admiral did not respond, leaving the air filled with a heart thumping silence.

"I mean this Keziah is obviously a delusional genetic oddity. What real harm can a child do?"

The Admiral slowly turned to face Mr Moogs and the White Coats. A tight-lipped frown adorned his pale decaying face.

"She tampered with state-run technology of the highest degree disabling our primary agent of mind control. She held counsel with The Res, our most ferocious enemy. She found the Saps hidden community. She is currently still at large, evading capture from the most skilled military on earth.

She has outsmarted all of you, the greatest minds the Upper Worlds has to offer. Someone is not doing their job properly and that someone is you."

"Your Excellency, I did not mean to question you, I, I, -" Mr Moogs stammered nervously.

The Admiral didn't have time for weakness.

"Seize him." He ordered disinterestedly.

Immediately four Elite Guardians tackled Mr Moogs by his arms and legs.

"Nooooo!" He screamed.

His colleagues side-stepped the desperate man and reformed the group as if he never existed.

Mr Moogs was dragged callously out of the room, to his doom.

Another White Coat, Dr Djaba stepped to the head of the pack as the new leader, seamlessly replacing the old one.

"Your Excellency what would you have us do?"

The Admiral spoke unperturbed by the commotion, "Never doubt the capabilities of a little girl. Capture her quickly, and annihilate her."

***

Philippe watched the digital news scrolling across the hallway in FB.

"Prophecy is fallacy. The Monrova siblings are still at large. Beware of false prophets."

Kid's 'delusional' face beamed from the report. She was the most famous person on the Upper Worlds, for all the wrong reasons.

340

"More like your 'facts' are a fallacy, fantasy is real," Philippe scoffed underneath his breath as he emptied his sports gear from his locker.

It had been a week, and TEN was still reporting the *'Keziah Monrova: Enemy of the state'* story. They had never run with a topic for that long. Luckily for him, the news had never released pictures of the rest of the crew and no one, but the Officials knew that they had ever been implicated.

Philippe slammed his locker shut and turned abruptly to leave. Someone rushed straight into him.

"Sorry." He instinctively held on to stop them from falling.

Philippe looked down. Mindy looked up.

They hadn't seen each other since that fateful night Ms Lush threw him out of her house.

Philippe released his grip immediately. Mindy lingered before letting him go. They faced each other uneasily. Then both attempted to talk at the same time.

"You first." Philippe offered.

"No, you first," Mindy insisted.

Philippe gazed at Mindy dreamily, a momentary lapse of weakness. He became sullen, "I was just going to say that," before he could stop himself he blurted out something he was not intending to tell anyone, "I'm leaving FB."

Mindy looked confused in only a way that Philippe could tell, to anyone else it just looked as if she was smiling as she always did.

"Why?"

Philippe didn't want to speak about this with anyone, but just looking at Mindy made him want to share all of his secrets.

"My parents thought it would be the best thing for me. After all the trouble with the Officials, they figured I was rebelling because they had failed me as Code Type parents raising a Tachion son. They said they didn't understand my, '*Tachion needs.*'" Philippe dryly air-quoted his parents.

"They think I'm confused about my identity, so they're sending me to Clapham House, it's the most prestigious Tachion boarding school in the country. They hope there I'll discover my '*self-worth.*'"

"Oh... My... That's unfortunate." Mindy was gutted, she had missed Philippe. She couldn't comprehend the thought of not seeing him at all.

"Yeah. I'm not stoked about the idea either. My mother -"

" - Well, well, what do we have here then?" Madeleine Stone and the Pretties interrupted the conversation. "My dad told me that you're all secret members of the TL and against the Upper Worlds."

"Like I've told you so-oo many times Madeleine we were, like, cleared from any anti-state activity. It was all a misunderstanding." Mindy tried to defend herself.

Madeleine had heard it before but carried on relentlessly,

"I heard you were a lieutenant in Kid's crazy army. I mean we all knew she was a loony tune, just look at the way she dressed! But you and

342

that twin of yours, masquerading as Aesthetic Code Types, you bring us all down, shame us all."

The Pretties tittered in agreement.

Mindy shrunk on the spot not knowing what to say or do. She had no comeback for Madeleine.

"You only wish your life was as popping as Mindy's." Philippe boomed making his way to the centre of the Aesthetic horde.

He angled his huge frame protectively in front of Mindy.

"Oh, I should have guessed you would stick up for her, you're just as bad. I heard you got caught up in the prophecy and - "

Philippe didn't let Madeleine finish. With one hand he grabbed her firmly around her tiny waist and lifted her effortlessly into the air.

"Put me down!" Madeleine squealed.

The corridor rush stopped to stare at the hulking Tachion, manhandling the powerless AE. The rest of the Pretties fled into the crowd frightened by his show of power. They had never seen Philippe do anything like this before.

"Look," Philippe growled lowly sticking Madeleine's face directly next to the digital news feed. " 'Prophecy is fallacy,' " he quoted the slogan which was plastered across the Upper Worlds. "So I suggest you quit tormenting Minds or you'll have me to deal with. OK?"

"Yes Philippe." Madeleine nodded quickly.

"Good." Philippe returned her to the floor just as two Elite Guardians, who had replaced the rickety old security, stomped up the hallway.

"What is the disturbance here?" They asked Madeleine, pop guns poised at Philippe.

Madeleine recoiled before responding in an uncharacteristically meek manner, "Nothing. He was just assisting me, to see something more clearly."

"Well if that's the case move on to your classrooms." The Guardians coldly barged students away from the scene before stomping off.

"Thanks." Philippe looked down at Madeleine, acknowledging that she had just saved him from being fuzzed.

Madeleine backed away slowly, genuinely frightened.

Mindy breathed a sigh of relief and placed her soft hand on Philippe's back.

"Thank you for sticking up for me," she fluttered her long eyelashes, "With you Philly, I always feel safe."

"I would do anything for you Minds, truly anything," he looked at her earnestly.

"I know."

"Sorry to go on about my folks."

"They're not always right you know, our parents. Take my mother; she's wrong like ninety-nine percent of the time. Sometimes you have to let them say whatever they are going to say and then make up your mind for yourself. That's what I do." Mindy bowed her head slightly.

Philippe thought he had lost something that night at The Twins house. A precious feeling that he figured would never return. But with Mindy standing before him, she gave him hope that there was a chance for love between him and the girl of his dreams.

"Mindy. I - "

"What's happening Big P? Long time no see player." Brad said emerging from the horde of students in the hallway.

The muscles in the side of Philippe's face rippled.

"Since you've been gone things are different around here," Brad said pulling Mindy in close to him. "The game has changed."

Mindy wanted to pull away from Brad but didn't. He was her boyfriend now, and no matter how she felt about Philippe, she had to put on a good show for the public. After all, that's what AEs were great at. Pretending.

Philippe's hearts thundered at the sight of the perfect Code Type couple. He needed to get away from them, and fast.

"Game on," he said through gritted teeth as he turned and walked away.

***

"...Jet's right," Sal agreed, "It's too dangerous to leave out yet, the Guardians, Orbs and Officials are everywhere.

"Dr Stoneway told me to listen to my dreams and follow my Inner G; so that's what I'm going to do." I insisted.

Sal folded her arms. Here Kid was again going on about her dreams. Kid spent so much time sleeping, and when she woke up, she would spend even more time by herself logging what had happened and writing secret plans. She said she finally understood that her dreams were guiding her on what to do next. But Sal thought there was a much more down to earth explanation for Kid's weariness. And that was, like everyone else, she was grieving losing Wain.

"I've seen a clock counting down and when it strikes four everything fades to black, and I wake up. Time is running out. I know it is. I have to complete the last mission, whatever that is, soon. Otherwise, all of this destruction and heartache will be for nothing."

We had been holed up in the TL HQ for too long. There were at least fifty members of the movement with us, all occupying the same cramped library filled to the rafters with books.

Jet looked up from the brown paper magazine he was holding. He had engrossed himself in faded publications from the olden times and was in awe of the past. Back then people lived with carefree abundance unheard of on the Upper Worlds. They acted as if the earth would never run out of resources as if not taking responsibility for their selfish actions wouldn't affect the future. How wrong they were.

"You heard what Skye said, she spoke to the Arcadians, the Urbanites will help us. We have to wait."

"But for how long?"

"As long as it takes." Jet said trying to keep reading and not get drawn into the conversation.

"Maybe they aren't coming at all. And the longer we wait more Tachions are fuzzed, more lives lost, like Wain."

My heart stalled. I couldn't bear to think about my friend. No matter how many people told me differently, I still felt that Wain's termination was my fault. He had decided to leave the safety of the library so that I would not be detected. I had devised a plan that he would throw the Authorities off the scent of the whole crew by telling the Officials that I was demented, a crazy person, on a mad mission. Now I wasn't sure if it was a cunning plan or simply the truth.

"There is a war going on outside. No Prophecy is worth this much sorrow."

Sal cracked her knuckles, "It's too late to turn back. We've come so far. You have to complete the mission."

"I can't stay here in safety any longer knowing the devastation I have caused all around," I said hopelessly.

"You haven't caused this. It was always the Authorities plan," Skye rasped. "Everyone in Zero knows this is just a good excuse for the Officials to put into practice the measures that they do on the sly anyway. Tachions live under the constant threat of being fuzzed for just breathing, this state of emergency is nothing new to us."

"And don't worry about the safety thing either," Jet said calmly. "Look outside."

A red lazer beam shone through a crack in the curtain, aimed directly at my head.

The old clock on the library wall struck four PM at the same time that an almighty siren wailed outside.

"Come out, unarmed and with your hands up. We have you surrounded." Came the sharp order from a loudspeaker system.

Jet finally put down the magazine. "Looks like you were right sis, our times up."

***

Bibi closed his front door and walked out to the garden leaving his wife, in a crumpled heap on the floor. Milan had been crying for so long he couldn't bear to hear her sob anymore. The doctor had said her breakdown was due to a complete sympathy and empathy overload. The only thing unusual for her Type was that this time she felt sorry for herself.

Bibi breathed in the crisp air. He could tell it was going to snow. Not because he had any psychic ability as he'd wished, but because at the end of every year the Authorities always provided two weeks of snowy weather for the Yuletide celebrations. It was meant to induce a sense of fun or some other concept that he did not understand.

Bibi knew this was a good opportunity to deliver the orders that had been sent from his superiors. He took a swig of moonshine from his hip flask, strode over to his next-door neighbour's house and pressed the bell.

Max opened the door.

"Dr Monrova, we were not expecting you. My parents are in the relaxation sector. I'll just call them for you."

"No, actually I've come to see you." Bibi shuffled.

"Oh?" Max said, growing uncomfortable at the sight of Dr Monrova's dishevelled appearance.

His beard was overgrown, his eyes bloodshot red and his white coat was creased and discoloured, a far cry from his usual, pristine appearance.

"Yes, I wanted to deliver the great news to you personally."

"What is this *great* news Dr Monrova?" Max asked cautiously, detecting an insincere tone.

"You've been fast-tracked. My superiors have checked all of your school records and have decided that you will be joining us at Techno Corp as an apprentice. This semester you'll graduate from Falconbrook High and will be our youngest employee to date." Bibi concluded with a tight smile.

Max was momentarily speechless. Finally, he was going to leave the small minds behind and was getting the recognition he craved. He would be able to put all of his inventions into practical use. This news eased the weird tension he had in his chest since Wain's annihilation. He had never experienced such a thing and couldn't explain it, so he had read up on the subject, and the closest definition he could attribute to the way he was feeling was the emotion, guilt.

"That is absolutely fantastic Dr Monrova." Max finally managed to say.

"Welcome on board. Keep this up, and soon you'll be my boss!" Bibi laughed heartily.

Max shifted uneasily smelling the banned substance of liquor on Dr Monrova's breath. He deduced that Dr Monrova was not joking. It was common knowledge that since Kid's disappearance, Dr Monrova had been demoted from his department and outcast by his colleagues. No one wanted to associate with the man who had raised not one, but two enemies of the state.

Max wanted to shut the door and run to tell his parents the good news, but there was something that didn't add up.

"Dr Monrova, why was I chosen to join the Techno Corp before the hundreds of older brighter minds the Upper Worlds has to offer?"

"Someone up there likes you," Bibi said, loudly as if being watched.
He leant in close to Max before uttering quietly,

"Stay on their good side. It's hell when they turn against you."

Bibi walked away.

Max closed the door frightened.

The Orbs watched their every move.

This is the final call,

For we are in distress.

Please heed our plea,

A personal S.O.S.

SIXTEEN

Urban Intervention

In the small grassy courtyard behind the library Jet, Skye, Sal and I kneeled, handcuffed, alongside members of the TL. The entire Authoritarian search had converged at this one point. Rows upon rows of Elite Guardians surrounded us, and Top Upper World commanders adorned every vehicle forming a blockade around the library.

"All of this for me?" I said, at the sheer scale of the operation.

"Don't take all the credit, sis. I was second on the most wanted list." Jet tried to joke about the dire situation we were in.

A highly decorated Code Type decked out in full warfare regalia pushed past the Guardians. He was flanked by other important looking CT militia Types. His badge read, *General Grey.* He didn't look like your regular army personnel; he was broad-boned and handsome. I figured he must have been born an Aesthetic or Athletic Type but didn't succeed in his predestined field. Maybe he had been regened, into a combat Type. I looked at him trying to figure him out.

General Grey shifted uneasily under Kid's stare, "So you're Keziah Eden Monrova, birth code GC 153 589, State enemy number one!"

"Who is this guy?" Jet sniggered in a desperate attempt to bide time. "Shouldn't he be hosting a TV game show or something?"

"Shut your mouth!" General Grey sneered, violently kicking Jet in the stomach with his steel capped boots.

"Oomph!" Jet fell face forward to the floor.

"Jet!" Skye screamed at an ear-splitting octave.

"Leave him be!" I tried to reach out to my brother, but the shackles rooted me to the spot.

General Grey yanked Jet by his hair. His nose was bloodied, his pride hurt.

"Know your place, Little Boy!" General Grey spat.

Jet hung his head doubled up in agony. Skye narrowed her piercing blue eyes. She was burning up inside. If she could free herself, she would have personally dealt with General Grey. The Authorities must have been aware of her Tachion ability because her handcuffs were emitting a gamma ray that drained her powers.

I remembered the teachings of Dr Stoneway and controlled my rising anger; it would not get the better of me. I calmed myself by looking at my inner eye. Concentrating on my Inner G.

"None of these people here with me have done anything wrong. I am the Soul Survivor. I am the one you want. Let them be!" I commanded.

I shocked myself with the power of my voice. I hadn't truly believed I was the chosen one until I uttered those words.

General Grey looked at me with sheer contempt, ignoring my declaration.

"Where is Jonsey?"

Jonsey, the leader of the TL, had left the safety of the library days ago to help fight the Guardians and rally more Tachion support. He had not returned. I thought he had been captured, but this was obviously not the case.

"What has Jonsey got to do with your search for me?" I said, confused.

"You ignoramus," General Grey spoke rapidly, "did you think all of this was really about you? You're a pathetic genetic oddity, media fodder." He pointed to The Eye Network helicopters circling overhead filming every detail of our capture. No doubt this would be breaking news on all media streams any minute now.

"The citizens have gotten behind you, it seems. They want a show they do, so we'll keep them entertained. Once you're annihilated, end of story. Our justice will prevail. Our authority will be upheld.

"This so-called Prophecy gave us the green light to smash the Tachion Liberation and all other enemies of the state. Like him, him and her." General Grey pointed furiously at the members of the TL kneeling in front of him.

They looked knowingly at each other and attempted to raise their fists in one last act of defiance.

"Tachion Liberation forever!" Lianda, a sweet one-eyed Tachion shouted.

355

A Guardian annihilated them all on the spot leaving three smoking heaps of ash.

"No!" I screamed.

Sal froze in fear. She was the next in the line-up to be terminated.

"Now where is Jonsey?" General Grey yelled raising his pop con.

I was not afraid for my own life, but my friends must be spared,

"He's long gone, you'll never find him, and you will never win. I see clearly now what you are trying to do, but you will never succeed, the people of the Upper Worlds have awoken."

"Shut up, you stem cell mess!" General Grey screamed blobs of spittle spraying from his mouth, "Or I'll silence you forever right now."

"General Grey, Sir," one of the officers in the line stepped forward, "we are waiting for all cameras to be in place before we annihilate her. The public is going to want to see her obliteration from every angle."

"How long will this take?" General Grey screamed.

Although he was supposedly in charge, his emotions ran wild and he was totally out of control. I was surprised at how at ease I felt. Yes I was staring death in the face, Jet had been hurt and my friends captured, but I was not afraid at all.

"Camera repositioning will take ninety seconds, Sir!" came the call from another Official.

"Arrrgh!" In frustration, General Grey launched his pop con at Maria, a thin pink Tachion. She instantly turned to ash.

"Hurry up." trigger happy General Grey raged.

Sal bit her lip hard to fight back her tears. She would rather die than show these Officials any sign of weakness. Skye, on the other hand, trembled uncontrollably. These were her Tachion brothers and sisters, and now they were all turning to dust.

Jet kept his eyes downcast, the pain from General Grey's boot still embedded in his stomach. He was trying to control his emotions, as Dr Stoneway had advised, but hate had replaced his fear, and that was the most dangerous emotion of them all.

There was nothing else I could do. I closed my eyes and practised Kimetic. I breathed deeply and focused my attention on my Inner G. Immediately my parents popped into my mind. It would be my sixteenth earth year in a few days, but this year there was no cause for celebration. I wondered what my parents would do without us, what they were doing right now. I hoped that when they fuzzed me, others would take up the cause and in years to come, I would be remembered in a way that would make my parents proud.

"Thirty, twenty-nine, twenty-eight - " General Grey counted down to total annihilation.

I wanted to turn and tell Jet how much I loved him. That even though I was older, I looked up to him for he was so much wiser than me in so many ways.

I wanted to thank Skye for risking her life carrying out all of my demands and always looking out for my brother. I wanted to tell Sal her friendship meant the world to me as she had stuck with me through the thickest of things. But I couldn't. I was lost in my inner worlds. My eyelids felt like they had been stuck down with glue. And then the slide show began, just as I had always heard, right before you die your whole life was meant to flash in front of you. And here it was.

Every moment of my entire life whizzed by at breakneck speed. The visions of the past now blended with those of the future. I saw Max as a grown man, marching at the head of a group of White Coats. Jet and Skye back-to-back fighting Guardians ferociously. Dai gave a Capsing pill to Cindy. Mindy held a newborn anxiously covering up the baby boy's chest, which beat with the force of two hearts. I saw myself slumped on a rocky floor.

"What is taking so long?" Came the sound of General Grey's voice. I saw it on the inner before he said it on the outer.

My eyes rolled to the back of my head, my body convulsed. Everything was being revealed to me on my inner screen.

"What on earth is she doing?" General Grey said in disgust as Kid convulsed violently.

"If the cameras are in place let's put this rabid child out of her misery."

"Wait! There's just one more thing." One of the highly decorated Sergeants stepped forward with long powerful strides.

"What?" General Grey demanded.

He wanted to get this over and done with, but he didn't want to miss his moment of glory. The TV cameras were of utmost importance to his ego. He would be canonised on the screens across the nation as the man who successfully captured Keziah Monrova. That would show everyone who mocked him when his tibia bone broke, and he didn't make it into the Allstar baseball team. He had the chance to be a hero again, even if it was through regen and with the military.

"What is taking so long?" General Grey demanded.

"This!" The sergeant held out his open palm and emitted a force so strong that the rays knocked the first circle of Guardians to the ground and they shattered into tiny pieces.

"Wh- what?" General Grey froze in horror.

The sergeant was now in full view. The highly decorated man wasn't part of The Admiral's Elite Military at all. It was The Res.

"Annihilate him!" General Grey wailed like a banshee.

The next round of Guardians launched missiles at The Res. With one flick of his hand, he sent their bullets flying back to them, and the Guardians exploded.

"Urbanites. Ante up!" Commanded The Res.

Urbanites appeared from every conceivable direction to attack the Code Type and robotic militia. They rose from potholes in the streets, descended from buildings and scurried from safety hideouts. Their crude weapons were made from broken bottles and rope; they wielded crowbars and slingshots. Anything that they could lay their hands on was now a fighting tool.

The Res and his imposter Urbanite army had infiltrated the Official Militia disguised as Elite Guardians. Now allies or enemies were impossible to tell apart.

"Tachions!" The Res bellowed to the masses of people who passively watched from behind the cordoned off areas.

"I know you are frightened, but isn't it time that you took a stand? Those in charge have led you to believe that you are inferior. That you are weaker. That you are defective. That is a lie. A lie that you have allowed yourselves to believe and it has kept you at the lowest rungs of society.

"The truth is we are *super*. Magnificent beyond our *own* comprehension. What we have are not defects. They are powers. Powers that they cannot control so, they will not let us harness.

"My brothers and sisters, cower no more. It's time that we stopped living in fear of everything, including ourselves! It's time that we rise. You are much stronger than they are. You can beat them. You must defeat them. Tachions. *Ante up!*"

The Res rallied the Tachions passionately while single-handedly taking out rounds of attacking Guardians.

A rapturous applause rippled like a tidal wave through the crowd. Many pumped their fists repeating the words The Res had said like an anthem,

"Ante Up! Ante Up!! Ante Up!!!"

Spurred on by The Res a round blue Tachion nodded contritely. He clapped his hands in front of him. A small cloud of frost emitted from his palms and icicles fell from his hands. He jumped back, afraid of what he had just created. He slowly raised his hands and tried it again. More ice cubes fell from his palms. He laughed, unbelieving what he was able to generate.

A Guardian menacingly approached him, pop con raised,

"You are breaking the first Truth. Halt that activity immediately or you will be annihilated."

The Tachion held up his hands in surrender. A thick sheet of ice shot from his hands, and with one accidental blast, he froze the Guardian in its tracks.

"Whoops!" The blue Tachion jumped back, looking at his palms in awe.

More Guardians ran towards him, and he shot out ice blasts freezing them instantly. The blue Tachion laughed maniacally shocked by his newly discovered Tachion power.

The Res snapped the chains from the crew as easily as most people snap their fingers.

"Thank you, thank you, thank you." Sal whispered as The Res released her.

Kid slumped to the ground as her chains fell away. The Res swiftly picked her up and carried her carefully like a precious jewel.

"Look after them, Skye." The Res commanded as he fended off more oncoming Guardians.

"Of course." Skye instantaneously created a force field protecting Jet and Sal from the missiles flying all around them.

Kid was still lost in her inner worlds being bombarded with the past, present and future happenings; Brad and Philippe in Kindergarten played catch. As small children, they were the best of friends. The image raced through time. Now Captain Brad led the National Football team. He ran onto a packed stadium of adoring fans. A red lazer beam targeted his back, Philippe held the gun. In adulthood, they were the worst of enemies.

General Grey launched a pop con missile at The Res. He was too busy shielding Kid and did not see it coming. The mighty Res was obliterated and turned to dust.

"Ha-Uh!"

My eyes sprang open. All around me was the carnage of war. Guardians were launching missiles, instead of Tachions running for cover, they were fighting back! Some caused explosions; others were hurtling through the air. The Tachions fought alongside the Urbanites against the Elite Militia. And they were winning.

"Nice to have you back." The Res said.

I didn't waste time. I had already seen what came next. I pulled The Res down and threw myself in front of him. The blast from General Grey's gun went straight to my heart.

Everything faded to black.

Choose wisely your time,

And with whom it you
spend.

For endings are inevitable,

And beginnings mark the
end.

SEVENTEEN

The Long Goodbye

"Where am I?"

My body ached. A loud whirling sound in my ears made my head throb.

"She's awake everybody. Kid's awake!" Jet rushed to my side.

Through blurred vision, I could see that I was laid on the floor of a makeshift tent. My eyes adjusted to the familiar friendly faces.

"Where are we?"

"The Outer Limits. How are you feeling?" Sal asked.

"I'm not going to lie, I've felt better." I croaked.

"You're unfuzzable!" Jet said excitedly, "You took the full blast from General Grey's gun and nothing! It just bounced off you."

"Thanks, Jet, but I can't take credit for stopping the bullet. It was this."

I fished out the crystal on the shoelace.

"The gamma ray struck it, instead of me. Lady Zono made me promise to wear it at all times; now I'm glad I did. She protected me with one of her magical crystals."

The Res peered at me with his sharky grin, "I thought I was coming to rescue you, but you ended up saving my life."

I smiled sheepishly, "I'm glad you came with the Urbanites. Without you, we wouldn't have made it out of Sub Zero alive."

"Zero will never be the same again." Skye whispered.

"I know. I feel so terrible for what the Authorities did there hunting for me."

"No, it's not that. The Tachions were *incredible*. They finally fought back!"

"What?"

"Yep," Skye beamed proudly, "I never thought I'd ever witness so many Tachions harnessing their powers."

"I wish you had seen it, Kid, the battle in Zero was epic," Jet said. "The Elite Militia retreated! Their guns and weapons were no match for Tachion power."

"All that the Tachions needed was the impetus for they did not know their worth. But now they have knowledge of their self, things in Sub Zero will never be the same again." The Res said.

"If all Tachions were ever to realise their powers, they would be unstoppable," I said. "No one should ever be forced to play down their talents. They should be encouraged to use them wisely."

I turned to the members of the TL in the camp, "But remember, two wrongdoings can never make a right. Violence to those who oppress you is not the answer. There are other routes. Have the courage to find them because if you do, no one need ever feel lost in our world again."

The TL nodded in sombre agreement.

Zen, a high-profile activist, spoke for the movement, "From this day forward the TL pledge an alliance with the underground dwellers and an allegiance to you and your crew, Keziah. I have never witnessed the bravery in the face of danger you all showed. And we will heed your words. This is my promise to you."

I smiled gratefully. The Prophecy had set our world alight, and change was on the horizon.

***

"...I can't believe you just said that." Philippe looked at Cindy, shocked.

School time was over, and they sat in the courtyard of FB on the Top Tables.

It was unusual that Cindy had asked to meet Philippe alone, they only ever hung out together with other people around. He knew something had to be up, but he wasn't expecting this.

"It's true! If I were Tachion, I would be part of the liberation movement."

"How can you even say that? You're an archetypal Code Type. They want to destroy people like you."

While on the run from the Authorities, Philippe had spent time in Zero. The Tachions had treated him kindly, but one thing he knew for sure was that there was no love lost between Tachions and Code Types.

"Not destroy, just be on a level playing field. I'd fuzz a few for equality."

"You don't know what you're saying Cinds." This conversation was making him uncomfortable.

"Yes, I do!" She squeaked, "I'm never taken seriously because of the way I look. But I have opinions too. Gosh! No one understands my PGP."

"What's PGP?"

"Pretty Girl Problems."

Philippe glanced at Cindy sideways, and a chill ran up his spine. Her smile was plastered across her face so broadly it just didn't add up with what she was saying. She looked pained, not pleasant.

"I never knew you felt like that. I thought you loved being an AE."

"I hate it," Cindy said flatly. "I mean look at how the Gold Star Code Types like me treat people different from them like you."

The muscles on Philippe's face rippled. No matter how hard he tried to assimilate, in the presence of Code Types, he always felt insecure. From the stares of strangers in the streets to the jeers from the jocks and his own parents' prejudice, Philippe was always judged by the Types.

"I don't see it like that," Philippe said masking his feelings.

"Well if I were you I would, like, totally support the TL all the way. I mean if you won't take a stand for Tachion rights, why would you expect anybody else to?"

Philippe's muscles tensed.

"I've got to go Cinds." He stood up to leave.

"Why what did I say?" She blinked.

"Nothing. It's just that I don't know anymore. I don't know what everyone wants from me. I stand out here on the Upper Worlds, and I don't fit in Sub Zero. Where am I meant to go? Who am I supposed to be?"

Cindy jumped to her feet to comfort him.

"I didn't mean to upset you," she said softly.

"It's ok, Cinds. I guess I just have to figure out where I belong."

Looking into her face, which was the same as the girl he loved, calmed him.

"And what about you?"

"Oh, like, I know where I'm *supposed* to fit in. I'm just not wiling to conform anymore."

They looked off in silence at the perfectly lined purple carnations in the forecourt. As the auburn and yellow leaves blew blissfully in the wind, they both knew that their lives were about to take an extremely different course and FB was behind them forever.

***

Sal looked up from the potion she was mixing, "Are you sure you want to do this?"

"Yes. I didn't send Skye into dangerous territory to get this stuff and not make use of it."

"But you've never Capsed before. You don't know what it will do to you."

"I have to see my parents and the only way I can do so is in disguise, so please let me have it."

Sal looked to The Res for back up, the only authority she believed could even try to challenge Kid. The Res stopped chugging on his pipe and blew blue smoke into the night air.

"If Keziah says she's seen the future then she has to do what she has to do."

"But Capsing can be really dangerous for a first timer," Sal said hoping to win The Res over to her way of thinking.

"Then you better make sure you get the levels right." The Res boomed sternly.

Sal got back to work, carefully adjusting the chemicals in her potion.

"Now I must return to my city. There are matters underground that require my immediate attention. Jahni and Pepo are my most skilled riders, and they will take you home. After that, you are on your own. As The Prophecy states, only the Soul Survivor can capture the three-eyed beast, only you know what you have to do."

I nodded, thankful that The Res respected my choices.

"You have discovered your purpose, the sole reason why you are alive. Stay focused and finish the job you came to do."

The Res extended his balled up hand to me, signifying the ultimate respect. I was honoured and quickly bumped his fist.

"Until we meet again." The Res bowed with his hand across his chest before disappearing into the darkness.

I looked wistfully after The Res. A lump formed in my throat. I had a sinking feeling that I would never see him again.

Sal tapped me gently on the shoulder and held up the mixed solution, "It's ready."

***

"Nightfall." Brad instructed, clicking his fingers.

On command, a myriad of twinkling stars appeared in the moonlit sky. A hundred-foot screen showed the latest blockbuster movie. Brad and Mindy were the only ones at the drive-in, parked in his convertible cruiser.

"Now we can really get comfortable," Brad said, gently manoeuvring Mindy towards him.

"Daylight!" Mindy said quickly, and the scene overhead changed to a bright blue sky with fluffy white clouds sailing sleepily across it.

She didn't feel romantic. But Brad didn't get the message.

"Nightfall." Brad instructed again, and the stars reappeared.

He held Mindy's hands staring longingly into her beautiful face.

"Minds so much has gone on over the past few weeks, but I'm so glad we've got each other. I would do anything for you. I don't care about anything else as long as I have you. I just want to tell you that - "

"Braddy, not now." Mindy interrupted him.

She feared he wanted to say those three special words to her, but she didn't want to hear it, not from him anyway. She had been trying to avoid this talk for a long time, but here, in a deserted drive-in, there was no escape.

"Daylight." Brad said, and the clouds reappeared. He wanted to see Mindy properly when he spoke the words from his heart.

"I can't keep it to myself anymore. We're special. We're perfect together. Even your mother says we were made for one another. Things couldn't have turned out any better."

"Brad! Like, how can you say that after all the terrible things that have happened?"

"Of course I'm not happy that Wain was fuzzed. Or that Kid is a delusional enemy of the state."

"We don't even know that to be true."

"Hush. Let's not speak about them. I don't care about them. I would have traded the whole lot of them in for you. *I love you.* I have always loved you and will always love you, more than you could ever know."

There it was, he had said it, and the words made Mindy's stomach churn. How could she profess the truth that she was in love with someone else, someone unsuitable for her? Someone who her mother despised and the rest of her world viewed as a genetic misfit. How could she explain to the hunk before her that if she could live her life the way she chose she would be with Philippe, instead of him. She wanted to say all of those things, but she couldn't. She was a Gold Star

Code Type, and she had to adhere to the Upper Worlds conventions. Here her life was predetermined to follow a path and this path led her right into Brad's arms, forever.

"Nightfall." Mindy instructed, and the stars once again sparkled above.

The weirdest sensation came over her. She had only ever felt it once before. But now she realised it was a feeling that was here to stay. She was relieved to be enveloped in the darkness because the shadows hid the solitary tear that slid from her eye and rolled down her cheek.

***

"Kid, you can't drink it all at once, it will give you a crazy head rush," Sal said nervously. "Actually," she took a beaker from the ground and poured half of the solution into it. "It's better this way, less potent, shorter lasting effects."

"Are you secretly a Cm like my ma or what?" I laughed.

"Better to be safe than sorry," Sal said handing me the half-full cup.

I downed the drink in one shot.

"Yuck." I spluttered falling to my knees gagging.

Sal crouched next to me, "I told you Capsing was no joke. To temporarily alter your DNA can affect you in so many different ways."

"What's going on with Kid?" Jet asked, rushing into the tent.

Sal cracked her knuckles, "I've just given her the formula to Caps."

"Whatever she does, so do I." Jet said grabbing the other beaker and downing it in one gulp.

"Arrgh." Jet fell to the floor.

Skye ran to his side but couldn't do anything to help as he squirmed and wriggled on the ground.

"Are they alright?"

"That's just the effects of their DNA structure reforming. They'll be fine." Sal said.

"They don't look fine." Skye rasped.

"I'm an expert. I've Capsed loads of times, many different ways. They'll be ok."

Sal had Capsed plenty but had never made a bespoke formula for someone else. Watching it was freaky.

"This is frightening," Skye said, her eyebrows knitted with concern with what she saw.

Kid's body began to stretch taller and widen thicker. Her once baggy hoody now fitting tightly around her new chubby torso.

Jet matured rapidly into adulthood. Lines formed under his eyes and a thick dark moustache and beard sprouted from his face.

Sal breathed a deep sigh of relief as the process came to an end.

"Where are the uniforms?" Sal asked.

Skye froze in awe, at her friend's new appearances.

"Skye! Snap out of it and get the clothes please."

Skye tentatively picked up her backpack and unfolded two satellite workers uniforms.

"Whoa. What a rush!" I said, sitting up in a daze, a deep male baritone replaced my normal voice.

"Look at you!" I laughed at my brother as a full-grown man.

"Well look at you!" Jet laughed throatily slapping my new broad back with his big shovel hands.

"Look at yourselves," Sal said, pulling out her IM and projecting our image back to us.

I touched my face not believing it was mine. My soft skin and feminine features were gone, replaced by a middle-aged man's face with a moustache and stubble.

"How long does this last?" I asked, marvelling at myself.

"Not long," Sal said impressed at her handiwork, "you'll have to be quick. In about three hours you will begin to change into your normal form. It will be too dangerous for you to be in the Upper Worlds then. Your image has been everywhere; you'll be recognised instantly."

"True." I agreed and changed quickly into my new clothes.

Jet continued to ogle himself, "I'm buff!" He laughed.

Sal smirked, and Skye giggled.

The roar of Jahni and Pepo's aero bikes ended our fun.

"The Res told us to get you to the Upper Worlds by nightfall. It's time we were leaving."

Jahni wasn't there to joke around. He had been given strict orders from The Res, and he would be a fool not to carry them out to the letter.

"Everyone Upper Worlds bound jump on," Pepo said, light-heartedly.

"You know the rendezvous spot, meet you there in four hours," I said to Sal.

"Yep," Sal said. "That should give us just enough time to carry out what you asked us to do."

"Be safe," Skye whispered to Jet.

"I'm a man now I can look after myself," he joked, "you take good care ok."

"Let's get going." Jahni beeped his horn impatiently.

Jet and I ran awkwardly in our new bulky bodies, to our transport. We waved one last time before we sped off on the back of Jahni and Pepo's aero bikes.

Skye and Sal waved back before picking up their backpacks and saying their goodbyes to the smattering of TL at the campsite. They had to be off too. They had an important mission of their own to complete.

Do you hear it beating?

The motor your blood runs through.

Your heart's wisdom is speaking,

To the very essence of you.

EIGHTEEN

Listen To Your Heart

Under the cover of darkness, two black aero bikes manoeuvred stealthily down Glycena Avenue. Jahni pulled his bike to a halt but kept the engine running; he didn't intend on stopping for long. Pepo followed suit. The Upper Worlds made the Urbanities feel uneasy.

"Number 25, we're here," Jahni said gruffly.

"Thanks for the ride," I said, taken aback by the masculine voice leaping from my vocal chords.

"Be careful now," Pepo advised, "you're our only hope."

"We'll do our best." Jet said in his new gravelly tone.

They saluted us both before riding off into the night.

As we walked to our doorstep, I relished the air of familiarity. I had missed home so much.

"What are we going to say to them? Jet asked.

I hadn't thought it through. I just desperately needed to see my ma and dad again. And I knew it was now or never.

Before we had time to concoct a story, the home security sensors read our eye scans.

'Access granted.' It beeped, and the front door slid open.

Although our biometric structure had altered and our appearance was different, our core DNA remained the same.

We cautiously stepped into our home.

"Who goes there?" Milan's small voice rang out as she shuffled towards the door.

"Ma!" Jet ran and swept her off her feet.

Milan looked bewildered but was not afraid, instantly recognising her son.

"Jet. But how? I don't understand?" She said gently holding his face. "Did the Authorities do this to you?"

"No, we did it to ourselves. We Capsed, so we could come and see you."

"Where's Kid?" Milan asked desperately.

Jet loosened his hug and stepped aside to reveal the other man standing behind him.

"Hello, ma," I said gruffly.

"Oh, my stars!" Milan exclaimed. "Is that you Keziah?"

I nodded, tears streaming down my face. I had not cried since Wain's death but now was as good a time as any.

Ma stretched her arms around Jet and me, and we hugged as if our lives depended on it. Tomorrow was my birthday, and I would be sixteen years old. Being at home was the only present I wanted.

"Where's Dad?" I asked, muffled. I wanted to see him too, to apologise, explain or something before I went.

Milan sighed, "He's working late, trying to impress his superiors, show what a good citizen he is. He's been doing it ever since you two..." she trailed off.

I didn't have to hear any more. I knew my father's Type. He would be doing everything in his power to make sense of this.

"Have we ruined his life ma?" Jet asked.

"You didn't ruin him. I think it was the opposite way around."

I took a step back.

"What do you mean by that?"

Milan looked up to both of her children then sighed even louder, "I never imagined the day would come where I'd have to tell you this, but it has. Follow me."

We walked into the kitchen, and ma rummaged about the old science books on the desktop. Jet and I looked at each other puzzled and perched awkwardly at the table.

Ma opened a handwritten book and pulled out a nanochip attached to the back inside cover. She blew on it to remove the dust, then placed it into the house operating system. A projection appeared at the centre of the room.

"Can I get you two anything to eat, some nuts, liquid calcium?"

"No, ma," I said anxiously. I just wanted to know what was going on.

A range of old images filled the room.

"What is this?" Jet asked.

"It's our family album," Milan said, zapping the projection. "But more than that it's our family history before you were born."

The recording displayed our dad as a child with his parents, and Ma speeded it through to his graduation before he enrolled into the scientific training institute at Techno Corp. He received his diploma and smiled proudly. He was the youngest student in the line up by far.

"Your dad was a brilliant man," Milan smiled absentmindedly, "So creative. He wanted to do good in this world. Not just create enhancers for people to alter their attributes as he does now. I married him because although he's a logical brain and I'm an emotional empath, we held the same vision; we wanted to make a positive difference in this world."

The image flicked to a teenage girl joining dad on the podium. He kissed her cheek, and the girl blushed.

"Is that you ma?' Jet laughed.

"Yes, that's me," Milan said cheerily.

I squinted at the screen. The old professor giving my father the diploma was small, white haired with a crook in his walking cane.

"Do you know the professor giving out the awards?"

"Oh, the ancient looking fella. He was a Dr something or other. He was your father's philosophy teacher. He would talk in riddles. I think he may have been a Sap."

Jet nodded at me as he too realised Dr Stoneway had ties to our family since our parents were teenagers.

Milan scrolled through a set of images, stopping at one showing the day I was born.

"When you were small your father would film everything. He didn't want to miss a single bit of your development."

A nurse handed the baby to my proud parents. I smiled to myself as I recognised Lady Zono. It looked as if the mystics had also been guiding and guarding me all along.

"Your father was sure that there must be a way to develop the missing Human element, the potential for infinite possibilities, back into our species. With that ability Code Types and Tachions would be able to think out of their pre-destined Type. Imagine what the world would be like if we had the gift of possibility."

Milan spoke in low conspiratorial tones as if William Admiral himself could be listening from the next room.

"This is, of course, in direct conflict with the Authoritarian ideals of the Upper Worlds. They want everything in a strict order. Even perfection is regulated. As long as there are Types, then people are kept in their place. If there is no Type then who knows what might happen?"

"So?" I asked.

"So, your father secretly engineered genetic materials at home. He wanted to see if he could reverse the evolutionary process. In essence, this would give our species the ability do more, like our forefathers, be more - "

"Human?" Jet asked beginning to understand.

"Yes. He wanted to see if his theory was right, but needed a living example. And what better variables to study than his own children."

"What!" Jet and I said together.

"He never intended to harm you, honestly. He just wanted to be able to create beings who could do more for each other, more for the world."

"What did he do to us ma?"

"He claims nothing," Milan said, scrolling the image further along.

The projection was of Jet and me as little children pushing each other on a hoverboard in the outdoor sector.

"And at first I believed him. Your father worked on both of you during the gestation period before your birth. I suspected that he might have tried to enhance your embryos with other hormones alongside those administrated to you by the state. When you were born he diligently observed your development.

"And." Jet said in his regular voice. Gone was the gravel tone, the Capsing effects were beginning to wear off.

"And nothing. Neither of you displayed a range of attributes like your father had wished. It was very much the reverse; you didn't develop a Type at all."

"That's why dad treats us like he does, he's disappointed his little science project didn't work out." Jet said bitterly.

I wasn't upset. Everything finally made sense to me.

"Dad based the success of his experiment on the wrong data. He expected us to be like multi-faceted Code Types. He didn't understand that's not what Humans are. Humans are regular. Humans are ordinary. And that's precisely what makes them so special. I doubt the Humans back in the day realised how unique they were. That's why they evolved themselves out of existence."

The events over the last few weeks slotted together, like a puzzle, to create the bigger picture. Unbeknown to my dad he had created the Humans the mystics had predicted, but he couldn't identify our potential because he didn't have it himself. *"Takes one to know one,"* Poppy had told me in Commania, and now I got what she meant.

"So do you have the Human element? Is The Prophecy real?"

"It's real ma."

"But how can you be so sure?" Milan sniffed as tears ran down her face. "I want to believe you, I do, but the Officials say this is all fiction, *'Prophecy is Fallacy'*, maybe genetically something is askew, you need help. Please let me help you."

There was nothing more my ma could do for me.

"Believe me ma. Believe in me." I said simply. "And tell dad that he didn't fail with his experiment. Jet and I are both beautifully Human."

It felt good to understand what that meant finally. Our predecessors may have wasted their gifts and talents, but I certainly wasn't going to.

Just then the front door flew open. Jet and I stood up on high alert.

"Hi honey, I'm *finally* home," Bibi called out wearily as he walked into the kitchen.

He stared at the two strapping men in his house. Jet and I stared back.

"So, Mrs Monrova, we can have your new Satellite system installed in the next twelve hours if you make the payment right away." I blurted out.

"What is this for?" Bibi asked.

"A new satellite system," I answered before ma could blow our cover.

"Our records show that you have the Neptune 80, an older style system, we could upgrade you to version 90."

After everything I had just heard I knew it wouldn't be wise to reveal our true identity to our dad.

"I am aware that ours is not the latest in home entertainment, but it works perfectly fine, so we'll have to decline your offer. Thank you." Bibi said rigidly, taking control of the situation like he always did.

"Well thank you anyway, Mr Monrova," I said shaking my dad's hand rigorously.

Jet did the same but ended his handshake with a hug.

Bibi looked quizzical about the sudden affectionate embrace from the satellite worker.

"We'll be going now." I strode quickly to the door.

"Thank you, Mrs Monrova, for everything." I said looking back at my ma one last time.

Milan managed a weak smile, "And thank you. May all things of love, beauty and joy walk with you all of your days."

I grabbed Jet's rocket sneaks, and as we exited our house I heard dad say,

"What was all that about?"

***

Jet wiped his teary wrinkled eyes with the back of his shovel like hand and sniffled, he wasn't one for all of that weepy stuff but seeing his parents again made him realise how much he had missed them.

"I'm glad we got to spend time with ma, now let's get out of here."

"I've got one last thing to do, which isn't going to be easy," I said looking next door.

"What last thing?" Jet hissed. "Ma might tell dad, and then there'll be Officials all over the road. We've got to go, *now!*"

"One minute Jet," I said, trotting over to Max's house.

Through the window, I spied Max downstairs with his parents.

"Kid, let's go!" Jet said as his burly muscles deflated rapidly revealing his puny arms.

The Capsing effects were wearing off fast.

"One moment," I said as I zoomed up the wall.

"Kid. Don't!" Jet whispered after me, but it was too late, I disappeared into Max's bedroom.

Max had been a faithful friend my entire life. In these familiar surroundings, I felt like a little girl again. Here I could zoom around in Jet's rocket sneaks and worry about why my Code Type hadn't kicked in, not save the world, from a negative force that no one even knew existed.

I typed a message onto Max's aero pad and projected the message into the middle of the room. I took one more fond look at Max's bedroom before climbing out of the window.

"Are you crazy?" Jet moaned as his body shrunk to normal size and his moustache and beard fell out to reveal his regular baby face.

"Let's go," I said, running across the garden into the darkness. Jet ran right behind me.

All the while the Orbs were watching.

***

Sal and Skye's first stop on the list of tasks set them by Kid was Philippe's house. They knocked the door once, and almost instantly he answered.

"Expecting someone?" Sal asked cracking her knuckles.

She and Skye were dressed in full Eee Cee shrouds, their faces heavily made up in white foundation and thick black eyeliner. Their identities completely obscured.

"Not you two." Philippe laughed and lifted them both into the air, carrying them inside to his room.

Skye giggled, and Sal cracked a smile. Philippe put them down gently.

"Like what I've done to the place?"

Sal looked around the empty room. Every item of furniture was boxed up in containers.

"Going somewhere?" she asked sitting on a box.

"Moving," Philippe said.

"Where?" Skye asked.

"Far."

"When?" Sal asked.

"Tomorrow." Philippe said. His one-word answers indicating that this was not something he wanted to talk about.

"Kid wanted you to meet her tomorrow," Skye said, "she knows it's a big ask, but she said she only needed one of the crew to meet her to complete the mission."

"Really? How is she?" Philippe lowered his voice.

"You know Kid, she puts a brave face on, and you can never really tell what she's thinking. So will you meet her?" Sal said.

Philippe's face rippled, "You know I've got so much love for Kid, but right now I've got a lot on. I won't be able to I'm afraid."

"It's cool. She'll understand." Skye said.

"So will your move affect school?" Sal asked.

"I've left FB."

Sal couldn't help but read his brainwaves. Philippe's parents had enrolled him to study at an exclusive Tachion boarding school. They thought it was best for him to be around others of his kind. He didn't want to go, but his parents were adamant. They expected him to leave immediately, but Philippe had other plans. Sal blocked out the rest; it hurt to read her friend's mind.

"Kid also asked us to give you this." Skye handed him a bag of chocolate drops and a new purple IM on a keyring. Skye meticulously double-checked that she had all the other multi-coloured keyrings in her backpack.

"Kid recorded a special message for you, but you can't view it yet. It's time locked." Sal explained.

"Seriously? What does it say?"

"I have no idea. The message will automatically be displayed, whenever the time is right. Kid says she's seen the future, you won't believe it now, but it will help when you need it most."

"I guess she knows best. And what are these?" Philippe asked holding up the bag of chocolates.

"Olden time edible treats," Sal continued, "we ate it in Commania and Kid loved the stuff, so much she wanted to share the feeling with everyone."

"So I eat all of this?" Philippe asked

"I'd give some out if I were you. It's mind blowing stuff, so don't eat too much ok?" Skye said.

"What does it do?"

"Kid wanted to give you something sweet to remember her by. She said she put a little of herself into each one, so you could see the world through her eyes."

"Maybe she has seen how it all pans out," Philippe said. "I sure would like to know the future."

"Just keep hold of that IM. I've even got one, see." Skye said dangling her bright yellow keyring from her finger."

"I will," Philippe smiled attaching it to his trousers for safekeeping. "So who else is on your list?"

"All of the crew. We've got treats for everyone." Skye sprung to her feet ready to leave.

"Oh. So you still have to see everyone else?" Philippe asked.

Sal rolled her eyes; she was never one to beat around the bush, "Have you got a message for her?"

"For who?" Philippe asked fooling no one.

"Mindy," Sal said flatly, "if you've left school I'm sure you miss her."

"I'm not really good with words," Philippe shrugged bashfully, "but just tell her that it's not her Code Type that makes her stunning, it's the essence of her heart and the magnitude of her soul where her real beauty lies."

Sal cracked her knuckles, "Anything else you'd like us to pass on. Something not so mushy."

Philippe looked up and smiled, "Well there is one thing..."

***

"What did she want from you?" Dr Djaba spat.

Max took off his specs and then put them straight back on again. He fidgeted nervously in the midst of a mass of White Coats and Officials who had converged in his room.

Another White Coat read the projected message again out loud;

"Max, I need your help one last time.
Meet me at our place in the woods tomorrow,
4 in the pm.
Come alone.
Come prepared.
Don't be a Neek all of your life."

"Where is your place in the woods?"

Max shrugged unwilling to let the White Coats into his and Kid's secret spot.

"What does that mean?"

Max shrugged again.

"Do you realise how important this is? That girl and her cohorts from the Underworld defeated our finest armies. She instructed the Tachions to break Truth One and use their powers against us. They are enemies of the state to the highest degree. This is no longer child's play."

Max never thought it was.

"If Kid instructed the Tachions in question to use their powers I can only logically deduce it would be in defence because - "

Whack!

392

Dr Djaba slapped Max hard across the face with his latex gloves.

Max held his cheek; the sting made his eyes water. He didn't need an excuse to cry. Kid had been here, in his room and he had missed her. And that hurt more than anything the Officials could ever do to him.

"We have invested in you, promoted you, fast-tracked you and you dare to take the side of public enemy number one!" Dr Djaba raged.

Max rubbed his face, remembering the words Dr Monrova had said, *'Stay on their good side. It's hell when they turn against you.'*

"Now Maxwell Schneider it's time for you to decide. Whose side are you on?"

***

Sal sat uncomfortably in the luxurious white leather seat of Brad's cruiser. Skye stayed on the aero bike a few feet away. She couldn't bear to be near him and breathe the same 02 he did. After finding out what he really thought about Tachions, they could never be friends again.

Brad, as always, was oblivious to the frosty atmosphere his deeds had created.

"You should've seen the game dude. I scored a triple double." Brad flashed a dazzler.

"You've always been a big time player," Sal said unimpressed.

Brad didn't notice her resentment, "Yeah baby. I'm taking this all the way to the interstate Championships and beyond!"

"Emm hmm."

"Seriously though, I can't believe you saw Kid."

"Briefly," Sal said quickly. She didn't know if he would contact the Authorities.

"That's cool, but I can't meet up with her at the cave, I've got a massive interstate B-Ball game tomorrow, so tell her I'm sorry. I admire you though, the way you stick up for your friends. They don't make many loyal Code Types like you anymore."

"Yeah, sure," Sal squirmed.

"So what did you say again? I play this now, and eat these in a few years?"

Sal shook her head. Some things would never change, and Brad would always be a bonehead.

"No, you eat the candy now, and the IM will unlock in a few days, months, years I don't know. It's a personal message from Kid. She said it would all make sense."

"Right, right. I miss her. I miss the whole crew. Boy did we have an adventure..." He trailed off as deep in thought as a jock Type like him could be.

Skye beeped the horn on the aero bike.

Brad looked her over scornfully, "Jet's little friend is so odd, what those Tachions can do still weirds me out."

"And on that note, I've got to go," Sal said ejecting herself from Brad's cruiser.

She didn't want him to say anything else that would offend her.

"When are you coming back to FB? I've missed that face of yours, even if it is all covered in that white scary stuff."

"I'll see you around for sure," Sal said knowing that the next time their paths crossed she would be in her full Tachion form and Brad would never want to talk to her again.

***

"I can't believe we've come this far and you took a stupid risk like that." Jet yelled.

We were back to our regular appearances trudging through the undergrowth to the rendezvous spot. Just like Sal had said, the Capsing only lasted a few hours.

"If Max wasn't there, why'd you have to leave a message for him?"

"Because if he comes to meet me, then everything will fall into place," I said quietly.

"What!" Jet stopped dead in his tracks. "Have you lost your mind? He can't be trusted. If you're ever going to complete the mission and escape to freedom, Max is the last person you should see."

I held my brother's face gently in my hands, the way our ma always did to us. It was a very calming feeling.

"That is the exact reason why I need him to come."

***

Mindy and Cindy sat wide-eyed on the bed trying to absorb everything they were being told. When Sal and Skye stopped speaking each blinked wildly and looked at each other and then to the bag of candy between them and then at the matching pink keyrings. Mindy's was a pale pink, Cindy's was a bright fuchsia.

"The difference in shades is so that you don't get them mixed up. Kid said that you would both like the pink, so I got different shades." Skye said.

"Like wow!" The Twins said in unison,

"This like has the future on it!" Mindy said excitedly.

"That is like so-oo cool," Cindy attempted to match her sister's enthusiasm.

"So do you two think you'll be able to meet with Kid or not?" Sal asked.

The Twins looked at each other before Mindy spoke for the both of them.

"A lot has happened since we first found out about The Prophecy, we're all very different now."

Sal nodded, she of all people knew about changes.

"We've got to like figure out what's going on in our own heads. We can't help Kid out with this one. But we miss her and wish her the very best."

"Fair dues," Sal stood up about to leave. "Oh yeah Minds, when we saw Philippe he told me to tell you something about your heart being prettier than your face," Sal said taking the whole romance out of the sentiment.

"Oh. Like, where did you see him?" Mindy asked trying to sound casual.

"We met him at his house. He was packing. He's leaving town tomorrow."

A million things rushed through Mindy's mind, but she could not think of anything else to say other than, "Oh."

"He said to give you this." Sal handed Mindy a nanochip.

"It's the receiver to his router. It will track wherever he is in the world. He said whenever you need him all you have to do is signal him, and he'll come running."

"Oh," Mindy said again.

"That's, like, the most beautiful thing ever!" Cindy gushed.

She wished Philippe liked her as much as he did Mindy.

"Oh," Mindy repeated in a speechless under drive. "Like, I mean wow, like…" she tried to think of something fitting to say to match Philippe's gesture, but couldn't.

And there it came again, strictly against her Code Type genetic programming, a solitary tear rolled down her face.

***

"I can't let you do that Kid, it's lunacy. You're the Soul Survivor; the whole world is depending on you. I won't let you jeopardise the entire mission because you want to see your neeky boyfriend."

"He's not my boyfriend," I said. "I'm not doing anything on a whim. It's all calculated Jet. You have to trust me."

Jet choked on his frustration as he tried to speak, "No good will come from meeting Max. He will lead you to harm. You can't," his voice broke, "you can't trust him, sis." He bit his lip hard to stop himself from crying.

"I'm the chosen one remember, and my decision is final," I said, turning my back on him.

I didn't want to hurt Jet, but I knew him to well. I knew it had to be this way. Predictably, his emotion switched instantly from sadness to anger.

"Well, you didn't get this far by yourself!" He snapped. "Skye helped you, Sal helped you – and they're risking themselves for you now. Wain helped you, and he's dead! Max, Philippe, The Twins, Brad, The TL, The Res, Dr Stoneway, Lady Zono, Ma, Dad - everyone along the way got you to where you are now. That shows you don't always know best!"

"I know they all helped me, but you forgot the most important person in all of this."

"Who?" Jet mumbled miserably.

"You," I said quietly. "You led me to Underground City, you began all of this, and you've been the catalyst every step of the way. Everyone's looking at me when I'm not even the most important part of The Prophecy. You are."

"What do you know that you're not telling me?" Jet asked slowly.

"Look," I said fishing in my pocket and pulling out a metallic keyring. "This IM holds a special message for you. I know it doesn't all make sense now, but it will. I've listened to my Inner G, and I know what I'm doing. I'm not the key to save the world. I just had to unlock the door for you to walk through."

Jet took the keyring. "So what happens with this?"

"When the time is right a message from me will guide you. It may seem crazy now, but I promise you it will all make sense."

"What do you mean? I thought the plan was that we leave the Upper Worlds together tonight? I thought we were all heading to Ethereal Bridge. Why do I need to read a special message from you? Where are you going to be?"

"Trust me, ok?" I said.

"But - "

Two aero bikes crashed through the undergrowth. They skidded to a halt inches from Jet and I.

It was Skye and Sal.

"Ms Lush called the Authorities. The Officials are after us. We have to get out of here right now!" Sal yelled.

Jet ran and jumped on Skye's bike. "You go. We'll run a diversion."

"How?" Sal asked.

Jet grabbed handfuls of chocolates from Skye's backpack and shoved them into his mouth.

"Jet, no!" Skye rasped, "I told you what eating too many would do."

For once Jet didn't listen to Skye and stuffed another handful into his mouth.

"What are you doing? This is not the time to get the munchies." Sal shouted.

Jet fell to the floor writhing in agony and began to change instantly. His braided hair unravelled and grew straight from his scalp. His limbs lengthened, his skin turned a few hues darker.

"What's in that stuff?" Sal called out recognising the Capsing process.

"Humanity," I said, running to Jet's side. "I asked Skye to get this particular candy made up from a dealer she knows in Zero. Each is laced with a trace of the essence that makes me wonderfully Human. Eating just one drop will give the taster a sense of what that means. No top scientist, not even my dad, could do that.

"I want everyone to experience what I have. To master themselves and unleash their Inner G. To be the chosen one isn't unique to me. It's a state of consciousness that anyone who truly believes in themselves can achieve."

I picked up Jet, and my mirror image stood in front of me.

"With this, you are taking on so much more than just looking like me. The identical appearance will wear off, but a special part of me will be with you forever. Are you sure you want to do this?" I whispered in his ear.

"Yes, Kid. I can handle whatever my part in The Prophecy is." Jet said.

"You're powerful beyond measure and more remarkable than you know," I told Jet as I pulled a band from my hair and tied his new long locks into a high side ponytail, just like mine.

We hugged each other tightly. Energy emitted from us so intense that we glowed.

"Go, capture the last eye. We'll run a diversion." Jet said.

I jumped on the back of Sal's Speedster. Jet saddled up next to Skye. The two aero bikes took off in different directions to face their destiny.

I took one last look at my brother and smiled. Jet beamed back. There was no time left, and in any case, nothing more needed to be said. At that very moment, we both understood that the power of love was beyond language or logic. And there was nothing one wouldn't do for whom they truly loved.

United as one we are unstoppable.

Together we can achieve the impossible.

NINETEEN

Me, Myself &...

Explosions erupted, setting the world ablaze as Jet squared up to Zyclon in an arena watched by millions of people.

"You impertinent fool," Zyclon warbled acidicly. He gnashed his pointed dagger teeth and flexed his talons menacingly, "Do you think you can defeat me?"

"Wrong question," Jet glared back, "Do you think *you* can beat *me*!"

Zyclon blasted Jet with an electric red force that sent him hurtling backwards, crashing through time and space.

"Finally. It ends!" Zyclon shrieked triumphantly.

Jet floated in the abyss that was the Vortex of Souls. As the book had taught him, there were levels to this game, and he had been in training for too long and sacrificed far too much for it to end here. The battle for planet Earth was not something he was prepared to lose.

In a flash of blue light, Jet burst back into the arena to face Zyclon.

"Level Up." Jet instructed, the energies from all of the life forces he had captured gave him the power to go one last round...

"Ha-Uh."

I sat bolt upright, awakened by the cold breeze that whipped around me. I rubbed my eyes half expecting to see Jet battling Zyclon by my side. But I was out in the woods, and there was no one to be seen for miles around but Sal.

Sal sat on a rock in the wilderness, stoking up the fire and keeping a watchful eye on me.

"I think you were having one of those bad dreams again," she said.

"No this dream was better. A major piece of the puzzle. It's what I needed to be sure of." I yawned.

Sal nodded and poked at the flames. The campfire blazed keeping us warm and the wild animals at bay. Many strange beasts were fabled to roam the Outer Limits, but we hadn't encountered any, except the gaggle of unsightly birds who circled our spot now and then.

"What a time we've had together eh?" I said.

"Unlike any other," Sal nodded. "It's a far cry from you worrying about fitting in with those awful Prees."

I cringed, "I can't believe Madeleine Stone and those mean girls were ever a priority."

"Don't worry. I gave you enough stick about it." Sal laughed.

I laughed too.

"You know I couldn't have done this without you, Sal. You being by my side helped me get through the toughest of times. I didn't mean to drag you into all of this. But I'm sure glad you came."

"Well, it gave me something to do," Sal smirked. "But seriously Kid, I know this Prophecy is yours to fulfil, but it's been a journey for all of us. No doubt it's been a hard road, but for the first time, I've felt worthy. You've made me feel special."

"Me? I didn't do anything. You risked your life for me. There's no way I can ever repay you for all that you've done."

Sal smiled crookedly, "I'm always here for you Kid; you know that."

I looked up at Sal perched on the rock. I knew I could count on her until the end. I hoped her feelings of worthiness would manifest in her finally being able to live her true identity.

"And look at this," Sal said, projecting a holographic map, "while you were sleeping I plotted the coordinates back to Ethereal Bridge; this time we'll cross over to the Great Unknown. We're not too far from it. I figure if we head due south, we'll get there within a few hours."

I heard what Sal said, but I kept looking off into the distance at the flock of birds high in the sky. It was late for them to be flying at this time I thought.

Sal started to clear the campsite, shoving her utensils into her backpack.

"I'm ready to go when you are."

I faced her slowly.

"This is it," I told Sal quietly. "It's the end of the line."

Sal stopped packing mid flow, "What do you mean? We haven't fulfilled The Prophecy. We still have one eye to get."

"I know. Where I'm going, I cannot take you with me. We must go our separate ways."

"Why are you ditching me? Was it something I said? Something I've done?"

"No Sal. You've played your role perfectly. I asked you to tell the rest to meet me for a reason. One of them will come by, and then I will complete my mission."

"What? I've got this covered, look at the map. See." Sal projected the way to the New World. "I've found our way to safety."

"Someone will come by," I repeated.

"I told you, none of the crew is coming to help you. I'm right here, telling you I've found a way out. Why aren't you listening to me?"

"I know this doesn't make sense right now, but it will. You have the keyring I gave to you. All you need to know is on it. Please don't worry. I know what I'm doing."

"If you know what happens in the future then just tell me, rather than acting so strange, you're freaking me out right now!"

"If I told you the future now, you'd try and change it. But we have to let what will be, be. Every single element of our life is an intricately woven masterpiece. You need every stroke of the brush to create the perfect picture."

"Are you okay? You seem like you're in a trance or something."

I fought back the lump clogging my throat. This was going to be hard on Sal and everyone else, but I couldn't let my emotion rule me at the last hurdle. This was what Dr Stoneway had warned me about, to quiet my feelings. All of my life had been leading to this moment. I couldn't falter now.

"To ensure The Prophecy is fulfilled, there is one eye I have yet to give." I managed to contain myself.

"Please stop speaking like a Sap!" Sal snapped.

"What I know is too dangerous to burden you with, but I am certain of what I am doing, and one day it will all make sense."

Sal shook her head, but there was no point in arguing. She had tried her best to prove that she was useful and worth keeping around. But her efforts were in vain, and once again she felt the humiliation of rejection.

***

Skye's aero bike tore through the terrain at top speed. Jet clung onto her for dear life, his long Kid-esque ponytail flapping in the wind. Skye was riding like there was no tomorrow, and if the pursuing Guardians caught them, there wouldn't be.

"They're gaining on us." Jet yelled in Kid's voice.

"I know that," Skye shouted back. "I'm giving it all I can. I don't think I can hold out for much longer."

"You have to; otherwise we're done for."

Jet wished he could protect them both, but there was nothing he could do. In comparison to Skye's Tachion power, he felt helpless.

The troop of Elite Officials blazed their searchlights menacingly. The intention was clear; annihilation would be the only outcome. The front section of the convoy launched another round of pop cons. Once again Skye powered up her force field. The missiles exploded on contact. This last burst of energy took its toll and Skye fell back unconscious.

"Skye!" Jet screamed, catching her from falling to the ground.

Now it was all down to him. He had to get Skye to safety. He grabbed the handlebars and steered with one hand holding Skye with the other. The long ponytail flailing from the side of his head shrunk down. The Capsing effects were wearing off.

"Aww man!" He needed to lose the Officials quickly; otherwise, Kid's cover would be blown.

The Guardians blasted another wave of missiles. Jet zigzagged across the air, dodging the onslaught.

His body shortened returning to his normal size, and he momentarily lost control of the steering. The bike swerved, and he careered into the window of a derelict building. A mass of

Guardians tailing him smashed straight into the wall.

Jet rode down the steps and out the door. He moved with expertise, skidding through the gravel. The cumbersome Official riders were no match for his agility and crashed into each other, grinding to a halt.

On street level Jet raced off towards the buzzing electric barrier of Sub Zero. The fencing was ahead, the Authorities hot on his tail. There was no way out.

Jet held Skye tightly. Slamming his foot on the accelerator, he steamed full throttle towards Sub Zero. The Guardians followed suit. Jet could feel the blazing heat from the red-hot electrical fence as he approached. He had only one course of action. The slightest error would mean certain termination from one direction or the other, but there was nothing else he could do. Just as the riders closed in, Jet popped a wheelie and skilfully flipped the aero bike backwards over their heads. The Officials couldn't stop quickly enough and crashed into the electrical wire boundary.

Jet watched as the fence erupted into a neon wall of fire, lighting up the night sky.

The explosion brought Skye back to her senses, "Are we dead?" she rasped, her bright blue eyes flickered red reflecting the blaze in front of them.

Jet pulled her close, "Nah, we made it Skye, we did it."

"You did it." Skye whispered.

Jet nodded. Nothing but his sheer Human determination had saved them.

"Let's just hope Kid and Sal can find their way to safety too."

***

Sal reluctantly rose to her feet and sauntered towards her bike. She dropped her bag of survival gear, "Keep this; yours is running low on supplies."

"That's kind of you, but you take it. You'll need it more than me."

I walked over and hugged Sal tightly.

"Thank you from the bottom of my heart. Whatever you do keep under the radar and stay safe."

"You know I will."

"And say hi to Deschanel from me." I smiled.

Sal shook her head, "Deschanel? When am I ever going to see him again? I wouldn't know how to find Commania even if I wanted to."

I raised my eyebrow, "What's yours will never pass you."

Sal shrugged shyly, "You know best, *Soul Survivor*."

With that, she jumped on The Speedster, revved up the engine and drove off without once looking back.

***

411

Jet powered down the aero bike. He and Skye had reached a clearing through the forest terrain that overlooked the ocean.

"Where are we now?" Skye yawned sleepily.

"This is the coast. We're near Ethereal Bridge. The Upper Worlds and all that we know is behind us. Across the water is a new world."

"So what do we do now?" Skye asked.

Beep, Beep.

Skye's yellow keyring buzzed startling them both. She untied it from her trousers and projected the message into the air. Kid's Vir Sim beamed at them.

"Nevaeh Skye, you are a Tachion Sensation, and you have no idea how much more powerful you will become. Keep training. Believe in your abilities. Harness them well.

Thank you for always having Jet's back. How beautiful your friendship is. Please look after him for me. You are all that he has now and the future of our world is in his hands. Keep each other safe. I'll miss you."

Kid's image digitally dropped out into the ether.

A plummeting feeling gripped Jet's stomach, "If only Kid could have made it here she would have fulfilled The Prophecy. Now all is lost. Everything was in vain."

Jet and Skye looked at each other sorrowfully and turned silently towards the rolling sea.

Skye linked her bony arm through Jets. Jet hung his head wearily. Neither knew what to do or where they went from here, but there was one thing they knew for sure. The weight of the entire world rested on their young shoulders.

"We're gonna be alright, aren't we Jet?" Skye rasped.

Jet nodded tautly holding back his tears. He protectively put his arm around Skye hoping to be the comfort that he also sought. He felt her petite frame soften in his arms, and he knew that he had to be doubly brave, for the both of them. But the lump welling in his throat exposed his fears. They were on the run, his sister was gone, and life would never be the same again.

Fin. Owari. Done. Quit.

Dit-dah-dit-dah-di-dit.

TWENTY

I

I powered down the rocket sneaks and wandered into the mouth of the cave. It was the stone cold rendezvous point I had asked all members of the crew to meet me. Now all I had to do was wait. If my Inner G was on point, then I would complete my mission.

I delved into my backpack and drew out the chocolate treats.

"Go, Keziah, it's my birthday." I sang scoffing handfuls of the stuff.

Most people hope to live a long life, until a ripe old age, like Grandma and Grandpa status. I just about made it to my sixteenth birthday. And the prospect of celebrating another year isn't looking likely. So, here we are, right back where we started. And this is the last entry I'm going to make to add to the Vortex of Souls.

The wind howled around me, and I took a step further into the cave to escape its frosty bite. It was the end of the year, that winter season again. Another chapter in the history of time coming to an end. A ray of light flickered behind me breaking through the darkness.

"Hello, Kid." A figure stepped out of the shadows.

I nodded expectantly, "I knew you would come. I knew it would be you."

***

Cindy sat alone in her darkened bedroom. She flicked through the TV channels staring absentmindedly at the screen. The pink blinds on her windows were shut, keeping the outside world locked out, just the way she had grown to like it. Her mother had stopped pleading with her to leave the house. And even Mindy, who never left her side, knew it best to give her space.

Cindy zapped onto TEN news. The report held her interest for more than the usual millisecond, and she stopped changing channels. The AE newscaster looked seriously into the camera as she continued the outdoor broadcast.

"...Sub Zero continues to enjoy the Yuletide season after the celebratory fireworks which could be seen for miles around."

Something about the news didn't ring true. It hadn't looked like fireworks like the report had claimed. It seemed as if the parameter fencing off Sub Zero was on fire.

Sal and Skye had said the Tachions in Sub Zero had helped Kid and The Res in defeating the Authoritarian Militia, by using their powers, but that wasn't reported. Why hadn't the news shown that? The news was meant to tell the truth after all.

Things weren't adding up. TEN had even stopped running the Kid story altogether. Last week she was public enemy number one. This week she was removed from all screens. It was like she never even existed.

Cindy fluttered her eyelashes. All this concentrating on something other than fashion

417

and celebrity gossip made her brain ache, but she forced herself to keep thinking. It was something her Type was not encouraged to do.

Cindy reluctantly flicked the screen past the shopping channel and stopped on a breaking news report. This time, a reporter who looked like a Brainiac took up the story in a very knowledgeable way.

"The militant, callous, anti-state, Tachion Liberation Movement have broken into the Nexus, the Nucleus that is the home of CAB - Confidential Authoritarian Business. This is an abhorrent threat to National security and your personal well-being. The TL is a dangerous threat. Their reign of terror must be brought to an end."

Cindy had been actively following the TL since Wain's demise. She hadn't known him that well, but the injustice of his termination had severely affected her. The militant Tachions fought because the Upper Worlds judged them by their imperfections. As a Gold Star Code Type, she was also judged by society for her perfection. To her, it was the same thing, but on the opposite side of the scale. Judging someone based solely on appearance was wrong whichever way you looked at it.

There was a light knock on the bedroom door, and Cindy quickly paused the screen. Her mother had already warned her to stop sympathising with the TL. If the Authorities found a Code Type empathising with their cause, they were liable for Regen.

"It's only me Twinny," Mindy peered around the door. "Oh, my, days!" Mindy gasped at what she saw.

Cindy was sitting on her bed, a pair of scissors in hand. Her long golden tresses lay strewn on the floor replaced by short spiking hair. Her face was blotchy red with spots, and she had gained more than a few pounds.

The look on Mindy's face said it all. Cindy looked far from beautiful. And this was her desired effect.

"I'll call mother. She'll get you a lazer treatment, and that acne sorted straight away and like, one pill can grow your hair back within the week."

"No." Cindy yelped defiantly, lunging to close the door. "Mother can't come in here!"

There was a silent standoff before Mindy sat gingerly on the bed. Cindy had been acting odd for some time now. She didn't understand why her twin was blocking her out like this.

Mindy reached over to fix her sister's boyish mane into some form of funky hairstyle.

"Leave it." Cindy hissed, through the brightest smile.

"Like, ok."

For the first time in their lives, Mindy felt distant from Cindy. Now they didn't even look like each other; it was as if they no longer had anything in common.

"You're changing Cinds," Mindy said quietly. "Buzz cutting your hair, bad skin, chubby-fat. Why are you doing this?"

Cindy knew that this day would come. She and Mindy had been inseparable their entire lives, and now it was time to be honest with her twin, no matter the cost. Sharing the same beautiful face as someone else, who was considered better in every way, had finally taken its toll on her.

"I need to be me," Cindy said sadly, beaming like a beacon.

"What does that mean? We're the same. Don't you like being like me?"

"That's just it! I'm fed up of being *like you*. I'm perfect, but you're perfect-er! I'm beautiful, but somehow you're more so. Everyone likes me, but you're still more popular. You're so right for this Aesthetics thing. The preening pouting perfection, you're so comfortable in your own skin. I'm not."

"So the reason you don't like being you is because of me?" Mindy asked blinking wildly.

Cindy hadn't thought about it like that before, but the simple answer was, "Yes. I guess so."

The Twins looked at each other long and hard. A feeling passed between the two that they had never felt before, or at least had never admitted. Cindy stared at Mindy and felt jealousy. Mindy stared back and felt pity.

The bedroom door knocked again, and Brad bounded in without an invitation.

"Your mother let me in," Brad said flashing a dazzler at his girlfriend, Mindy.

He followed her gaze to Cindy and total horror spread across his face.

"Jeez! What happened to you?"

Cindy hid behind her hands. Although she was adamant in her decision to change her appearance, she was not prepared for Brad's response. No one had ever been disgusted by the way she looked before.

Mindy hastily ushered Brad out of the room, "Let's go, Braddy. Cindy wants to be left alone."

"Why in the world would she do that to herself?" Brad asked horrified.

"Because she hates me." Mindy said closing the door.

Cindy turned woefully back to the television. She had never crossed words with Mindy in her entire life. Their negative exchange made her miserable. But she had chosen to conceal her Type, like the Eee Cees, and would have to deal with the consequences.

The news report continued with the breaking story of the TL infiltrating the Nexus. Through her sadness, Cindy tried hard to focus her attention back on the screen.

Orbs captured the images of the four members of the TL in blue balaclavas smashing into the Nexus. There was no mistaking Jonsey, the known leader of the TL. His red face and long plaited locks flowed behind him. Masks obscured the other two assailants faces. But there was something about the fourth perpetrator. He was so huge that his blue TL uniform was ill-fitting. Cindy figured that they didn't make revolutionary outfits in Quadruple extra large sizes. For the briefest moment, his mask slipped.

The Brainiac reporter continued;

"This is the most brazen attack on the Nexus recorded in the history of the Upper Worlds. If you have any information on these criminals, please contact your local Authority immediately. It is your civic duty to do so. You owe it to your fellow man. You owe it to the state!"

The still images of the four culprits lingered onscreen. Cindy paused the report and zoomed into the last assailant. For her, there was no mistaking the muscular veins, which crept up the right side of his face. Philippe's poorly disguised figure rang out from the TV screen.

***

In the mouth of the cave, a small fire roared.

"Your outdoor skill and ingenuity with those bits of wood are outstanding," Max said making a note of it on his aero pad. "I've only read about such amazing feats."

"I learnt traditional fire making in Commania. They make everything from the nature around them, food, clothes, shelter, everything. I learned a lot from the Saps. They even made your gift box." I said gesturing to the small hand-carved wooden box I had given to him containing his silver keyring.

"The IM has a time encrypted message for you. Keep it safe." I reminded him, not that I needed to. He wouldn't forget.

"Fascinating." Max said, looking at the handiwork of the container, "And very kind. Thank you. I would have loved to have accompanied you to Commania and studied the ancient Sap variables. I - I mean people."

"I wish you were there too. But it just wasn't meant to be. I'm glad you're so interested in what I experienced. It's important for you to know that it isn't just people in the Upper Worlds that have phenomenal talents and skills. And knowledge doesn't only come from books and screens."

"That's very philosophical Kid. I guess you learnt that from the Saps too." Max said, pushing his specs up the bridge of his nose.

"I figured that out on my own. But their way of life has taught me many things, like trusting my instinct. That's why I asked you to come here."

Max avoided direct eye contact, and his demeanour dropped, "I'm so sorry about what happened to Wain."

I swallowed hard, battling to control my emotion.

"Fulfilling The Prophecy has brought challenging times for all of us, this journey was never just mine to take, and I appreciate you more than you'll ever know for helping me carry the load."

Max looked at me through his fringe, "You're so different Kid, so self-assured. What happened to you? Did your Code Type kick in?"

"I'm not a Code Type, Max. I'm Human."

"Human?"

"Yep. Beautifully so." I spun around so he could take in the splendour of what it meant to be a real-life Human being.

"But how is that possible? They're extinct!"

"There are many things in this world above your genius level of understanding, Max."

He pushed his specs up and nodded slowly trying to take it all in.

I sat next to him and held his face in my hands, "Whatever has happened and whatever will happen I don't blame you. You know that don't you?"

Max looked directly into my eyes, "Why did you do this Kid?" He took off his specs and wiped away his tears. "Why did you insist that I come here? You are public enemy number one. You know I couldn't logically come to meet you without the Authorities finding out."

"That's the logic of your mind Max, but what would your heart have wanted you to do?"

"I'm a Brainiac Kid, not some airy fairy Type like your mother. You should have gotten away when you had the chance. You shouldn't have made me do this!"

Max grabbed my arm and plunged a serum into it.

"Ow!" I pulled away from him.

"Why Kid? Why did you make me do this?" Max wailed uncontrollably.

The effects of whatever Max had given me took hold instantly. I nodded my head feeling woozy.

"I didn't make you do anything, but I knew you would betray me, Max. It had to be you."

"I'm sorry, I'm so sorry." He turned away, shamefaced.

"The Prophecy of the Soul Survivor is real. This is the last piece of the puzzle. For the beast with the three eyes to be captured there is just one eye to go. The last eye is me. Myself. I."

I stumbled, feeling my essence begin to drain away. I grabbed onto Max and looked him square in the face. This was something he needed to know, something he must never forget,

"It's not your Type which determines your life, but your choices. Even when a situation seems impossible, there is always a choice. You can break out of the box they put you in and be whatever you want to be. Your life belongs to you. Choose well."

Max cowered at the fierceness flickering in my pupils; I half smiled before my eyes snapped shut.

Kid fell to the cold rocky floor.

"It's done," Max whimpered quietly into a lapel mic.

Within seconds Dr Djaba, surrounded by dozens of White Coats, tentatively made their way into the cave as if about to face the most hideous of creatures, instead of a sixteen-year-old girl.

To prove his leadership, Dr Djaba took charge and grabbed Kid's lifeless body. As he did so, a brilliant bright light illuminated her.

"Arrrgh!" The White Coats screamed as the glare stung their eyes.

Dr Djaba trembled but did not relinquish his grip, "We've got you, we've finally got you!"

The light faded and the cave was once again a hollow dank space.

Now that the Kid no longer posed a threat, more Officials and Guardians swarmed in.

"Dr Djaba, what shall we do with her?" A White Coat asked fearfully.

"Keep the body on ice and take her for testing. The Admiral himself wants a report on every line of her DNA code."

Max watched pitifully as White Coats rushed around Kid carrying out his orders.

"Boy, what are you staring at? Get him out of here." Dr Djaba commanded.

Two White Coats ushered Max roughly from the cave towards a waiting vehicle. Rows upon rows of Elite Guardians lined the hilltops surrounding the cave. It was a mission of gargantuan proportions.

"State your name and business here." A Guardian aimed a pop con at Max.

Max nervously stumbled, dropping the ornate box containing the silver keyring to the ground. The parcel landed softly in the brown mud.

"Step down! He's the bait; he led us to her." A White Coat snapped.

"Yes, sir." The Guardian made way for the White Coats to march Max to his vehicle.

Max looked desperately towards the box, it was in touching distance, but there was no way he could pick it up discreetly.

"What are you waiting for? Your job here is done. Get going."

The White Coat pushed Max into the back of a cruiser, and it drove off but not before Max caught one last glimpse of Kid's limp body being hauled ruthlessly out of the cave. He sucked on his lower lip to fight back his tears.

"I'm so sorry Kid." He whimpered. "What in the world have I done?"

All the while a peaceful smile stayed fixed on Kid's face. She had fulfilled her role, and the baton had been passed on in the form of eight special keyrings. Now everyone else had their part to play in The Prophecy, and only time would tell if they would.